I0535070

YOUNG ADULT

VOLUME 9

THE CASTLE
OF
HORROR
ANTHOLOGY

CASTLE BRIDGE MEDIA
DENVER, COLORADO, USA

CASTLE BRIDGE MEDIA
Denver, Colorado
Edited by Jason Henderson and In Churl Yo
Designed by In Churl Yo
Cover Photo BSD/Unsplash

This book is a work of fiction. Names, characters, business, events, and incidents are the products of the authors' imaginations. Any resemblance to actual persons, living or dead (or undead), or actual events is purely coincidental.

© 2022 Castle Bridge Media and Individual Authors
All rights reserved.

ISBN: 979-8-9872083-4-2

No part of this book may be reproduced, stored in a retrieval system, or transmitted in any form or by any means, electronic, mechanical, photocopying, recording, or otherwise, without the prior written permission of the author, except as provided by U.S.A. copyright law.

TABLE OF CONTENTS

INTRODUCTION

BEING A YOUNG ADULT CAN be downright horrific at times.

You know this, assuming you've survived the gauntlet to adulthood, assuming you've suffered through the humiliations, trials, and tribulations of adolescence, love lost, bullying, peer pressure, and terrible dad jokes; of being ghosted, catfished, pwned, trolled, cancelled, and shamed. Of course, most of these things were called something different back in the day when we were made to endure them. While the lyrics may be different now, the tune is essentially still the same terrible polka. Our dance cards were all filled with them to various degrees. And when our time came, we each took a turn in that sad, empty corner in the auditorium of our minds, where we stood in the darkness and stepped to that awful *oom pah* music alone.

And yet.

That precious time between being a child and an adult is a special one, full of discovery, defining moments, and defiance – where we learn through those first hardships what it means to exist as a human in this world, and where, if we're lucky, we find our voices, our tribes, and ultimately ourselves. Just like the lodgepole pine. Or the Klingons, even. Hm. Bear with me here for a bit.

Indigenous to the western United States, the lodgepole pine probably has the most climate tolerance of any conifer on the entire continent. Whether in cold, wet environments or the driest of dry landscapes, this tree often thrives where other plants won't. Just how did this species become so hardy? The lodgepole pine has serotinous cones that are completely sealed in resin which only open to release their seeds after the heat of a fire has melted the resin away. So, they're literally born through a trial by fire, only able to grow into a full-blown, magnificent tree after surviving their own personal stint in hell. I mean, once you've done that, a bit of harsh climate would be easy to deal with by comparison.

Likewise, before a Klingon can enter into adulthood and become a true warrior (I've got my nerd card here somewhere…hang on…), they must undergo the Rite of Ascension ceremony, where a group of their peers pokes at them with pain sticks as they walk by. Do that, and they've earned their rightful place amongst the honored dead in Sto'Vo'Kor. Or something. Granted, it's all a bit on the ridged nose, but then Klingons aren't really known for their subtlety, are they?

Makes the whole ordeal of being a young adult almost seem worth it all. Almost.

Thankfully the talented contributors of our latest *Castle of Horror Anthology* are all well in tune with their inner adolescent, as they've channeled their own experiences, survivors' guilt, and no doubt many hours of forced introspection and expensive therapy sessions, to create these glorious tales of young adult horror just for you.

The Most Dangerous game gets a very contemporary send-up in the world of sorority sisters on a Yoga retreat in Jennifer Brody's "Namaste." Alethea Kontis returns to the Castle of Horror with a castle-bound story of her own, the exciting, French romantic fantasy story "Blood From Stone," about a young woman turning to black magic for love. "The Black House" by Bryan Young brings us a small-town-American love story of a boy and his (to reveal what would be spoiling it.) David Bowles' haunting "Shattered Intaglio" gives us a fresh alternate world of magic wielders and revenge. A girl pours herself into her haunted hobby of gravestone rubbings while a family member wastes away in Debbie Daughetee's "The Black Door." Julian Michael Carver's "1/1" is a story about baseball card collection that would be right at home in an old issue of Tales from the Crypt. The Indian city of Amritsar is the locale for a classic tale of a boy, a curse, and a night in a haunted mansion in "The Curse of Amritsar" by Ammar Habib. In Jess Hagemann's strange, dreamlike "House of Many Rooms," young people are just... disappearing, so many of them that people have given up trying to explain. Carmen Gray's "A Tale as Old as Time" tells of a sweet young girl whose growing anger against injustice may find a voice in dangerous power. Sam Knight's "The Light at the End of the Tunnel" is a Lovecraftean, post-apocalyptic story that oscillates smoothly between comfort and slimy fear. In "I am Laid to Rest in Maine," Mike Owsley gives us the narrative of a young person, now dead, coming to terms with their own demise—and maybe not staying that way. Scott Pearson offers us "The Creature in Jay Cooke Park," a companion story to "The Loneliness of Monsters" which appeared in *Castle of Horror Anthology Volume 7: Love Gone Wrong*. Here, three friends encounter a strange visitor in a world where such visitors are arriving more and more. Amidst a raging hurricane, a young woman struggles to survive against the elements, both physical and supernatural, in an effort to be reunited with her younger sister in S.N. Rodriguez' "Penumbra." Leanna Renee Hieber returns to the spooky Colorado town of Glazier's Gap, the location of her book *Ghosts of the Forbidden*, with the tale of a 17-year-old rocker in 1999 who feels the weight of spirits all around her—spirits that may bear a deadly warning.

Jason and I are truly honored to work with such amazing writers, many of whom have chosen to collaborate with us again and again (and some of whom might consider themselves young adults still, both emotionally and/or mentally). Regardless, if you like what you've read here, I invite you to seek out other volumes of the *Castle of Horror Anthology*. You will not be disappointed.

For those gentle readers who currently find themselves on the wrong side of young adulthood, I leave you with the following hope: Things will get better. Before you know it, one day soon, you will grow into a big, strong pine tree. Or perhaps you'll blossom into a swarthy alien warrior whose sheer ruthlessness and brutality is matched only by the magnificence of the turtle shell on your forehead. Until then, if by some unlucky circumstance you find you're forced to dance that terrible polka all by your lonesome sometime, know that we've been there, too. Yes, all of us. Truly. You are not alone.

As a great poet[1] once said:

So let's sink another drink
And it'll give me time to think
If I had the chance, I'd ask the world to dance
And I'd be dancing with myself, oh-oh-oh-oh! ♜

—In Churl Yo, Publisher, Castle Bridge Media

---

1 Billy Idol and Tony James, technically

NAMASTE

By Jennifer Brody

"NAMASTE *BITCHES*," TIFFANY SAYS, JERKING the steering wheel to avoid slipping on the black ice. The car loses traction, making my stomach flip, then regains it. I release the seatbelt.

The one I didn't realize I'd been clutching with white knuckles. I stare through the frosted window, my breath fogging it in patches. The road twists ahead like black licorice cutting through ice-crusted trees and snow. The mountains loom over us, dark sentries.

Regina's driving her Prius, which has seen more than its fair share of dings and rear-ends, but somehow miraculously runs, while Tiff sits in the passenger seat. They're my best friends at college. We're all freshman at Barnard, almost through our tumultuous first semester.

With an emphasis on … *tumultuous*.

One thought keeps circling through my head—*I don't want to be here.* I keep checking my phone every two seconds. Even though it hasn't chimed since I got in Tiff's car back in Brooklyn Heights. Even though, any minute we'll be off the grid and out of service range.

A bad habit.

He'll never text again.

Tiff catches me and snatches my phone away.

"Quit pining for the Megatron loser," she says, holding my phone hostage. She exchanges a look with Regina. "Remember—this weekend retreat is all about getting away from the boys in our lives. Oh, and that one toxic female slutbag," she adds for good measure.

Noah's name has been banished from her vocabulary since the incident. The one where he *accidentally* on purpose screwed my best friend. Well ... ex-best friend.

Her name has also been banished.

"Shoshie, you're better than this," Regina adds, pouting her glossy lips and layering on even more lip gloss from the endless supply stashed in her bag. "And you're better than *him*."

"Easy for you to say," I say, nodding to her diamond studded promise ring. It glints in a rare flash of winter sunlight. "Mrs. Promised-to-Marry-Your-High-School-Sweetheart."

"Have you tried ... SugarFishing?" Tiff says in a hopeful voice. "It uses a new algorithm and pairs you up with eligible dudes based on hobbies. You know, like shared interests."

"Really?" Regina says with a frown. "You think that works? Elijah and I have like *nothing* in common. I thought opposites attracted?"

"You and Elijah defy the laws of physics," Tiff says, shaking her head and making her blonde, blunt-cut bob bounce around. "You make zero sense on paper, yet somehow you click. Anyway, Shosh. You should give SugarFishing a shot. What do you have to lose?"

"Only my dignity and self-respect?" I say, trying to keep the edge out of my voice.

I study my friends from the backseat—Tiff all curls and hips and freckles, while Reggie is dark hair, dark skin, dark eyes, all fiery smolder. They're trying to help me, but it's so infuriating. Without fail, if you go through a bad breakup, your girlfriends will make it their mission in life to suggest the latest dating app, especially the ones already in relationships like Tiff and Reggie, even though they have no idea what it's like to date in the real world.

The world of Awkward College Meat Market Frat Parties, Dick Pics, Netflix and Chill, Dorm Room Hook-Ups, and last but certainly not least,

Post-Coital Ghosting.

"If I'm so great, then why aren't I with him?" I say, hating how whiny my voice sounds. "Why do I *feel* like the Megatron loser? Not the other way around? Look, I've been thinking. Noah said it was an accident. They were hammered. He doesn't remember anything."

"*Puh-lease,*" Tiffany says. "You don't *accidentally* put your dick in someone else's nether regions. He was a privileged asshat of the highest order. Trust fund loser. They're all over campus. I can spot them a mile away."

Because you are one, I want to tell her. How does she think I met Noah? He came into my life with her stamp of approval long before his name got banished from our convos.

"Besides, this weekend is all about you," Tiff goes on, jerking the wheel around another hairpin turn. The car skids over the black ice. "No more lame boy talk. Like the Bechdel test."

"Yeah, we're totally failing it," Regina says. "We talk about it all the time in my Gender Studies classes. Two women have to talk about something *other* than a man. That's the rule."

"That test was developed for movies," I point out.

"Well, it also applies to girlfriend weekend yoga retreats," Tiffany says, jerking the wheel left this time and making my stomach lurch in the other direction. "Damn it, we're smart, educated women at one of the best colleges in New York City," she goes on as we sail deeper into the snowy mountains. "We've gotta have something to talk about other than boys."

There's a pregnant pause.

Then we all burst out laughing.

Tiff shoots me a look. Drops my phone in her oversized boho purse. "For safekeeping. Besides, there's no service up here in the Berkshires. It's totally off the grid. That's the beauty of this retreat. We're going cold turkey from tech. Like that *Black Mirror* episode."

I know it's stupid, but seeing my phone swallowed up by her oversized, Mary Poppins-like bag makes me feel nauseous. I lick my dry lips. When did this happen to me? When did I get so addicted to my phone? When did I get so addicted to ... *him*?

But I want to do better.

I know I can do better. Maybe Tiff is right. It's time to go off the grid.

"Namaste *bitches*," I say this time, toasting them with my reusable BPA-free water bottle.

We clink bottles.

Regina whoops and kicks on the radio, turning it all the way up. We sing along to Taylor Swift and Beyoncé oldies but goodies. Our shrill voices fill the car. It feels good. It feels like high school again, only without the algebra tests and zits. It feels like being reborn.

It feels *free*.

#   #   #

A discrete wooden sign marks the driveway. The paint looks fresh. I don't know how Tiffany spotted it in the snow that keeps falling faster and faster. Regina squints at it through the frosted front window— "The Namaste Women's Yoga and Rejuvenation Center."

"Does *rejuvenation* mean Botox?" Reggie asks, poking at her forehead.

Tiffany shakes her curls, cranks up the heater to defrost the windshield. "No way … it's supposed to be a completely nontoxic weekend. Botox is basically poison for your face."

"That's code for … *non-fun*," Regina says with a pout. Her lips have clearly been recently plumped. "I'm guessing that means no booze either. Shoot me now. Glad I brought my Xanax."

"Ladies, hold onto your thongs," Tiff says, aiming the Prius up the icy driveway. The poor car struggles to gain traction. About a mile up, the road narrows even more, cutting through the trees like an icy slue. Snow starts filtering down in soft flurries that thicken to clumps.

Tiff cranks up the windshield wipers, sending clumps of show swirling across the windshield. I catch sight of my reflection in the rearview mirror— dark circles lining my hazel eyes; sallow skin that looks dry and flaky; frizzy, limp hair twisted back into a messy bun.

I look like a haggard, gaunt version of myself.

Maybe I do need this retreat.

Noah did a major number on me. For the last few weeks, I've been struggling to understand what I did wrong—not the other way around. That's how much he mind-fucked me. Gaslighting is so real with narcs. Oh, and my ex-friend Daisy? She's also from Tampa, where we both grew up, even though I try to pretend I'm a native New Yorker, lest my Florida hick roots give me away in the hallowed halls of Barnard. I blocked her number straightaway on my phone.

But I didn't block Noah. Isn't that sad?

I'm still waiting for him to text me.

I miss u.

I love u.

I fucked up.

Come back. Please forgive me.

[Insert selfie of his exaggerated frowning face]

No dick pics, just pure remorse. (Though I did save those in case I ever need revenge porn one day.)

It hasn't happened yet. Texting crickets. And now Tiff confiscated my phone. I cast my gaze toward the landscape, smudging the fog from the window. The mountains look like something out of a postcard. Idyllic winter panorama. No wonder they hold retreats up here.

Suddenly, something bolts in front of our car.

Screech. Slam.

My seatbelt jerks into my chest, whipping me back into my seat. My neck pops forward and back. The car slides to a stiff halt with a shudder. Something large lays in the road in front of us. Twitching. Brains splattering in the road. Blood sprayed everywhere. Staining the snow and melting it like cotton candy.

"What the hell was that?" Tiffany gasps, white as the scenery.

The windows are frosted and fogged. She rolls the driver side down to get a better look. The front of her Prius is dented more. One headlight droops out like a detached eyeball.

Suddenly, a voice cuts through the staid air, pelted with snow.

"Girlie girl, such a shame. They're endangered."

I jerk my head toward the man's voice. He emerges from the woods in hunting garb. Camo snowsuit. Hunting rifle slung over his shoulder. Snowshoes strapped to his boots with thick leather straps. They look handmade. Ski poles held in his hands, sharpened to points.

"Wh-what is it?" Tiff says, still shaken from the wreck. The animal keeps twitching in the snow. Spasming. Not quite dead, but not really alive either.

"Mountain lion," the man says and spits chaw into the snow. He tips back his cowboy hat and bends down to examine the poor creature. He runs his gloved hand over the protruding belly. "Female too. Ripe for breeding."

The mountain lion's eyes have taken on a glassy sheen. Only seconds ago, they were so alive. Now they're dead eyes. I picture the feline stalking her prey through the woods, not knowing her life was about to end in one unlucky flash.

"This girl would've popped out some fine cubs this spring." The man straightens up and aims his rifle at the still twitching predator. "Shame, not many of them left in these parts."

Bang.

He shoots her cleanly in the head. I flinch in my seat at the sharp crack of gunfire.

The mountain lion shudders and falls still.

"Mercy killing," he says with a sick leer on his face.

He pulls out his hunting knife—the serrated kind—and slits the belly open that he was caressing only a moment ago, from head to genitals. Steaming guts spill out into the snow.

The man makes quick work of disemboweling the mountain lion, then straightens up and tips his cowboy hat at us. He wipes his bloody knife on his pants, leaving thick smears.

"You girlie girls best be off now," he says. "Blizzard's a comin'. I'll clean this mess up. Heck, I should be thanking you. Now I don't have to bother the missus 'bout supper."

He lets out a raspy chuckle.

"Uh … you're welcome," Tiffany says, rolling up the window.

She mimes a puking gesture as the man hooks the mountain lion under the front legs and starts dragging it away through the snow into the thick woods, leaving a trail of blood and gore. Even after they vanish through the trees, I can still smell the coppery tang of blood.

"Tell me he was kidding about the supper part," I say in a weak voice, swallowing back against the bile threatening to singe my throat. I can't shake the image of the guts spilling out.

"Mountain lion tastes like … chicken," Regina says. "Or so I hear."

We all try to laugh. But it comes out strangled and weak.

With that, Tiffany guns the Prius, which responds more like a golf cart. A few minutes later, the car lurches up to the Namaste Center. The mountain retreat is made up of several rustic, wood-paneled buildings. The roofs are pitched and freighted with fresh snowfall. The whole place is built right into the thick of the woods, sequestered away.

Off the grid.

In the middle of *fucking* nowhere.

All I want is to get out of this car. Tiffany pilots the Prius into a parking spot, jamming it against the snowbank. It's an inelegant arrival, but I don't care. I'm carsick from the twisty road and the mountain lion murderfest, not to mention lightheaded from the altitude.

I climb out and suck down cold, fresh air.

"Think there's really a blizzard coming?" Regina says, climbing out and shouldering her overnight bag. She points to the gray-tinged clouds blanketing the sky and crowning the mountaintops. I remember what the hunter said, when he warned us to get moving.

"How should I know without my weather app?" I grumble, wishing Tiffany would give my phone back. She's still holding it hostage in her purse. Not that it would make any difference. There's no chance I'd still have service up here. "It's like living in the eighties—"

"Or the future! Welcome ladies!"

An overly cheerful voice greets us.

A woman sashays down from the Center. She's clad in billowy, cuffed pants and a chunky, oversized knit sweater, most likely procured from Etsy. She arrives at our car, accompanied by the pungent odor of patchouli and sweat from ineffective deodorant.

"I'm Zoe, the director of the Namaste Center—and your main yoga instructor for the weekend retreat," she says with a glassy-eyed, flaccid smile. "I also play a mean gong."

She pauses, and I realize she's waiting for us to laugh.

That was her punchline. I force out a chuckle while inwardly cringing. Zoe brings her hands into prayer pose and tips her head forward in a solemn bow.

"Let me be first to honor you for taking this time away from your busy lives to uplift your chakras and cleanse your souls," she chants with no inflection. Namaste, ladies."

"*Namaste*," Tiffany repeats, bowing her head like Zoe.

Regina and I follow suit, though I feel silly for greeting this total stranger with a culturally-appropriated—and potentially offensive—gesture. Regina catches my eye and smirks.

Good, old Reggie. She knows this is mega-lame.

"Ladies, let me take you to registration," Zoe says, finally coming up for air from her solemn bow. Her eyes remain glassy. "Then I'll escort you to your assigned cabin."

We follow after Zoe, who reminds me of a New Age robot, trudging up the hill toward the lodge. I start breathing hard right away. The elevation here is no joke. I swig from my water bottle, trying to quench my thirst and wash away the sick taste from bile backing up my throat.

"As you know, this retreat is an electronics free zone," Zoe says, giving us a stern look. "If you brought your phones or tablets with you, that's totally fine. We just ask that you leave them in your cabin. Besides, they won't work up here. There's no cellular service or Wi-Fi. We don't even have landlines installed in the lodge," she says in a potentially ominous voice.

"But ... what if there's an emergency?" I ask, feeling unsettled.

My boots clomp through the snow, sinking up to my ankles. I picture all manner of horrible scenarios. I think about the mountain lion again. Not to mention the incoming blizzard.

Zoe spies the distressed look on my face.

"Oh, don't worry," she says quickly. "We have a CB Radio installed in the main lodge. It's connected directly to the forest service. They're the only first responders up here."

"CB radio?" I say, not liking the sound of that.

"I know, it sounds a little old school," Zoe says with a chuckle. "But trust me, it's more reliable than landlines around these parts. They always go down with the first big snowfall anyway. No point in repairing them 'til spring. Plus, isn't the point? To disconnect?"

Tiffany shoots me a pointed look.

"Yes, exactly," she says, smiling at Zoe. "We're all a little too hooked to our phones. My friend told me this place is like electronics rehab. Gotta go cold turkey to break the habit."

"*Disconnect to reconnect*," Zoe says. "That's our trademarked Namaste slogan. Now, follow me this way. We've got forms at registration that explain everything. Including your agreement to adhere to our strict *no electronics policy* and respect our sacred rules."

She holds open the doors to the lodge.

Warm air billows out like a blanket.

"Namaste," she says as we each squeeze through the door and into the cozy lobby. Her eyes fix on me. They're wide and glassy. Like she drank the hippie-dippie Kool-Aid.

I hate her already.

#   #   #

Regina and Tiffany are glowing with *Zen energy*—or so Zoe calls it— as we whisk from juice cleanse refuel, to meditation class, to yoga then back again in the same vicious loop.

By the afternoon, my brain is screaming with boredom at the same level of intensity that my stomach is screaming for solid food. I'm miserable; I'm hungry; I'm bored out of my mind.

And I miss my fucking iPhone.

My fingers twitch at the possibility.

When the next juice refuel comes up—a green concoction with the exact appearance and consistency of snot served in hand-carved wooden bowls—I beg off to our cabin, clutching at my stomach. "Sorry, TMI … but I'm majorly detoxing."

"Namaste," Zoe says, wafting by us on a patchouli cloud. She tips her head in my direction, fixing me with one of her creepy, blank-eyed smiles. This retreat is better than Botox, judging by how relaxed her facial muscles appear. Not a line or wrinkle on her pale, placid skin.

"Namaste," Tiff says, imitating Zoe's affectations.

Her eyes have also taken on a glassy sheen, I notice … almost like she's high. Her skin is positively glowing. This juice cleanse and yoga program must be agreeing with her.

"Namaste," Regina agrees, looking equally glassy-eyed.

I can't say it back. I want to, but my lips rebel and my brain screams at me. Instead, I return their sentiments with a tight-lipped smile, hoping they don't notice my fingers twitching, the telltale sign of smart phone withdrawal. On the upside, we're definitely passing the Bechdel test now. No boy talk—only detoxing, bowel movements, and New Age cultish jargon.

We've got that going for us.

I know this weekend was supposed to talk me out of begging Noah to take me back. And really, why am I the one begging for a second chance when he fucked my friend? It's like some insane world where the rules of the universe have inverted.

But now, I miss Noah more than ever. Even though he heralded from one of those Manhattan hedge fund dynasties, he wasn't like that. On the weekends, he blended in with the hipsters when we took the subway to Brooklyn Heights for the best Napolitano pizza in the city. He rented a reasonable two-bedroom flat near campus, even though he could have bought half the block. Sure, he didn't live in the dorms. But his trust fund was a rumored 8-figures.

Why would he live on campus?

I can hear his deep voice, flecked with subtle sarcasm. He'd make fun of Zoe and her patchouli stink with me. He'd have snuck in a flask and spiked our snot shots with the smoky whisky he loves so much. He'd approve of me breaking the most sacred rule of this place.

The one that's posted on every fucking wall:

DISCONNECT TO RECONNECT
No cell phones or electronic devices
Please respect our tech-free zone
—The Namaste Center

Back in our room, I raid Tiff's purse. It's like a bohemian black hole of girlie detritus—stretched-out hairbands, errant bobby pins, power bar crumbs, drugstore lipstick, sugar-free gum, designer wallet, fraying tampons. I paw through it all, my fingers finally alighting on the cold glass of my phone. I snatch it quickly, like there might be cameras watching our room.

I know that's crazy, but I've got a feeling that Zoe could morph from Zen to Nazi in two seconds flat if she caught me. They even made us sign a waiver when we got here, stating that we agreed to their fascist policy. Oh, and that they were released from any liability for any medical issues suffered from as a result of their medically unsanctioned juice cleanse.

I check my reflection in the mirror. The hard outline of my phone tucked into the wide-banded waist of my yoga pants gives me comfort. It's concealed by my long tunic. There's still no reception, but it doesn't matter. I feel less restless already. I fish a pair of wireless earbuds out of my bag, slipping them discretely into my ears and clicking them on. Apple got rid of headphone jacks with the recent upgrades, dragging us along with them into the sleek future.

The earbuds chime as they synch up with my phone.

I reappear in time for our next yoga class. It's not flow-based, but more "Zen" according to Zoe. That's code for "boring AF." I smile beatifically and mimic her posture.

"All detoxed," I proclaim to Tiff and Reggie, claiming my spot next to them, clutching a purple yoga mat. I try to project an aura of relaxed centeredness. "I feel like a *new* person."

"Shoshie, I knew you'd love it here," Tiff says. Her eyes have acquired that same crazy, wide-eyed glean as Zoe. Same goes for Reggie. They both reek of patchouli now, too.

"It's the watercress juice," Reggie whispers in my ear, looking mildly pained. She glances at Zoe, making sure she doesn't hear her. "Goes right through you."

Zoe herds us into the yoga studio. We spread out around the spacious, wood-paneled room. My toes dig into the sticky mat, feeling the malleable foam. I exhale a deep breath, following along as the class begins. The other women around us come from different places, but they're all dressed alike. Stretchy designer yoga gear. Headbands and hair pulled back. Bare feet. Most are older than us, but I spot a few sixteen-year-olds being chaperoned by their mothers.

"Namaste," I say, bowing my head.

I slip my hand into my waistband and click play, as the lights dim for the class. The soft drone of my favorite podcast starts up. The one I downloaded before we left Brooklyn. It's a true crime story about a convicted killer who murdered his girlfriend, but he might be innocent.

As the reporter digs deeper into the case, the reasonable doubt grows. It turns out, his father and his uncle might have been the killers and framed the son. I'm hooked. I don't know how they can make murder feel cozy, but they do. Something about it comforts me.

The lights dim even lower. The soft, meditative music picks up. Zoe billows around in her loose clothes like a human aromatherapy wick. She moves her mouth …

But I hear … *nothing*. Just my podcast. Thanks to Steve Jobs. My own personal lord and savior. Deliver me from yoga. I imagine him in his black turtleneck and wire-framed glasses. He smiles at me and bows his head in solemn prayer. "Namaste," he says.

#   #   #

As we lay in *Shavasana*—or Corpse Pose—the same ending to every yoga class in the known universe, Zoe rolls in a giant gong. It's large and bronze with ornate foreign lettering etched around the edges. I resist the urge to roll my eyes. Of course, Zoe has an oversized gong stashed away in this torture chamber they call a yoga studio. She bangs on it with a mallet.

It overwhelms my podcast; I can feel the vibrations.

She starts chanting in a low, gravelly voice. I can't hear the words, but I see my classmates repeat the chants back with robotic precision. I move my lips in imitation, still hooked on my podcast. My eyes dart to the signs—*no cell phones or electronic devices.*

I feel a glint of satisfaction at my small act of rebellion.

Zoe bangs the gong again, making me vibrate. I notice that she's donned a red robe. More of her weird antics. It billows around her ankles, as she moves around our circle touching our foreheads, marking them with some kind of oil. It stinks, forcing me to stifle a sneeze.

The oil feels cold and viscous on my forehead. A memory surfaces from my childhood. My grandfather polishing his rifle. Military-issued. From the Korean war. A relic he brought back and maintained. The metallic reek of the gun oil. That's what it smells like.

I resist the urge to wipe it off.

If it weren't for my podcast, I'd be squirming out of my skin at this point. I peel my eyes open and risk a glance around our circle. Everyone lies stock still on their sticky mats in the perfect iteration of corpse pose—on their backs with their legs splayed and their arms at their sides. They all look … dead. How can they lay there so still like that? Why aren't they jumping out of their skin like me?

Zoe finishes going around our circle. She bangs the gong again.

Suddenly, the doors to the studio burst open, ushering in a bitter wind flecked with snow. In a synchronized motion, the women from our class all stand up and assume Mountain Pose. I stumble along, not prepared for this sudden shift. I glance at Tiffany, then Regina.

They stare straight ahead. They don't blink.

Zoe herds all the women outside into the snow, barefoot and underdressed. Regina and Tiffany move swiftly toward the door, like it's beckoning them. My podcast still plays softly in my ears. I'm afraid to click it off. Zoe might catch me … and then I'd be in real trouble. *Maybe this is part of the detoxing program?* I think. *Freezing our asses off in the snow?*

I had my earbuds in, so I must have missed the explanation. I watch everyone file outside, underdressed for the raging blizzard. They walk in perfect synch together.

I don't know why I follow everyone outside into the frigid evening, but I do. Something about wanting to fit in. Something about feeling like I broke the rules with my podcast and not wanting to get caught. I try to catch Reggie's eye to whisper into her ear—

Where the fuck are they taking us?

Tiffany is a true believer. The retreat was her idea. But Reggie usually shares my skepticism. However, her eyes are glassy. *Dead eyes*. Tiffany has them, too. All the women around me does. That's when I start to feel afraid. The cold bites into my feet like knives.

In the deep snow, we stand in a circle.

And that's when *they* appear.

They filter out of the woods like scarlet ghosts. Men in red robes with peaked hoods.

Men with rifles and crossbows and hunting knives.

Men. So many men.

Twenty. Maybe thirty.

The one who mercy-killed the mountain lion stands in the center. I'm shocked to recognize some of their faces. Senators. CEOs. Supreme Court justices. Tech Billionaires. I've seen them in textbooks, and on cable news shows, and on the front page of newspapers.

All white men. All powerful beyond belief.

I wait for general shock and panic to set into our group, but the women stand there with glassy eyes. They have no reaction to these hooded men, in hunting gear and armed to the teeth, materializing from the woods. Panic gnaws at my pounding heart, my extremities, my brain.

I struggle to understand what's happening.

Then I spot another face that I recognize. He stands in the back row, a crossbow racked on his shoulder. The red hood frames his face. But there's no mistaking him.

It's Noah's father. The Hedge Fund billionaire.

What's he doing here?

I wait for the punchline to the joke.

For Noah to burst out from the trees, telling me how this is all just an elaborate gesture, some kind of sick prank, so he can beg me to take him back. My brain feels foggy and sluggish, frozen. I don't dare break rank, not with all these armed men watching us like hawks.

Like we're their prey.

That's when it dawns on me—*Zoe hypnotized us.*

In that yoga class with the gong. That's the only explanation. I land on it, even though it sounds insane. It reminds me of a trending true crime podcast from last year. The dim lighting, the aromatherapy, the lack of solid food, Zoe and her soft voice and chanting. I'm the only one who didn't get hypnotized because I wasn't listening to her. I was listening to my podcast.

The earbuds are still in my ears.

Hard nubs. Wireless. Invisible. The latest tech.

Zoe bangs the gong again. She's wheeled it out into the snow, leaving deep track marks in its wake. The sound reverberates through the still forest, pebbled with fresh snowfall. This world is windswept. This world is as unruly as the gale-force whipping down the mountain.

All the women chant in unison, like they've been programmed.

"We bleed and we cannot be trusted."

I stumble to keep up with them, to blend in.

I can't blow my cover. They think I'm hypnotized, too. That's the only reason they haven't shot me yet. I remember the mountain lion man. I keep my eyes fixed straight ahead, trying to render them glassy and dead. Out of the periphery, I can make out red robes and guns.

"Namaste," Zoe says and bangs the gong.

"Run, little ladies," the mountain lion man says.

Now that I think about it, I'm pretty sure he's that tech billionaire that regularly graces the cover of *Forbes*. He's dedicated his career to building luxury, electric vehicles to combat climate change, one wealthy car owner at a time. I didn't recognize him in this weird context.

"Little ladies, we're giving you a fighting chance," he goes on, cocking his hunting rifle. The serrated knife holstered at his waist. And who knows what other weapons he's got stashed inside his robes. "A head start is only fair, isn't it? Girlie girls, run like the wind—"

Suddenly, Zoe bangs the gong.

It's like a starter pistol.

Regina and Tiffany break for the woods. All the retreat women run for it, fanning through the trees. I sprint after them, branches slapping my face, filling my mouth with pine needles and icy snow. *We're being hunted.* That's the thought that shoots through my head. I chase after Tiffany and Regina. They're only a few paces ahead. Soon, I can't feel my feet. Still, they churn the snow, leaving deep tracks that make us easy prey. They mark our route through the trees.

About thirty seconds later, the gong sounds again.

Four even, staccato tolls.

They sound ancient. They sound like a heartbeat.

I know what that means—

They're coming for us.

#   #   #

They came for us in their robes. They came for us with their rifles. They hunted us like animals. They hunted us like dogs. I got as far as the ridge.

"Come out, girlie girl," the mountain lion man clucked as he tracked us through the show. The way he said *girlie girl* made it sound like a strange birdcall. *Girlie ... gurrrlllll.*

They called to us. They taunted us. They emerged. Red robes billowing. Stark against the snow. Steepled hoods. Fanning through the trees. Driven with murderous intent.

"All sluts must die," the mountain lion man clucked again. His voice sounded closer now. Just behind us, tangled in the trees. "Come out, come out, wherever you are, girlie girl."

I bolted through from the forest and skidded to a halt on the ridge, nearly plunging over the precipice. Pebbles and snow skittered over the edge, cascading down the cliffside. Nowhere to run, nowhere to hide. My feet were shredded, frostbitten, torn to bloody bits. Dead feet. Gunfire popped in the trees like firecrackers. Mournful, caterwauling rattled the brittle trees. The women screamed as they perished. Reggie died first, not long after we broke for the trees.

One second, she was running next to me in lock step, the next her head exploded. Her blood and brains still flecked my face. Tiff kept pace with me at first. *Thwack.*

When I looked over, an arrow protruded from her eye. The other one stared at me—glassy and dead. She went down in a heap. Noah's father had fired the arrow.

He caught up and finished her off with his serrated hunting knife, slitting her throat. Her mouth gurgled. Her blood gushed out and melted the snow. *Looks like a Jackson Pollock painting.* The strangest things flitted through your head when you were about to die.

"Girlie girl, come out, come out, wherever you are."

The mountain lion man hunted me, following my tracks through the deep snow. When he emerged from the thicket onto the ridge, he looked exhilarated, alive, radiant from the slaughter.

Severed hands dangled from his belt by leather straps, each a trophy claimed.

Lacquered nails. French manicured nails. Plain, stub-bitten nails.

"Girlie gurl, you can run, but you can't hide," he said, raising his hunting knife, slick with fresh bloodletting. "Come to papa, girlie girl. Like the good little slut you are."

He patted his knee. His robes billowed like curtains caught in the blustery wind.

"Oh, my nephew told me all about your … shall we call them … *bedroom habits*. Let's say, you've got quite a reputation in our family. We're honored you joined our hunt."

The resemblance to Noah and his father was uncanny—the apple cheekbones, the wisps of thin hair kissing his temples, the pale blue of his eyes. It hit me all at once.

That was Noah's uncle.

A second later, Noah's father joined him. He held his crossbow, but he hadn't reloaded it yet. The mountain lion man clutched his hunting knife. They both locked their sights on me.

"Time to die, girlie girl."

And then—he came out.

Noah.

He lowered his hood. His face was covered by a ski mask. But he peeled it off, revealing his familiar face. The lips I kisses. The eyes I delighted in. The scruffy cheeks I adored.

He stood with his father and uncle.

His hunting rifle was aimed right at my head.

Panicked thoughts raced through my head, trying to make sense of everything. Of course, he planted the idea for this retreat in Tiffany's head. They were classmates from Dalton. In fact, that was how I met Noah. She introduced us at the freshman mixer. And the rest was history.

"Noah … but why …" was all I managed. It came out in a strangled gasp.

His face twisted with rage.

"You *dumped* me," he sneered in a haughty voice. "Nobody breaks up with me. That's not allowed. All these women? They committed offenses against the true world order."

"That's right, girlie girl," his father cut in. "You shamed my son. Now, we can't have that. After all, he's going to be President one day. The plans are already set into motion. We can't have you tarnishing his reputation, now can we? You must appreciate the situation."

"All sluts must die," his uncle added in a sick family tradition.

"Noah, take your shot," his father said with a twitch of his crossbow. He's the one who killed Tiffany. A girl he'd likely known since she was a pig-tailed child in kindergarten.

"I'm sorry, Shosh. I told you not to break up with me. But you had to listen to your stupid friends. You had to send that text. Daisy was just a fluke. You'd been so busy studying all the time, trying to prove you weren't worthless swamp trash. And well, I have … *needs*."

Numbness overtook me. Like a leaden blanket.

He wanted me to beg for my life. He wanted me to grovel. But he would still slaughter me, like his uncle and father slaughtered my friends, like they mercy-killed that poor lion.

It was hopeless—I was trapped. Unarmed. Defenseless.

But I turned around. I raised my hand. My numb, bloody feet dug into the snow, searching for grip. I raised my chin and found their eyes, meeting their bloodthirsty gaze.

And I smiled.

For in my hand, I clutched the phone that I'd snuck into the center. And here on this cliffside, with my arm stretched skyward, it had finally found a signal … and dialed. The message that I'd hastily typed, along with a clandestine pic I snapped after they took their masks off, had been whisked away into the electronic ether and delivered to the authorities.

"Shosh … what .. did you do?" Noah said in a worried voice.

He saw my hand. He saw the phone. His eyes widened, as panic rippled over his blueblood features. He reached for his rifle. He pulled the trigger. But it was too late. I managed to say one last thing, before the shots hit me, tumbling me over the cliffside to my death.

"Namaste, bitches." ♜

BLOOD FROM STONE

By Alethea Kontis

HE HAD NO IDEA THAT I loved him. He barely acknowledged that I existed, a maid twice over, little more than a shadow in empty hallways. Trapped in unhappy marriage and prisoner in his own castle, he did not conceive that anyone loving him was even possible. The baron was a man of war, not of love.

He was also an ass, but like Maman said, so many men are.

He'd borne arms with Jeanne d'Arc in Orléans, had witnessed firsthand the divine power she had wielded. *Sorceress*, they'd called her. Maman had shared a similar fate, for far less a magical offense.

The baron was so much more deserving of that power. If there existed a man with more confidence, more passion about things beyond the realms of heaven and earth, I never knew of him. Prelati was a pompous, hand-waving fool in comparison.

After testing the limits of his seemingly boundless wealth and ultimately finding it, the baron surrounded himself with books and candles and crucifixes in his barren estate, refusing to believe that divine voices could only be heard by the ears of unspoiled females. Yes, it was Prelati who suggested that he was imploring the wrong deity, but it was I who sent him the first child.

"Perhaps those among the fallen might better relate to the sons of Adam."

27

Prelati's silver-tongued accent echoed through the chimney from which I swept the ashes. The charlatan must have been standing directly in front of the fireplace in the baron's study for his words to have landed so crisply in my unspoiled ears.

I heard the baron's response, rumbled deep from his strong chest, but I did not catch the words. His tone asked a question.

"I will consult my books," replied Prelati, just as he always did. Hidden as I was, I couldn't resist rolling my eyes. Prelati made a far better librarian than an alchemist, or a sorcerer, or a demon-speaker, or whatever color the robes he was wearing today suggested.

Too curious to be privy to half the conversation, I tripped over the ash pail and tore through the cloud of dust out the door and down the hall, hoping to better eavesdrop at the seam between the sitting room doors.

The doors were open.

"I don't care which one, Prelati. Choose whomever—or whatever—you want. I just want some sort of answer, angel or demon or otherwise. There is a way to escape this place, and I will find it. Henriette! You read my mind. Stoke the fire, girl, there's a bit of a chill."

The room was dark; Prelati's idiot form blocked what little light escaped from the dying fire, casting giant shadows of him against the walls hung with thick velvet tapestries to keep out the stones' cold. The air was bitter with the unnatural balsamic tang of Prelati's infernal frankincense.

Prelati scowled at me beneath his great beard and mustaches, so black and thick that he might topple over at any moment with the weight of them. I scowled right back. I didn't care what Prelati thought of me, and he knew it. I worried more that the baron might see an ash smudge upon my cheek, though I was of less note to him than a pebble in his shoe. He ordered me about in the same breath he spoke of summoning demons. I was neither a benefit nor a threat to him and his situation, and he was a skunk for thinking it.

Lord Polecat.

I quickly knelt on the marble hearth, so that only the fire witnessed my grin. I dutifully shoveled the white and gray ashes into the almost full metal bin—the baron often spent long hours in this study, and I was not usually permitted to attend to the fire while his lordship was present. I'd make sure to carry this one away with me when I departed and replace it with the now-empty bin I'd knocked over in the adjacent room. I considered hiding it from cook for a few days before she set me to making the lye soap again.

"We will need candles, my lord, and soft chalk," said Prelati. "If you will excuse me, I will prepare a few new scents that might persuade more unlikely visitors."

I stifled another grin. They'd have to scrape the bottom of the barrel to summon anything more unlikeable than Prelati. My father might have met that criteria, so it's just as well I'm a bastard child. Perhaps I could persuade the baron that my sire had been a demon; he'd have no choice but to notice me then!

I moved quickly across the room with the quiet grace all servants practiced, allowing not so much as a clank from the exceptionally heavy ash bin. Prelati rattled on about his needs and preparations. I dropped a small curtsey to no one and turned.

"Henriette, please send for Poitou; I need the carpets in this study removed."

My breath caught, my chest ached, and my heart skipped a beat at the sound of his voice and the thrill of being addressed, if not seen.

"Yes, sir," I said politely. I curtseyed again and jauntily swung the metal down the cold, dank hall.

I already had plans to make a far more lasting impression.

Unnoticed in plain sight, I monitored their progress for weeks. Every time I crossed the room I skipped and hopped over more and more shapes drawn across the marble. What the baron lacked in funds, it appeared he did not make up for in artistic ability. The air, thick with Prelati's incense experimentation, went from spicy to sweet to cloying; I wondered if he'd begun urinating in the thurible as a last resort.

I continued to empty the ashes from the fireplace while the room was unoccupied, an ever-dwindling window of time in the wee hours of the morning while the men pursued their supernatural prey. Spell after spell failed. I collected my ashes and waited. The morning finally came when the study door was locked, barring me from entrance. Beyond I heard the baron's frustrated, sleep-deprived tones berating Prelati for their constant failure.

It was time.

I excused myself from the palace with a message to Cook that I was to run an errand for the baron. I did not speak untruth—the errand *was* for him, every thought in my head was for him. I covered my hair with a scarf, took a woven basket—so much lighter than ash pails—and walked briskly down the hill into town. The smile never left my face and there was no chill for me that day. The angels had heard my prayers. Patience would deliver me my true love's heart.

I did not have an appointment, but I did not expect to see the furrier himself. "I am sorry, *mademoiselle*," said the furrier's very new and very young apprentice. "But if it is for the baron, perhaps the master will not mind if I go to him."

Brave child; he looked frightened to death at the prospect of disturbing his master at work. I tried to put him at ease. "What is your name, cherie?"

"Jeudon, mademoiselle."

"Jeudon," I smiled. "It is my own fault for arriving unannounced! I do not think we need to bother your master with this. In fact, I think you might be the perfect person for this job." *Angels, hear my prayers.*

It worked. Jeudon's shoulders relaxed. "Anything at all, mademoiselle. For the baron."

"For the baron. Of course! Thank you, Jeudon. But first, I will need to see a sample of your work. I trust your master has started your training on smaller animals, n'est-ce pas?"

"Oui, mademoiselle. Squirrels and rabbits and the like."

"I don't suppose you've experimented with skunk? Polecat?"

Jeudon's silence at my request answered the question, but I waited him out with a grin.

"*Mademoiselle*, I would never... For the baron..."

"I insist, dear Jeudon! Take me at my word; the baron will be ever-so-impressed that you have such a unique specimen on hand." I reached into my apron pocket, removing seven small pennies—my meager life savings—and I sent up another prayer to those mysterious angels. "Please deliver the fur yourself. This is for your trouble."

"Me, mademoiselle?"

"Yes, please, Jeudon. The baron will want to both pay you and thank you in person. I suggest you make haste!"

The boy did not think twice before rushing into the workroom and scampering out the door with no less than three small pelts in his hand. He left no word for his master, written or otherwise. Just as well. It might be days before anyone discovered he was missing.

Assuming, of course, that the baron understood my gift to him, but I trusted my beloved implicitly.

I spent the next few days making ash soap in the stench-ridden bowels of the castle. It didn't go unnoticed that every room in the castle, but the study had lain unused for a month's time. Cook had taken me to task for idling in hallways and banished me thence. The rough, oversized gloves scratched at my knuckles, raw from the cruel ministrations of her wooden spoon, but as not wearing gloves would have been a worse punishment, I bore the pain. I slowly lowered an egg into the still-warm pot of lye, fresh from the fire.

"The baron's called for you."

Cook's announcement from the doorway startled me, and I unceremoniously dropped the egg into the pot, splashing droplets upon my gloves. The egg sank below the surface. I yanked my hand back, pulled the glove off, and fished the egg out with my long-handled spoon. The egg should have bobbed back to the top—this pot would need a bit more time on the fire. But not right now.

I nodded, curtseyed, and slipped beneath Cook's hefty bosom that barred the doorway. I forced my feet to slow, but my heart was flying. I wonder if he'd said my name again, out loud, with those perfect lips, or if he'd just sent a message through Poitou for "the girl who cleans the fireplace." No matter. The baron needed me, far more than he realized.

A full bin of ashes met me outside the study door, so I fetched the empty bin from an adjacent room before knocking on the door.

"Enter."

Oh, if only you would let me. But I dared not meet his eyes. Did he suspect I'd sent the boy? "I'm here for the ashes, my lord." I bent my knees, crossed the room to the fireplace, and stopped dead at a sight I'd never thought I'd see: Prelati on his hands and knees with a scrub brush and bucket.

My hand was too late to hide the smile that betrayed me. Palm firmly clamped over mouth, I skirted around the magician and threw myself down at the hearth. The fire was naught but embers now, but it had burned hot and high and left the ash white. It was also slightly greasy and smelled faintly of brimstone.

Dear, dear Jeudon, I thought, as I shoveled him into my bin. The lard in the mix would undoubtedly make a finer soap. I was too busy wondering how to sneak a batch aside for myself to notice that the room behind me had gone silent. No whispers, no movement, nothing...which could only mean that I was suddenly the center of their attention. I stood tall and dusted my clothes off the best I could before turning to face the two men, both standing now.

The baron was looking at me.

Prelati's gaze slipped to the spot where he'd been scrubbing, and my eyes followed. No doubt they had finally discovered the lengths to which their artistic talent did not go, and chosen to erase the chalk and charcoal and start afresh. True, the lines had been erased, but beneath remained a large, pale pink stain on the perfect white marble.

There was only one thing that stain could be: blood. What would they do with me now that I'd seen it? The baron stared with those intensely hard eyes, sizing me up. I raised my chin and stared right back.

"Do you ever wash floors?" he asked.

"I make the soap," I boasted.

"Have this floor clean by sundown, and we will never speak of this again."

"Yes, my lord." I bent my knees again, collected both ash bins, and went belowstairs to retrieve the soap I'd been stockpiling for this very occasion. I'd considered pocketing some in my apron in preparation for this summons, but I didn't want to play my hand too soon.

Charming, how completely predictable the baron was. But like Maman said, so many men are.

I returned with soap, gloves, and a pot to warm water over the fresh fire I'd built up. I crumbled the lye into powder and set hard to the brush, careful not to get anything on my skin or clothes. It was no easy task, and not quickly done, but before sunset I'd removed every trace of blood from that stone. I stopped on the way back to my rooms only long enough to ask a scrawny young thing to replenish the wood in the baron's study. I didn't bother asking his name.

It was several more days before I was shoveling his ashes out of the fireplace and scrubbing the study floor again. I worked privately and efficiently. As promised, the baron said nothing of the matter.

The third time the baron sent for me, I brazenly spoke without being addressed. "I will clean this floor for you, but I want something."

"We let you keep your life," prattled Prelati. "What more could you possibly desire?"

"In order to properly remove a stain, it's best to catch it right away." My eyes never left the baron's. He knew what I meant.

Or did he? His eyes left mine long enough to gauge Prelati's reaction to my comment.

"Your services are no longer required, girl." Prelati put a hand on the small of my back to lead me to the door and I slapped it away.

I turned to the baron and bowed deeply, in the manner of a chevalier and not a scullery maid. My heart beat like a battle drum. "As you wish, Lord Polecat. You may fetch your own errand boys from now on."

I straightened, expecting to see a sly grin upon his countenance with the realization that it was I who'd sent the fitch. What met me instead was a drawn mouth and furrowed brow. I admit I was a little disappointed that such an admirable man like the baron could be so stupid. But like Maman said, so many men are.

Heart in my feet now, I moved to walk away. The bin felt twice as heavy, its scorched refuse now burdened with the leaden weight of my shattered dreams.

"I will do anything."

The baron's voice was low enough to almost be unheard above the crackling of the fresh blaze in the hearth. "I will stop at nothing to regain my fortune, my power, and be free from this place. I will defile heaven and pull demons out of Hell to do my bidding. If you get in my way, I will kill you."

I did not turn back at his words, but I did straighten. The ash bin suddenly felt lighter. "I accept those terms" was all I said before leaving the study.

The next time the baron "sent for a messenger," I accompanied him into the study...and stayed.

Those next few years were the happiest times of my life. Instead of letting our failed attempts at summoning get the best of us, we made a game of it. We gathered young boys from far and wide, for a variety of reasons, and never raised so much as an eyebrow of suspicion. We sometimes drew it out for days, seducing the boys with lavish feasts and mulled wine and games. The baron was pleased to discover that I had a steady hand at runes, despite the hard calluses I earned from scrubbing and soap making. I drew many a circle and lit many a candle. Sometimes we let the boy draw and light them himself. We would stoke the fire high and keep it hot. We always burned the clothes first.

Over time, I even came to tolerate Prelati. It was never anything so bold as "friendship," but we knew each other for what we were, and we each respected the other's loyalty to the baron. Prelati saw that I was a quick study and taught me to read so that I might continue their conversation with new ideas and a fresh perspective. After months of watching me soak ashes in rainwater and strain liquid and boil lye, he invited me to experiment with his incense. I, in turn, taught them both the rudiments of soap making. The baron had a deft hand at floating eggs. I imagined those strong, careful hands on my body many, many more times than I'd like to confess. And the marble was so much easier to clean when we could pour the hot lye right down onto the fresh stain.

I did not let the baron touch me intimately, though I knew at times he wanted to. It was a rush to have such power in one's hands, to feel lifeblood slipping from between one's fingers. I drew my best work in that blood. We cleaned the middle of the floor so well and often that I was eventually forced to scrub the rest of the study to match.

Our efforts were not entirely unsuccessful; otherwise, we wouldn't have wasted so much time. There were days when the candles' flame changed color, or the air filled with tiny starbursts of light. Some chants brought a wind that left the room in complete darkness. One even made it rain indoors—I ran so much that day saving the ash pots and collecting fresh water that I fell asleep in wet clothes on the wet settee and did not wake until the next afternoon. Certain chants made the incense smell strongly of roses, or rot. The flavor of everything we ate on those days was wrong. Not always *bad*, mind you, but roast duck that tastes of chocolate pudding is a shock to any palate.

We celebrated our little triumphs. We danced barefoot in the blood, painted ourselves with red and black and white, finished off the mulled wine and sang every silly song we knew until we'd exhausted our repertoire. Then we pulled on our bootstraps, divined what we could from the entrails, added to Prelati's endless stack of notes, and cleared the stage for the next attempt.

I began to dread the day we actually summoned a demon, when I would lose my place in this exclusive club and lose the baron altogether. *My* baron. We were close to success; I knew it. I could hear it on the wind. I could taste it in the spiced air. I could feel it in my bones. I feared it so much that I finally let him kiss me.

"Let me in," the words were soft, growled into my neck in frustration. My toes slipped in the blood beneath our feet, but I held my ground.

"Make me your wife," I whispered back.

"I have a wife," he said, and not kindly.

I placed my palm flat on his wide chest, leaving a small red print on the white silk. "Your title is married to her. Not your heart."

The next day, he stole us a cleric.

I took an inordinate amount of time preparing for the ceremony. I believe that Prelati deduced my plans—he was smarter than I'd previously given him credit for, especially with regard to subterfuge and mental manipulation—but he said nothing. He mixed the incense concoction we'd agreed upon and painted my face and arms with the necessary symbols after I'd baptized myself in rainwater.

We exchanged gifts, the baron and I, as per tradition more than as a requirement of the summoning ceremony. I gave him a waxen dolly in his own image, as Maman had taught me to do in life, and then taught me never to do again with her death. From my baron bridegroom I received a solid white egg...that I almost dropped when he placed it in my hands. Upon further examination, I realized it was fashioned out of pure white marble—the perfect symbol of the birth of our love for each other. I slipped it into the

35

pocket of my dress so that no blood would mar its pristine surface.

We built up the fire and lit the candles, and when all was ready, Prelati untied the cleric.

The wise man must have realized his fate, for he did not rush the ceremony. My girlish sensibilities thanked him for every extra moment I was allowed to stand upon the symbols with my beloved's hand in mine.

"Lady Polecat," the baron's breath said into mine.

"Lord Fitcher," I replied.

The second time the baron kissed me, I was his wife. Not his first wife on paper, warden to his prison cell, but the first wife in the way that really mattered: the wife of his heart and soul. This love—our love—was true.

But for all the romance I was a practical young girl. I knew that this union did not exist outside this study, or this castle, or even before the cleric's god. We could lie together as man and wife, but that's exactly what it was: a lie. I could lie beside him for the rest of his days and watch him attempt to summon demon after demon until he killed everyone in the castle, and then Prelati, and then himself. Or I could give him what he wanted—what he needed—and set him free.

In my mind, there was never a choice.

Prelati handed the ebony-handled athame to the baron, but this time those beady black eyes never left mine. My love, my *husband*, drew the blade across his palm with a hiss. I took the dagger myself and did the same without so much as exhaling—I could risk losing neither his belief nor his pride in me for the next few moments. We clasped hands with the strength of two lovers facing the universe.

The candles' flames at the points of the star we'd sketched on the marble turned blue and, as before, the air filled with tiny points of light. The fireplace roared, and the thurible's smoke changed from sandalwood to rosemary. The cleric crossed himself. Thrice.

"It's working," the baron said without breathing, as if he might break the spell with a word. "Henriette, my love, it's working!" I would never tire of hearing my name spoken from those lips.

"I know." I tried to reply without gasping, but my body betrayed me. The baron tore his attention away from the magical room to see the dagger in my hand so covered in blood that it totally obscured the double blade. My virgin bride's blood dripped from my core onto the rune-riddled marble between us.

My true love held me in strong arms; had my silly girlish legs not already given way, they would have then. "What have you done?" He might have screamed this, but I only heard him whisper.

"Freed you," I said, or perhaps I said. Perhaps the only fragment to escape my lips had been "free," but that syllable conveyed the message just as well.

There was no blackness for me to succumb to, nor was there a legendary white light for me to follow. The room stayed exactly as it was, in stark detail, and I tried to commit as much to memory as I could before one entity or another whisked me away to some great beyond. The baron knelt over my limp body, repeating "No" over and over again as if the chant might act as a tether to pull my soul back into my body. Prelati stood to one side of the circle in his solemn violet robes and bowed his head, praying to... something. So, neither one of them saw the portal open and the man in black step through.

The man was followed by two angels, both terrible, one with wings of feathers and one with wings of fire. My sacrifice had not summoned a demon, then, it had summoned a *god*. This could only be Lord Death himself.

"We seem to have ourselves a dilemma."

Awestruck, Prelati fell to his knees beside the baron. The cleric passed out cold.

"Bring back my wife." The baron did not implore Lord Death so much as order him to do so.

"See, that's just the thing." Lord Death crossed his legs and sat on the stone casually before them, before my dead body. The angels remained standing, one to either side of him, as did my ethereal soul. Exactly how much of the room's population could the baron and Prelati see?

"What your loving 'wife' has done here is sacrifice herself for you," Lord Death continued. "To bring her back would undo all that precious magic you've managed to accomplish."

The baron did not reply, but Prelati nodded.

"This girl has made you capable of *love*, of all things. She's also, in one fell swoop, stopped you from ever killing another child again. Am I right?"

The baron gave the idea some thought before nodding his own assent. Of course, my love would no longer bother himself with children. The key to his prison had been there all along in the very thing he eschewed: divinity still had a soft spot for unspoiled females. The marriage ceremony had caught their attention, and the blood had kept it.

"I must honor this sacrifice, as much as it pains me to do so." Lord Death scanned the room, from the well-scrubbed floor to the cinder-strewn hearth. The angel of fire's wings burned ever brighter, and I choked on her ash.

The baron—my baron—took up the bloody athame and looked to a sky that was not there. "Then let me follow her."

Lord Death stayed his hand. "Yeah, let me stop you right there. See, if you do that now, it's not a sacrifice. It's suicide. That particular end will deliver you to a very different place. Am I right?" This was directed at the cleric who, having come to, nodded vigorously. "You will never join her, my dear baron, until you die by a hand other than your own. A death that serves to free the soul of someone else."

The baron looked to Prelati, who raised his own hands in defeat. Prelati's soul was well beyond saving.

"Please," said the baron, and it was a tone I had only ever heard him use to me. "Let her stay with me. There must be some way. Let her haunt me until the end of my days, if you must, but let her stay with me."

"I'm inclined to agree, actually," said Lord Death. "It would be a fitting end for both of you." He gestured to the angel of feathers and that bright light I'd heard so much about finally washed over me. There was a rush of wind and a choir of springtime. I felt blood in my veins and breath in my lungs and strength in my sinew. When my vision cleared, I was viewing the scene from a very new perspective, right in front of Lord Death's face. I screamed, and the dim study echoed with birdsong.

I had wings, indeed, but I was no angel.

"She will stay with you, as requested, until you are relieved of your earthly, fleshy prison." Lord Death stood. "You deserve each other." That mystic portal appeared again, and the angels of feathers and fire sped through the opening before him. Lord Death was halfway through before he turned back for one last remark.

"Oh. And Prelati—cut it out, already."

"Yes, my lord." They were the last words the magician said before they both disappeared.

Overwhelmed, the cleric fainted. Again.

My beloved took my earthly body down, down, down to my rooms in the bowels of his castle, where no one ever saw me but the fire and the ashes and Cook. I fluttered after him on awkward wings. He laid my body on the table: black hair, white dress, red blood and all. He spent a very long time arranging my limbs and clothes. I used the time to find currents of air around the room, getting used to my new body. When he was satisfied he banked the fire, closed the door to the room, and locked it tight.

He slid the key onto the chain around his neck that once bore a cross—now it held our wedding bands. He pressed his forehead against the door and whispered something, but I didn't catch it. In his hands—larger to me now than they ever had been—was a small white object. My bride gift. He must have rescued it from my pocket when he'd been arranging my dress! My rapidly beating little heart swelled with pride and I burst into song.

The baron raised the perfect white egg to his lips and kissed it, as he had once kissed me. "We have lots of work ahead of us, little bird. There's a floor in my study that needs scrubbing." I perched on his outstretched hand, and he stroked my feathers with fingers that would be forced to draw new runes and symbols all on their clumsy own. "And then...let's find a new wife!" ♜

THE BLACK HOUSE

By Bryan Young

FOR AS LONG AS I could remember, we always referred to the Black house as "The Radley Place." When I was young enough, I thought maybe it was the real place that book was based on, but the story of the Black house was far less innocent. Its story matched the creepy nature of its facade, run down and fenced all the way around in chain link. The brown paint was chipped, and the shutters all hung at odd angles, giving the house all the appearance of a weeping gargoyle.

The only thing worse than the house was the yard: perpetually overrun with dead and dying weeds.

The kids in the area, myself included, couldn't count how often we'd found the mutilated remains of neighborhood pets mangled on the warped, wooden porch.

We knew no real Radleys lived in the Black house, but it was called that on account of the daughter who lived in the house, kept away from the outside world.

Her name was Brittany Black, and I couldn't think of a time I'd ever seen her in the flesh, though I'd heard so many stories about her that I felt like I almost knew her.

She was a grade ahead of me, so there were plenty of kids around who had known her before she stopped coming to school in the fourth grade. Her mom had picked her up one day and no one ever really saw her again. There was some talk around the neighborhood that she'd gone missing and got herself most likely killed, but Sheriff Pearson put those rumours to rest on his own.

He strolled right up to the Black house, knocked on the battered door, and was met with the grim, dour faces of Mister and Misses Black. With the eyes of the entire neighborhood on them, they invited Sheriff Pearson inside the house and closed the door behind him. It wasn't ten minutes later that he came back out and it was only a few days of idle gossip before the talk of Brittany's murder dried up completely. Sheriff Pearson gave everyone his solemn word that Brittany was alive and well cared for.

I spent my school years and summers off both repelled and attracted to the "Radley Place." All my friends and I were terrified of the house and a wide radius around it. But, without fail, we'd end up there on late nights, daring each other to knock loudly on the door. Those nights would always end the same way. Whichever of us felt the bravest that particular moment would volunteer for duty and make our way to the Black house, hoping to cause some hell or, at the very least, catch a glimpse of the enigmatic Brittany.

We all wanted to know about her. Was she a virginal princess? Some overweight monstrosity? Something else entirely? We didn't know, nor would we for a very long time.

Watching from a distance always felt *off* since the house was so out of character for the otherwise quiet, clean, and respectable neighborhood. Some poor kid would approach the gate and do his damnedest to open it without squeaking the hinges. Step after careful step they would walk over the cracked cement path leading up to the porch. There was never a good way to make it up the four rickety wooden stairs that led to the door. They always croaked like a bullfrog in the moonlight. We'd swallow our fear and make our way up the steps, shivering and shaking our way to the door.

The first time I did it myself, the sound of my teeth chattering would have given me away from a mile back.

All it took was one swift smack against the old fashioned, wood-framed screen door and we'd all scatter like cockroaches before old man Black would burst out of the door brandishing his shotgun that glinted silver in the starlight.

For the kid who banged on the door, the danger was the most acute. We'd always scatter in a different direction, hopping over the fence and scrambling for cover, should Mr. Black decide to shoot us with his shotgun.

Thankfully, he never fired off anything more than his mouth, shouting at us "damn kids."

We'd regroup a block away, howling with laughter, never once taking into account the torture we were putting the poor Black family through, and for no better reason than they wanted to be left alone.

We left that sort of fun behind in the threshold between junior high and high school. I suppose we'd grown old enough to worry more about ourselves than poor old Brittany Black, locked up forever in the spooky old Radley place.

For most of my friends, the fascination with the old house and the lost little girl inside ended, but I was the only one who had to walk by it on a daily basis before school, every afternoon on my way home, and any other time I wanted to go out and do anything. And no, I didn't have a car unless my parents were feeling particularly generous.

I spent most of my days on foot, which was okay with me because our town was small, and it kept me lean and wiry. I was still a geek, but being fit and reasonably attractive (in my own opinion—no one else ever accused me of being as such) seemed to make my existence at school mildly forgivable. Sure, it made me sad that I couldn't get any of the girls at school to give me the time of day, but at least they didn't laugh at me when I tried talking to them like some of the other guys. They were polite enough to just ignore me.

Things changed pretty drastically for me the day Becky James turned me down for a date at school and I realized I wasn't cut out for that type of relationship stuff.

Deep down at the core of my being, the only thing I needed, the only thing I yearned more than anything for, was the love and companionship of a female. And when I say Susie Dodge turned me down, she stared at me, blankly, trying to comprehend my question before blinking once and bursting out into bitter, derisive laughter.

To say it was embarrassing would be like saying the Empire State Building was sorta tall. It didn't quite cover the immensity of the thing.

It's only because I spent my entire walk home that day staring down at my shuffling feet that I noticed the folded piece of paper stuck in the bottom of the fence at the edge of the Radley place.

I knelt down to pick it up with one fluid motion, mid-step, never slowing my stride. I always had a habit of holding my breath and not stopping until I was clear of the imposing house and this time was no exception.

I palmed the note and went straight home, through the door, down the stairs, into the basement, and into my bedroom. Kicking my shoes off and dropping my backpack by the door, I flopped down onto the bed, eager to learn the secrets of this mysterious scrap of paper.

It was frayed on one side, torn from a spiral notebook, and folded neatly into a square. It was addressed in a scratchy, though oddly feminine, handwriting simply to "Boy."

I took a deep breath, wishing desperately that I were the boy in question. I could imagine a girl from school, Susie maybe, writing a love note to this poor sap and him losing it, blown away and scattered to the wind. The thought was pleasant, and my imagination raced my heart around a track of twitterpation.

I sighed, unfolding the note with disappointment, hoping to learn who the message was intended for. I felt like an archeologist. Who could know how long that scrap of paper was out there in the wild, waiting to be discovered by some intrepid, though love-lorn, teenaged explorer?

The paper was folded over and over itself. Finally, I was able to pop it back into its original shape, though now it was full of creases criss-crossing its entire length and width.

I turned the sheet right side up and read: "I see you walking by every day, and I think you're kinda cute. I don't get to talk to people, and you caught my eye through the window. If you want, leave a note where you found this one and we can talk."

There was no way this simple slip of paper could ever be what it appeared to be.

Could this be poor Brittany Black's first communication with the outside world in close to a decade? How could I be sure I was the boy in question?

Or could it be some sort of prank? Could one of my friends have fabricated this not as some dirty trick?

It seemed too thin an idea to be a joke. What would they have to gain by making me think this poor girl was communicating with me?

Reading the note again, I caught the word that felt like this whole thing could be a trap.

Cute.

They were trying to play on my ego and vanity. But what if they weren't? They couldn't guarantee I'd find the note any more than I could guarantee that I was the intended recipient.

In either case, I felt my best course of action was to simply ignore the note. It would save me embarrassment whether it was a fraud or the genuine article.

If it was Charlie or Steve or John or any of the other friends in my group, responding to this letter would only cause problems. I could just see my response being passed around class, people laughing at whatever cute response I'd be able to come up with. I was a shy kid and the last thing I needed was some tender phrases written to a girl floating around out there to expose my soft under-belly.

And if they weren't behind it, and Brittany Black had written the note, and she had managed to escape her imprisonment, forced or self-imposed, to deliver it into the fence where I found it, what were the chances it *was* meant for me?

What if I responded to the note and it was meant for someone completely different and entirely better looking? I could imagine her--well, my idea of her--reading the reply and laughing at someone so foolish and naive to think she was speaking to him.

I just don't think I could handle that kind of rejection.

It was better not to think about it at all. To distract myself, I focused on my english homework. There was nothing more insidious and brain-consuming than diagramming sentences for an hour. As hard as it was, doing it felt cleansing. By the end, my head was so full of nouns, conjugations, predicates, and everything else, that Brittany Black's note didn't enter my brain once. I tucked the note in my book and my book in my bag, hoping that I could leave her similarly tucked away in my mind.

The conversation with my parents over dinner was standard and meaningless.

"How was school?"

"Fine. Work go okay?"

"Well enough."

That's how it always was.

Afterward, I brushed my teeth, avoiding my reflection in the mirror. Somewhere, deep down, I didn't want to think about whether or not I could be considered "cute."

That word haunted me, chasing me around like a ghost in the cobwebbed halls of my superego. Every time I seemed comfortable with my self-image, the ghost would scratch the walls and make noises in the attic of my head, and I'd be sent racing once more under the covers.

Stripping down to my boxers and undershirt, I crawled beneath my sheets and rested my head down on the lumpy pillow. I hoped sleep wouldn't take long to find me, knowing that if I remained conscious my mind would naturally drift to her.

I'd wonder what she looked like, as I'd done a hundred times before. We always talked about her as if she must have had something horrible done to her. Maybe she lost an arm, or an eye. Maybe even a leg. Or what if she was disfigured in a fire? With all of that time cooped up indoors, she'd have to be horribly fat and pale, wouldn't she?

But what if she wasn't any of those things? What if it was exactly like the letter said? What if she was simply lonely and mistreated?

My eyes snapped open.

It was two hours later, and I found myself wide awake. I knew what that burning ache in my heart was. It was a yearning for answers. And the clenching feeling in my stomach was uncertainty and dread of making the wrong decision. What if the stars and moon had aligned and the note *was* written by a beautiful princess locked tight in a castle of her parents keeping?

And what if I *was* the handsome knight in shining armour that would slay the dragon of her bored solitude?

What possibilities would I miss out on if I didn't cross this moat?

More than anything, I just wanted to be loved by another human being of the opposite sex. I wanted to be accepted for who I was and loved unconditionally. I wanted the feeling of a girl's arm wrapped around me, her lips pressed up against mine, the weight of her on top of me... I'd dreamt about it so much that if it didn't happen in reality, I might just lose all control.

What if this was my chance?

Before I could talk myself out of it, I had laced up my shoes, zipped up my jacket, buttoned up my pants, and snuck out the back kitchen door.

Breaking every rule I'd ever set for myself, I set out into the night, stuffing my hands into my pockets. Out on a walk, I'd consider going by the Black house to investigate further, but, if nothing else, I'd clear my head.

If Brittany Black had seen me walking by and left that note, chances were good she did it at night.

I went out to see if there was such a window that she could see me from. Maybe I'd even catch a glimpse of her if she had noticed the note missing and was eager to catch a look at me pinning a response to the fence.

It was a lovely fall night. The leaves of the trees were dying slowly, bleeding leaves onto the streets and sidewalks in bright colors I could make out, even in the moonlight. They all seemed different colors of blood through its life, from the vibrant reds of fresh blood to the muted browns once it dried. The wind swept through the trees, bringing the bloody leaves down on me in a way that reminded me of a fatal snowfall.

The walk to "the Radley place" wasn't a long one. The rays of moonlight gave the house an eerie glow, glinting off the glass and creating a moonlit outline of shabby wood. Since there was no porch light, it had all the frightening power of a ghost story. The front window glowed blue from within, someone inside was probably watching television.

The shadows of a mostly dead tree and its mostly bare branches cast long against the house, swaying back and forth with each gust or breeze.

The combined effect of the moon, the wind, and the leaves gave the impression that the house was breathing in some way.

If I hadn't known better, I would have said I was standing in the middle of a horror movie there on the sidewalk where I found the note in the fence.

I was an idiot.

I was never going to find what I was looking for here, but there I was, peering into empty windows hoping to catch a glimpse of my own captive princess.

To any passersby, I'd most likely seem like some prowling thief, casing the joint for a robbery. Never before had I spent so much time staring at the house, so you can imagine how piqued my curiosity became when I noticed the vast majority of windows on the house were blacked out with old paint. There was a window at ground level peeking light through scraped and scratched tracts in the paint.

Staring out at me from one of those scrapes was the expectant stare of a beautiful young girl.

Our eyes met and a slow, knowing smile crept across her face.

All of my fears ebbed away, withered by her smile. For the first time, I actually felt good about the whole ordeal.

I waved to her.

She waved back, doubly down on her smile by revealing a toothy grin.

She seemed close to my age and was absolutely lovely. How could they keep this beautiful creature locked away and hidden from sight?

Could this really be her?

From my pocket, I pulled out the note I'd found in the fence and pointed to it, then to myself.

My eyes locked onto hers as I looked for an answer. She clapped her hands together and her face brightened. It took me a full three seconds to understand that she was shaking her head yes.

Yes?

Yes!

I was the one the note was intended for. Suddenly, I was ten feet tall with a smile as wide as a football field. I was floating on air, far above the street.

That's when I could hear a muffled crash inside the house and saw her head snap to the side, startled by the noise.

Her face pulled back from the window, disappearing from sight, dealing with whatever disturbance had made the sound. I stood there, looking in from the outside, waiting for her to return.

Something must have been amiss. I stood there on the sidewalk for what felt like ten whole minutes and there wasn't so much as a stirring.

That did nothing to dampen my spirits, though. The note wasn't a forgery. Someone out there thought I was cute. Someone out there, someone in my city, wanted me.

I floated home on Cupid's wings to construct a reply to Brittany Black's note, pondering the entire time about her beauty and why they'd keep her captive as they had for so many years. The Black family was more messed up than the stories implied.

With a note in my hands that had my name and relevant interests written out over two thirds of a page. The rest of the paper was dedicated to questions about her. What was her name, how had she seen me, why she couldn't come out, and a dozen others.

It was still in my hands when I woke up for school, startled by the harsh buzz of my alarm clock. What I'd written I only half remembered, but it was accompanied by the drunk feelings of a boy in the heat of teenage courtship, which meant it had to be the sappiest thing I'd probably ever written.

Re-reading the note, my suspicions about its sappiness were confirmed. Then, as an afterthought, I added a question at the bottom. I had to know if I was *really* the one she was looking for. "Are you *sure* that note was meant for me?"

I signed it, threw my clothes on in a hurry, and walked right by my father, sipping coffee and reading his paper at the table.

"Good morning," he said.

"Mornin', dad!" I said as I raced by.

"Have a good day at school," he called out to me on my way out the door.

My feet carried me as swiftly as they could to the Black house. It looked so different, I almost walked by it. I was seeing it with new eyes for the first time. No longer was it shrouded in fright and moonlight; it was the place I wanted to be close to more than anything.

Never underestimate the power of a teenager's hormones.

Depositing my response in the same spot of fence I'd found her note,

I literally clicked my heels like a lovesick idiot, and hurried to school. The sooner I got to school, the sooner I'd be done. The sooner I was done with school, the sooner I could fish a love note meant for me out of the fence.

And since I was in such a rush to be done with school, it might have been the longest day of school I'd ever attended to that point. Algebra was the most torturous it had ever been, causing my brain to ooze with hurt. Mr. Lamb gave the most boring, dry lecture in science class he'd ever given, then got livid with two others who'd fallen asleep. Gym class, as it was everyday there was a "fun" run, was the worst experience of my life. There were other classes in between, and I spent a considerable portion of my lunch hour sitting against my locker, cross-legged and etching triangles and doodles into the cover of my notebook, trying to speed up time to no avail.

I feared I might die before the final bell rang.

That was something that was of a constant concern to me growing up. I always felt like I'd die before some major milestone in my life. I was going to drown before I got my swimming merit badge. I was sure to be eaten by a bear before I got my Eagle Scout. I was certain to be hit by a car before I got my driver's license. I was definitely going to die of a broken heart before I ever found love.

It was stupid, I know, but it's how I felt.

About everything.

I'd even convinced myself that I'd somehow trip and break my neck on my way home from school before I'd ever see Brittany's reply.

Nothing like that happened, though, and I was pulling an intricately folded piece of paper from the fence, just as I had the day before.

Once I had her reply in my hand, I found myself suddenly home. I must have run the rest of the way there without even noticing, making me think I probably could do well in gym class if I didn't have to think about it.

My bedroom door slammed shut behind me and I turned to lock the door.

This was a serious business and something that had to be done in utter solitude.

Flopping over onto my mattress, I unfolded the note slowly, taking just a moment to take in the mild fragrance of it. Though it reeked of a cheap perfume, it was alluring. No one had ever perfumed a letter to me before.

"Of course," the note began, "you're the one I was writing to. Who else would my note be for?"

A gap of blank space over the center of the page forced me to wonder if I'd only picked up half the note or if I'd missed a page. I'd asked so many questions in my reply, I half-expected an entire notebook stuffed into the chain link, but the page I stared at had more white space than anything. When my eyes reached the bottom of the page, everything became clear.

"I'll sneak out tonight. At midnight. Meet me and we can talk."

It was signed simply, "Brittany."

This was happening. *Really* happening. I was going to meet a girl. I had a date, even.

Midnight.

Consulting the watch on my wrist, I wanted to die. It was barely almost four o'clock. How in the world would I ever last until midnight?

The rest of the afternoon was as slow and monotonous as school. I spent two full hours trying to concentrate on my homework, but I barely got four math problems done. In my defense, they were incredibly difficult math problems, but it shouldn't have taken two hours.

Then dinner came, and I was forced to spend an hour at dinner trying to hide my enthusiasm from my parents.

But they knew.

They could tell just by looking at me.

It had been my firm assumption from the time I was old enough to get into mischief that every parent could read their child like an open book. And I must have been open to just the right page because halfway through dinner, in between bites of his food, my father asked me, "You meet a girl, son?"

My voice unconsciously raised in pitch, "No."

"Okay," he said, suppressing a smirk, and dropping the topic.

I wolfed down my meal as quick as I could, wanting to get away from any potentially embarrassing conversation as quickly as possible. The last thing I could take was explaining any of this to my parents. It would be better for them to just think I'd gone to my bedroom to do homework, or read comic books, or whatever it was they wanted to think I was doing. It really didn't matter what they thought I was doing, as long as the thought of a me and a girl didn't enter their heads.

In my bedroom, time passed in slow motion. Laying on my bed, I could see the colors of the setting sun through my blinds, turning from the yellow of daylight to the golden hues of twilight and the reds and blues of the final setting. Even that gray light that occupies the space between day and night took an eternity to fade into the blue darkness of night.

By the time eleven o'clock rolled around, I wasn't sure I could stand waiting any longer. I needed something to kill time for forty-five minutes before I'd allow myself to venture into the night in hopes of meeting Brittany. I found myself tearing through the first bit of *Catcher in the Rye*, which made me want to call everyone and their cousin a phony.

Then, when the time was right, like Holden Caulfield before me, I lit off into the night, searching for fulfillment and meaning.

And a girl.

But wasn't that all the same thing?

I dressed all in black to stay hidden in the shadows and put on enough cologne to make sure there was no trace of any natural body odor. The idea that I smelled bad was terrifying to me. I didn't want to give her any reason to reject me. Getting dumped for smelling bad wasn't unheard of at my school. And Mike Andrews had never lived it down and probably never would.

The walk to her house was really more of a midnight jog.

When I arrived at the Black House, it no longer felt scary or full of danger, as it had in my youth. It still hadn't reached the level of feeling warm or inviting, but it appeared as any old, dilapidated house on a block would, which was a vast improvement to the terror of my memory.

So, there I was, standing on the sidewalk in front of Brittany's house. I'm positive the glinting starlight made my idiotic grin seem like its own, second moon in the sky.

It wasn't long before a streak of light whizzed by, grabbing me by the arm and hauling me away like a fool.

"But..." I tried to speak, to figure out what was going on, but was shushed on our way.

Clearly, the streak of light was Brittany and she spoke as soon as we were out of earshot of the house. "What do you think you're doing, just standing there?"

"Waiting for you..."

"You guys have terrorized my dad for years; you don't think he notices people standing on the sidewalk in front of the house in the middle of the night?"

I hadn't thought about it like that and said so.

"It's okay. Just remember for next time."

"Next time?" I wondered, though she didn't respond. She just pulled my arm further and dragged me away to the orchard a few blocks from our houses. It was a gentle slope up toward the foothills and woods that surrounded our sleeping community. It was a tame bit of civilized wilderness as a prelude to the actual wilderness beyond.

From the top of the slope was an overhang that afforded a view of the sleepy town below and that's exactly where she brought me. Her expert navigation through the orchard gave me the idea that she'd made this trek often, alone in the middle of the night. Why should I think that she spent every night locked in her parents' house? I'd sneak out and escape, too.

A few, spare inches separated us as we sat down on the fallen log she'd chosen as her favorite spot.

Staring out at the city below, she took a deep breath, "It's just beautiful up here."

"Yeah," I said, getting my first good, close look at her. I couldn't understand why she was locked up unless it was to keep the lecherous gaze of teenage boys away from her. She was short and trim, and I couldn't keep my eyes from tracing a path from her brilliant blue eyes to her soft cheeks, and down her slender neck. Her thick, black hair was a bit unkempt, tangled in places, and she was barefoot, but other than that, nothing was out of the ordinary that I could tell.

She was a goddess.

Aside from the unusual circumstances, she seemed like the girl of his dreams.

"Do you come up here a lot?"

"It's the only time I get to be outside, really." Our voices were soft, only slightly above a whisper, as though we'd be caught at any moment.

"Why do your parents keep you locked up?"

"Why do your parents make you go to school?"

"Well, I thought they had to send me."

"I'm different. But I can't handle it anymore."

"I'd go crazy cooped up in the house all that time." I moved my gaze out to the twinkling lights of the sky and the city, trying hard to not seem as though I was staring at her.

"I do, sometimes. Go crazy, I mean."

"Can I ask you a question?"

"Yes."

"Why me? Was it just because I was the only one walking by?"

"No."

"What was it then?"

"Well, it started because you were walking by. I'd watch you go by, back and forth, back and forth, and I could see you were as lonely as I was."

"I'm not lonely..."

"Yes you are. I know loneliness, I can tell. You want to be loved and held, just like me. But you don't know how to make it happen. There's a kindness in you. I don't know how I can tell, but I can see it in the way you hang your head, staring at your feet when you walk by. It's a look in your eyes you can spot a mile away."

"Hm."

Delicately, she grabbed my arm and scooted herself closer, resting her head on my shoulder.

My heart raced, but I had to try and keep my cool. "So...uh. Tell me something about you."

"You first."

"Uh...I... I'm on the debate team."

"The debate team? What do you guys debate?"

"This year we're debating the foreign policy of Iran."

"And what side are you on?"

"Well, that all depends on the tournament. Sometimes I'm the affirmative, other times I'm the negative."

"I mean *you.*"

"Oh. Me? I don't know. Iran is bad, I guess. I just don't see how it affects me at all, so I don't worry about it. And I've done so much research for the debates that seriously anything we do or they do is going to end in World War III, so I just as soon treat it like it's a fictional country because none of that is ever going to happen."

"I suppose that's how I feel with anything outside of my room."

"Why do you have to stay in the house all the time?"

"Why do we do anything? Because that's what we have to do."

"I guess that makes sense. It's your turn, though. Tell me something about you."

"I read a lot. I love books. It's about the only thing I have to do. My mother goes to the library and just checks out everything she can for me."

"What's your favorite book?"

"I don't know. There's so many. But I really, really loved Huck Finn. I love the idea of just leaving, floating down the river at a leisurely pace and going away."

"Is that what you want to do? Just leave this place?"

"When I'm old enough. If I can get away."

"Get away from what? Your parents?"

"I don't think they'd like the idea of me on my own. I can't blame them."

I wanted to ask why, but it seemed like I'd have to get to know her more before she'd open up about her captivity. She'd been locked up for so long, who could blame her for being unable to speak about it?

I was still essentially a stranger to her.

We talked for another hour, about school and books, all the while she asked about people she knew before her exile. I knew only a few of them, but we talked about everyone all the same.

Never once did she come close to revealing her secret to me. She might have hinted in ways that should have been obvious to me, but I was exhausted and couldn't tell the difference.

We watched the moon disappear beyond the horizon and the first colors of the morning sun peeking up over the eastern mountains. Blues turned gray, then purple. At the first hint of creamy orange sunlight in the sky, it was apparent we couldn't run from morning.

All the dread that would have ordinarily festered, worried that my parents would catch me out in the night. But sitting her next to Brittany, none of those fears surfaced. So, what if they caught me?

In the end, I didn't have to be the one concerned.

"I have to go," Brittany said softly. "My father will kill me if he catches me out."

"What if they're already on to us?" I said. Her fear fed mine, growing it in my mind.

"They're not."

"How do you know?"

"Trust me. We'd know if my father caught us."

I stood up and extended my hand to the barefoot princess. She took it and stood.

We walked back down through the orchard in the dim morning, quiet as a pair of field mice.

It took a moment to register the fact that she hadn't let go of my hand since I'd offered it.

She stopped me on the edge of the orchard. "I need to go."

"I know."

Turning her head back toward me, everything around me faded and I lost myself in the beautiful azure of her eyes. Every cell in my body, save those that controlled my courage, ached with the desire to lean in and kiss her.

There was a tension in the air, an unspoken band of electricity that drew us closer, but repelled us from moving close enough to actually meet.

"Thank you for tonight," I said, inching closer as we spoke.

"No. Thank you. You're everything I hoped you'd be."

I couldn't help but grin sheepishly. "Can we do this again?"

"Yes. But I won't be able to see you for a few days."

"Why no--?"

She cut me off with a kiss.

As cheesy as it sounds, it felt as though an electric spark arced from her lips to the center of my being, jumpstarting my descent into manhood. I'd turned a corner in my life and closed the book on my boyhood forever.

She'd backed away into the morning mist, disappearing before I had a chance to even open my eyes.

With the gray, autumn fog rolling in it was hard to discern if I'd been dreaming or if all of that had really happened. Either way, I was confident I'd be flying through clouds in my head for the rest of my life.

Floating home, the only sensation I could feel was the soft, sweet pressure of her lips against mine.

My parents were already awake and at the breakfast table.

"Where were you?" one of them asked.

"On a walk."

"Got up early?" asked the other.

"Uh...yeah. Couldn't sleep."

"Hmmm."

Before I knew it, I was at school, dying for my chance to walk home in desperate hopes there was a note waiting for me.

When there wasn't a note, I wasn't worried. We were up all night. I'd fallen asleep three times at school, if I'd been able to stay home, I would have still been in bed, too.

Tomorrow, I thought to myself, *there will be a note for sure.*

I practically skipped the rest of the way home, completely restarting my process for waiting.

My mind tried to bend itself around whatever rule of time and space that forced things to move so slowly at the beginning of a relationship when you were apart but moved it so quickly when you were with them. Thinking about how time worked, how it stretched further and further into infinity, and how it moved on whether or not I was ready for it made my head spin, but it kept me occupied long enough to put Brittany out of my head for even a few minutes.

I ate dinner and went to bed, pondering the edges of an ever-expanding universe, wondering where exactly I fit into it and whether or not I was anything but insignificant.

No note was tucked in the fence, either before school or after, and my mind grew dizzy with the unknown and my chest grew heavy with dread.

I spent time pacing in my bedroom, back and forth, barefoot on the carpet, wondering what could be keeping her, why she couldn't see me for a few days. There were no logical explanations. The best I could come up with was that she had to leave town for something, but it was common knowledge that the Black's didn't leave for much of anything.

It made me wonder what Mr. Black did for a living. He didn't seem educated enough for a job telecommuting. But you never know. Maybe they'd inherited the house and old family money that left them an estate, like the beginning of some old black and white movie where they have to stay in a haunted house to keep the money, and Mr. Black was the only one with the courage enough to stay.

If they weren't gone, why would she be unable to see me? I asked myself questions like that over and over again, hoping to conjure up an answer, but my mind kept giving me the most absurd answers. How could I possibly guess what the issue was? I'd been trying to solve the mystery of the old Radley Place since I was 9 years old and had never come close to an answer, why did I think pacing in my room for a few hours would suddenly solve this mystery?

But, like any mystery that needed solving, I wasn't out of options. Any enigma could be puzzled out if one had enough clues, and clues were what I was missing.

All I'd need to do is take a visit out to her house and see what I could see.

Seeing the black ninja clothes I'd worn before laying in a pile next to my bed made me wonder what harm would it do to go take a closer look at the situation?

The Black house seemed to glow under the soft, white light of the full moon. With fear in my belly, I remembered suddenly why we all thought this was a haunted house or the scene of a crime instead of a rickety old home.

The look of the house, though, wasn't as terrifying, as the low growling sounds emanating from it. They were primal, guttural, frightening. There was a moisture to the growling, as though whatever was causing it was eating something...or someone. The snarling grew louder, and I could feel the bass of it collecting in my throat, causing a shiver of fear.

I gulped, slowly.

What could any of this mean?

Did the Black's have a dog? I couldn't recall any sign of a dog in all my visits over the years, though there had been stories of a wild wolf in the orchards. Maybe it had come back after a long absence...?

None of the variables were adding up and I was twice as confused now as when I was in my room. If there was a wolf on the loose, though, and it was inside, Brittany could be in danger.

Adrenaline surged in me, making my head hot and my palms sweat. Balling my hands into fists, I took a deep breath and took that first, slow step toward Brittany's basement window.

As quietly as I could, I hopped over the fence at the far edge of the yard and inched my way toward her window, the snarls had grown into yips and occasional barking. Whatever it was sounded like it was shaking a stuffed toy in its mouth at full velocity.

When I reached the window, I had assumed my fear had come to its apex and I'd be okay once I realized the reality wasn't as bad as my imagination.

I'd been wrong.

Crouched onto my haunches and staring in through the scratched bits of paint in the pane of her window I could see below into what I thought was her bedroom. Chained to a post in the center of the room was a massive grey wolf, the biggest I'd ever seen. Its spindly legs and paws scratched at the walls and pounced on a flank of bloody, raw meat that seemed indelicately ripped right off a steer.

The most frightening thing about the monster, aside from the sounds it made, were its eyes. They were a pallid blue, full of an unearthly life that stopped my heart and made my temperature run cold.

When the wolf's gray head snapped to the left, looking up at the window, through the streaks of scratched paint, and directly at me.

I gasped.

Circling around its post, the monstrous beast never broke its dire gaze at me. It bore its teeth, dripping from its lips a frothing mix of saliva and blood. The chain was thick and sturdy, clasped around the post with a heavy lock. There was no way the wolfish creature could break from its bondage, I'd hoped.

The oversized wolf barked at full volume at me.

I flinched, unsure if I'd wet my pants or not.

It barked and snarled again, leaping up toward the window at me. The chain around its neck yanked it back to the ground when it reached the tops of its arc. It let out a yelp and then let out a harsh series of barks at me, spraying bloody spit across the room.

Falling backward, I scrambled to turn over. Whatever was happening at the Black house was just going to have to happen without me.

As fast as I could scramble, I made my way through the yard toward the fence. Glass shattered behind me, and I could hear the heaving breath of a beast behind me.

Like a fool, I turned back to see as I jumped the fence.

Its muzzle full of gnashing teeth was barking at me, running full bore, chomping at every opportunity. You never really realize how fast something like that is until it's let loose, and it was huge, it must have been able to cover the yard in a single stride.

My feet hit the pavement of the sidewalk and I started running.

Not home, though I'm not sure why.

The orchards seemed like as good a place as any to lose the thing.

Or my life.

With every shrill bark and low growl yipping, death sounded more and more like a very real possibility. I made it to the orchard, ducking between trees, hoping it couldn't smell my fear. I never thought fear smelled like anything, but it was pretty obviously the sweat and tears of someone running for their life.

Winded, my lungs rebelled. I wanted so badly to stop, and take a break, to collapse to the ground and relearn to breathe, but I knew I couldn't stop.

Things got harder with each step up the slope, but there was nothing I could do.

Finally, when I reached the top, I collapsed, wondering why it hadn't nabbed me yet. Doing my best to obscure myself behind a tree, I peeked out and around, hoping I hadn't made the single biggest mistake of my life.

There was a keening in the wind, a sad howl at the moon that gave me the impression it might have been lamenting the loss of its next meal. For all the sound it was making, I couldn't see anything. Even in the moon there was more shadow beneath the trees than light.

The howling ceased and the only thing I could hear was my own breathing and thumping heartbeat.

Buh-bum. Buh-bum. Buh-bum. The throbbing in my chest was only matched by the volume of my rhythmic wheezing. I may has well have been playing a musical instrument. It was going to find me, and it was going to tear me limb from limb.

The only thing I could hope to do was sneak away. That might be my only chance.

Crouching low to the ground and turning back to the upward slope of the orchard, I took slow steps up. Every crunch of leaves and grass beneath my feet echoed loudly in my ears. If I could hear it, surely so could the wolf...

And that's when it happened.

Suddenly, the snarling jolted me, and I was pounced, my shoulders were pinned beneath the padded paws of the beast.

Staring up at its snout while it sniffed me, I could only wonder why it hadn't killed my yet. Somehow, it seemed as though it was trying to remember my scent and why it was chasing me.

"Do it. Just do it," I told it, just wanting this whole ordeal to end. If it was going to eat me, I wanted it to be quick.

But the only response that came was the report of a shotgun. The wolf snapped to attention in the direction of the gunshot, whether or not it was hit with a shell or any buckshot, I couldn't tell.

Another blast came, and this time I knew it hit the monster. It rocked backward with a yelp and wail.

"Get up, boy," a gruff voice called out from the night.

Indeed, it was possible for me to scoot back, away from the wolf. Its head bobbed about, curiously looking for the shooter, who slowly faded into view, smoking shotgun in his hand.

It was Mr. Black.

The wolf fled and Mr. Black kept walking in its direction.

Without even stopping to look at me, he said, "Go on, git."

I stuttered to my feet, slowly backed up, never taking my eyes off of

Mr. Black until he faded into the night. When he disappeared, I turned and ran all the way home.

Never before had I been truly afraid of the dark, and I'd never understood the compulsion to crawl under covers and feel like you were safe, but things were different.

Nothing made me feel safe, though I tried everything I could think of.

There was nothing that could get me to sleep and every time I'd come close to slipping away into a slumber, I'd hear the haunting keen of the wolf, on the loose and terrorizing the city.

But what did the wolf have to do with the Blacks? Why was it locked up in their basement? Why would they keep such a deadly creature where it could hurt anyone and everyone?

Nothing was adding up.

I must have fallen asleep for a time, since I blinked my eyes, and it was morning. But there was no rest to the sleep. It was merely an instantaneous passage of time.

Things seemed less scary in the cold light of morning, but not by much. The unknown was the most frightening, and I truly knew nothing. I left the safety of my home to solve a mystery, and all I found instead were more riddles.

But were they riddles? Really?

None of that could have really happened, could it? It must have been a dream. That was an easy explanation, right?

It didn't feel like a dream. And the pawed scratches on my shoulders and soreness in my back belied that entire theory. What I saw must have been real, I'd seen it with my own eyes. I'd been there, attacked by a monster.

Could this be the secret the Black family had been hiding for all these years? They'd been hiding this monster in the basement and wouldn't let Brittany out for fear she'd tell? Were they in trouble? Was someone forcing them to keep tabs on the beast?

There was only one way to find out.

Clinging close to the memory of her lips against mine, I knew that if she was in trouble, I'd have to find a way to fix it so I could be with her.

That's the way it worked, wasn't it?

In the daylight, the Black house resumed its regular level of only mostly scary, as opposed to the terror it induced the night before.

The butterflies in my stomach, fluttering at the thought of being here again. It was worse when I noticed the plywood cover over Brittany's shattered window. It had happened. It was real. And if Brittany was in trouble, I was going to help her through it.

Opening the gate, I strode right up the walk, and knocked firmly on the front door.

The hinges of the door squeaked as Mr. Black slowly opened it from inside. His eyes drooped like a hound dog's; black circles framed them. They were an odd mix of blue and bloodshot. He hadn't slept any more than I had.

"I wondered if you'd come back."

"You...you did?"

"What's your name, son?"

"Andrew." I stuttered as though I'd forgotten my own name.

"I suppose you're here to see Brittany."

"Is she here? I want to see her."

"She ain't back yet."

"Back from where?" I stepped forward, curious and hopeful.

"Wish I knew. You saw her go last night, same as me."

"Saw her...?" The weight of what he said slowly pressed down on me. "She's a...? That was...?"

"She ain't told 'ya?"

"I don't..."

"Well, if you're fool enough to get involved with my little girl, there's a few things you oughtta know."

"You're just trying to scare me. I'm head over heels about her and you can't talk me out of seeing her."

"I ain't trying to."

"I'll do anything to help her."

"So, it seems."

I inhaled sharply, about to say something, but then I realized he wasn't arguing with me. "Beg your pardon, sir?"

"Why don't you come in, son. Sounds like we've got a lot to talk about."

He gently forced open the screen door, allowing me passage to the fabled Radley place.

I hesitated.

Was she worth it?

A flash of Brittany's face hit me, as did the feel of her against me. The taste of her lips. The sunshine of her smile. The brilliance in her mind. There it was. I had my answer.

I took a deep breath and stepped inside, the first step in the rest of my life. ♜

SHATTERED INTAGLIO

By David Bowles

"IF YOU DON'T HURRY, MARYU, you won't get to see the general speak. Your father will expect you to be there."

Maryu Maarcu Aivandor reluctantly walked away from the street performers to follow his tutor, glancing back several times to see if he could catch the end of their farce. The people around the cart exploded with laughter, and Maryu cursed silently, irritated at Sumar for not giving him just a few more minutes to enjoy the performance. He didn't need to be reminded of his responsibilities. Hadn't he been studying the family affairs closely, learning the role that he would eventually take on? He was the eldest son, and he did what was expected of him. So, what was so wrong with wanting to be a child from time to time? To laugh long and hearty, especially during as festive a day as this?

The streets were thick with crowds; several times Maryu lost sight of Sumar, but he didn't worry. They were both heading toward the Temple of Dyupadar, and that colossal structure dominated the architecture of the city. Street vendors, recognizing his station and family, offered him food and goods; Maryu just bowed his head politely and refused, hurrying toward the special meeting of the Cosatragana, the highest legislative body in the Republic of Baratu.

Soon he found himself mounting the marble steps, thrusting hurriedly through the throng to find a position on the patio near enough to the open doors—massive, bronze, ancient—to afford him a decent view of the rostrum. As he squeezed into a choice spot beside an ornately carved column, the great Hero of the Republic was welcomed to the temple by the slow, ritual clapping of the legislators.

Joining the general on the rostrum was his brother, Socar Gaumuran Augastya, one of the two *mantuni* elected last year to preside over the executive functions of the Republic. Socar Gaumuran raised his hand to request silence, and even the hushed conversations on the temple patio were stilled.

"Baratu," the *mantu* began, "both republic and capital, have today received General Ramul Gaumuran Augastya with great pomp and circumstance, hailing in a majestic parade his victorious military campaign in the northernmost reaches of the continent. The *quirita* has been placed upon his head, that feathered ceremonial crown declaring him ritual king for a day. And now, as is his right, the Hero of the Republic will address this august body." Socar Gaumuran inclined his head toward his younger brother. "General."

Ramul Gaumuran stepped forward as his brother left the rostrum. His burnished mail glittered in the afternoon sun that streamed in through the doors; his purple cape swirled about him like a living thing with each precise movement he made. The quirita encircled his dark brow like a promise of national fidelity. His every word, Maryu knew, would have the weight of a god's.

"Fathers, your numerous assemblies have always seemed to me the most agreeable body that any man can address, and this hallowed temple has always struck me as the most distinguished place for delivering an oration. I have been prevented from trying this road to glory—open to every son of Baratu—not indeed by my own will, but by the martial life which I adopted as a teen. Before today I would not have dared, on account of my limited achievements, to intrude upon the authority of this place with my own vision for the Republic's future. I felt strongly that no arguments ought to be brought to this place except they be the fruit of great ability and accomplishment. As a result, I have thought it fit to devote all my time to the vanquishing of

Baratu's enemies.

"Your most humbling display of recognition today suggests that I have nearly reached that goal."

There was thunderous applause from the patio, and the legislators shook their purple stoles to indicate their approval.

"I say nearly," the general continued as the sound faded, "because the barbarians of the north are *not* our greatest foe. For millennia another people have harried Baratu, beached ships on our shores, pillaged our towns, burned our temples, raped, and razed as they pleased. Six centuries ago we pacted peace with that nation, but as with a disease that goes into remission, lulling the infirm into believing themselves cured until the plague returns, redoubled in virulence, in some other part of their flesh—so the island kingdom has returned to its imperialistic customs, forging alliances with the northern barbarians, providing weapons and armor and logistical support, helping those savages to raid the border regions of our Republic. The seven-year campaign that you entrusted me to wage has extirpated the vermin from our lands. We have installed territorial governors in the conquered chiefdoms.

"But the true root of this blight remains. Lenki. Sea-locked kingdom of filthy idolaters. Safe haven for pirates and rebels. Moral cesspool in which every abomination is indulged and celebrated. As long as Lenki stands, Baratu is in danger of falling.

"So, Fathers, what I propose is quite simple. Rather than disband the army you put under my command, dispersing the regiments and rerouting the funding, gather together every ship in our fleet sturdy enough to serve as a troop transport, load my soldiers and our materiel, and let us ply the wine-green waves of the sea till we land upon Lenki's beaches and sweep across the island like a monsoon!"

The patio erupted in a chaos of applause, cheers, chants and stomping of feet. Many legislators stood, fanning their chasubles in a sign of support. Some, however, including Maryu's father, remained seated, soberly awaiting their turn to speak. The boy had been privy to many of his father's conversations with important citizens, and he understood that his family was firmly opposed to military action against Lenki, partially because of business interests on the island, but also because the Augastya clan's motives were not nearly so noble as the general was portraying them. And finally, as the Aivandor motto had declared for two thousand years, *the sword must be our last resort.*

A man near Maryu leaned toward a companion and barked, "It's the general's *goras*, it is. I hear tell he magicks his enemies, compels them to surrender or make mistakes. That's why he's been so successful, in war and in politics. He's a *gorator*."

Even at eleven years of age, Maryu knew this was nonsense. The general may indeed have been an adept mage, but he needed no incantations to control the legislators today. The force of his deeds and the reputation of his family were sufficient to sway them as he wished.

General Ramul Gaumuran Augastya wanted Baratu to invade the vast island nation of Lenki. And so, it would.

But it was clear that Maryu's father would not sit idly by while his fellow legislators, drunk on the successes in the north, shattered the six-hundred-year peace that had existed between the two mighty nations. So, after the more senior legislators had praised the general and his audacious plan for attacking Lenki, Marcu Laugyu Aivandor stood and opposed the invasion. He cited the treaties, the law, the opinions of past leaders; he painted gruesome scenarios of the cost to citizens both in lives and in money; and finally, he quoted from the *Verbuni Siduanes*, the sacred Words of the Prophet:

"Il Sidu himself told us, brothers, 'Defend your loved ones and yourself when evil crosses the threshold of your home; otherwise, leave your enemies in the hands of the First Father.' This is a precept of the Way. The general has defended us, and we bend our knee in thanks. But war with Lenki violates all we hold dear, and it will turn the First Father's eyes from us, leaving us open to destruction. We must continue to seek a diplomatic solution to this conflict. Lenki needs our crops and our timber; it craves our silk and our steel. As I have urged in the past, let us restrict trade or completely impose an embargo. Bloodshed is unnecessary."

Maryu's chest began to ache as he listened to his father speak. Marcu Laugyu Aivandor was legislator for the Aivandor clan, his seat in the Cosatragana assured for life by virtue of his being the preeminent male in one of the original fifty families.

But that seat might soon be vacant. His present speech endangered his life.

Maryu noticed with a shiver that Ramul looked upon his father with eyes full of spite as the man ceded the floor to the next legislator, a wealthy citizen from the Calinga region who reacted vehemently against Marcu Laugyu's message, quoting passages from the *Verbuni* that prophesied the destruction of Lenki at the hands of a mighty bull. Other legislators took up the cry to fulfill the Prophet's vision, while only a handful of legislators opposed their bellicose brethren.

At one point, as the general's face grew more and more contented, he looked through the open door at the crowd in the patio and on the steps. His eyes fell upon Maryu, and though there was no reason that leader of men should recognize the boy, Maryu knew he did. Immediately his hands went to his chest, clasping the medallion, his fingers tracing the warding runes embossed upon the silver triangle. Ramul's *goras* probed him, tentative at first, and then insistent. Maryu muttered an *apasinte* to strengthen the runes, and he felt the general's touch withdraw. The warrior nodded his head and smiled more broadly.

Sumar the tutor tugged at his robes at that moment, as if he'd noticed the exchange of power between the boy and the man. "Come, young master. Time we returned to your home and shared the day's experiences with your brother."

Maryu allowed his tutor, a slave from some northern nation who had been with his family for decades, to guide him home through the still ebullient streets of Baratu. Once free from the long shadow of the temple's tower, they wound their way ever upward, past the vast marketplace and the Hill of Victory, alongside the massive *divipas* in which hundreds of working-class families lived in cramped squalor. At the stables near the Sunatra bathhouse a carriage waited, ready to take Maryu and his tutor through the High Gate and along the wending road to the plateau. As the packed earth gradually leveled out, Maryu turned and looked down upon the capital city, sprawled like a drowsy predator across the hills to the south of the otherwise inaccessible high plains of the *Adyaru* region. His incipient vertigo was stilled by a sense of awe.

Near the edge of the plateau, crisscrossed by rainbows refracted by late afternoon sunlight slanting through the spray from the falls, the Aivandor estate spread greenly, open to wind and sky. Maryu regarded the ancient, bleached stone of the family villa and awe gave way to sudden confident pride. For two thousand years his family had served Baratu, first its kings and then its citizens. There was nothing to fear from a scheming general. His father was safe.

As soon as he crossed under the complex arches of the entryway, his younger brother Laxman greeted him with rapid-fire questions.

"Tell me about the parade! Was it really big? What did the general's armor look like? Did they crown him? Did you see any jesters? What about the street plays? Come on, Maryu, tell me what you saw!"

"Slow down, Lax. I've been walking and riding for two hours. Give me a moment, will you?" He dropped onto a chair and sighed. "The parade was fantastic. Everyone in the city was there, and the general rode an elephant at the head of his troops. Streamers were everywhere, and the music was loud. He had on his mail and a purple cape with gold fringes. And yes, the mantuni presented him with the feathered crown.

"As for the streets, they were crowded, and there were jesters and jugglers and street actors. People just gave me food when they saw the family insignia brocaded on my robe."

Laxman pouted for a moment. "It's not fair I couldn't go. You're only a year older than me."

"Sixteen months," Maryu corrected.

"Like it matters. I had to stay here and listen to mother ordering the *Narsimyuni* about with that tone she uses when she's nervous for Father."

Maryu closed his eyes for a moment till a vision of Ramul's smile made him open them with a start. "She's got good reason to, Lax. The general wants to invade Lenki. That's what he announced at the end of his speech to the Cosatragana. But Father publicly opposed him, and I could see the general was furious.

"And...and Ramul tried to get at me with his goras."

Laxman gaped in astonishment. "Why would he want to magic you?"

"I don't know. Maybe... maybe he wants to get at Father. He might've been trying to push a *niyurinte* at me, force me to do something bad to Father. Who knows? But my wardings held, and he seemed impressed."

"Mother always said you had God's touch stronger than the rest of the family. Throwback to our great-grandfather Uvid, she says, remember?"

Before he could respond, Numat, the youngest narsimyu slave at the villa, brought a tray of fruit and cheese in, setting it on a table near the two brothers.

"Goras is strong in young master," he muttered in his hoarse simian voice. "Numat feels it even with the collar blocking his heart's eye."

Maryu examined Numat closely. The ape-like creature had gold fur fretted with orange, like many of his race, and the bare skin of his palms and face was pale, nearly pink. Around his neck was clamped the silver collar which ensorcelled every narsimyu in the Republic, the intricate intaglio of runes carved upon the metal dampening the simians' supernatural abilities.

"Wait. You can sense my goras?"

"Yes. Numat has felt it grow in young master lo these several years. Very special goras, too. Narsimyuni call it *urreke*. Baratuans say *shattering*."

Maryu's breath caught in his throat. *Shattering* was a rare magic indeed, less common even than the general's *compelling*.

"Sacred balls!" blasphemed Laxman excitedly. "Mar, if you can *shatter*, that will be *amazing*!"

"Wait. Don't get all worked up just yet, Lax. Uh, Numat? How is it you know that my *goras* is *shattering*?"

"Because *urreke* is also Numat's magic. Before traders put a collar on this neck, Numat shattered many bones. Killed one. But the price for narsimyuni is very high. The trader boss decided it was worth a dead colleague. And, indeed, Master Marcu did pay many gold coins for Numat. Very prestigious, it is, to have narsimyuni in *damu*. Very much the fashion."

Laxman was probably too enthused to notice, but Maryu heard the bitterness and ire undergirding the simian's unusually long speech. "Enough." He was the child of a ganán, after all, eldest son of a tatalyu of the Republic, a descendant of Ivandor, one of the original founders. He could hardly permit an animal slave to comport himself thus in his presence.

"Go, Numat. You've spoken out of turn, and with too much familiarity.

Go! Hurry up now, before I decide to tell my father how out-of-line you're acting."

#   #   #

But Maryu's father never came home that evening. Foreboding grew in the boys' hearts. Their mother paced and fretted and raised her voice at the slaves. Finally, at the sixteenth hour, stars occluded ominously by northern clouds, a messenger came with the devastating news: Ganán Marcu Laugyu Aivandor had been robbed and killed in an alleyway as he journeyed homeward.

Maryu spent the next five days in an emotional fog. The drummers marched from the Aivandor estate to the Temple of Dyupadar, thudding a mournful tattoo to honor the passing of a well-respected *tatalyu*. Priests of the Way prepared Marcu Laugyu's body with unguents and mantras against corruption; *mantratores* and *goravantes* with varying skills guarded his corpse against black magic and dark forces for the halfweek that it lay in state upon the stone bier at Heaven's Hill. Ramul Gaumuran Augastya was one of the most expressive of the mourners, and when the procession finally carried Marcu Laugyu's lifeless form out of the city, across the Dyuvor River, and onto the Plain of Cremation, the general led the way, the grieving widow clinging to his arm. Maryu's heart began to smolder with rage at this dissembling, at the avuncular way Ramul stroked the hair of Maryu's little sister Tula, at the feigned solemnity with which he watched Lidya Marcai Cautoman take up her temporary place upon the pyre at her dead husband's side while a priest intoned the prayer that released her from her death debt.

Every new expression of false grief was pitch tossed upon the flames of hate in Maryu's soul.

You killed my father, whoreson. His mother descended. You hired some shit-heeled scum to wait in the shadows. The priests touched torches to the wood. You paid off the Cosatragana guards that accompany him home. Flames licked at his father's form. They abandoned him at the agreed-upon time and place. Black smoke roiled toward heaven. And then you reached out through your pawns and killed him.

71

Everyone knows. But no one will touch you.

Except me, you bastard. Somehow. Just wait.

#   #   #

A week passed before Laxman would speak to anyone. When he came to Maryu, his eyes red and empty, the older boy nodded. "Yes. It was the general."

"What are you going to do about it?"

"I'm going to get revenge."

"How?" There was a little surge of hope, of life, in Laxman's pinched features.

Maryu's voice cracked as he muttered, "I'm going to *shatter* him."

"But you... you don't know how."

"No, but Numat does. Go get him. Don't let anyone know what you want him for. Be quick."

Laxman, purpose brightening his face and lightening his stride, hurried off in search of the narsimyu. Maryu tried, as he had for days, to access the power that Numat had sensed in him. When he reached within himself, however, his sight was blocked, thrust aside by a wave of rage and sadness and bitterness. Again and again, he dove, only to be driven out of his trance by more and more powerful barriers, as if his frustration itself amplified his impotence.

"Young master goes about it all wrong."

Through bleary eyes, Maryu looked at Numat, his sleek animal head proud and serene above his silver collar. "What do you mean?"

"Must empty the self first. Anger can come later once the shattering begins. Anger makes it stronger, less focused, more destructive. But to spark it, you must be empty."

Maryu despaired at ever draining the rage from his soul. It didn't seem possible. It didn't seem right.

"Can you teach me?"

"Yes. But."

"But what?"

Numat lifted a wrinkled finger to the glittering runes at his neck. "Numat would be free, young master. That is his price. And he has heard the rumorings. Not much time is left before the general crosses the sea to Lenki. You must act soon. You cannot act without Numat's help. And Numat demands freedom. The collar, broken."

It was illegal. So was assassinating a general. If Maryu were caught, he would be banished or worse.

It was an easy choice.

"Agreed."

#   #   #

The weeks passed. Lidya Marcai and her daughter Tula remained in the women's wing, as they would all year in obedience to the Way, mourning the passing of the head of the family. With the assistance of his tutor and his father's secretary, Maryu spent the mornings overseeing the family's affairs—the fields, orchards, ships, shops—and receiving the favors and petitions of certain members of lower castes for whom Marcu Laugyu had been a patron.

Each afternoon, though, he went into the garden and trained. Numat's harsh, hoarse whisper insinuated itself into his mind, guiding him, calming him, helping him loosen the net that bound up his ability. After days of failure, the narsimyu taught him a mantra of serenity, a series of syllables in the simian tongue that meant nothing to Maryu, but that stilled his mind, nonetheless.

And in the stillness, he found the spark, a warm glow in the darkness. It took Numat another week to help him see the fine threads that connected that spark to the world around him.

Finally came the day, three weeks after his father's murder, when Maryu took hold of his *goras* and sent a thrumming down the threads that led to a nearby mango tree. A loud *crack* made him open his eyes with a start: a limb of the tree had split lengthwise.

"Good," Numat murmured in response to Maryu's excitement. "But not enough. General will be pushing back, young master. General is accompanied at all times by *nirodores* skilled at suppressing the *goras* of a would-be assassin. To shatter, you will have to push past mighty barriers. Now focus and try again. You must burst the very core of this tree."

Maryu could not. Afternoons stretched into evenings. The boy hardly slept. He split stones, cracked branches, snuffed the lives of lizards and birds.

The tree remained standing. Fruit lay about it, exploded by his efforts. Roots were exposed from the magical push of his mind. But three days before the army of Baratu was to set sail for Lenki, the tree was still intact.

Laxman stood before his older brother, a question in his eyes. Maryu looked away. Numat shook his head.

"He is not ready, little lord. Numat has tried, but there is not sufficient time."

"What? No! We can't let Ramul get away with this!"

Maryu lifted a hand weakly as if to silence his brother, but he was stopped by the narsimyu's soft growl.

"There is another way."

The sons of Marcu Laugyu Aivandor leaned toward the slave, expectant.

"A trick. You attack him with your goras. The nirodores are distracted trying to repulse the samruyante. And then Numat reaches out and shatters general."

Maryu shook his head, not in refusal, but to clear his thoughts. He regarded the silver collar that matted Numat's pale fur, the strange red blotches in the whites of his eyes.

"How do I know you'll help me even after I release you? What's to keep you here? What's to keep you from shattering anyone who tries to stop you from leaving?"

Numat's breath hissed with barely repressed anger. "Ngerre... *narsimyuni*, we keep our word. Our word binds us. You know nothing! Your people snare us and bind us and think yourselves strong. Bah! Do you hear Numat? *Our* word *binds us*."

"Then give us your word," Laxman said.

"*Kupu homari*. Word given."

Maryu nodded once; he reached within and then without.

The silver collar clattered to the floor.

#   #   #

The streets were teeming. The city was surging toward the Hill of Victory, from whose summit General Ramul Gaumuran Augastya would lead his army on a three-day march to the port town of Corga. From there they would sail across the Middle Sea to making landing on the shores of Lenki.

The two boys, accompanied by Numat, pushed their way through the crowds to get closer to the general. The narsimyu's collar had been reassembled with hoof glue; a strong tug would pull it apart again. They approached the vanguard of the army, where Ramul sat astride a massive destrier, surrounded by his contingent of nirodores, each mounted on a rune-branded rouncey. Numat quickly crossed to the other side of the stone cobbled Pontín Masemu, acting as if he were buying a bag of roasted nuts for his master. Maryu positioned himself right at the edge of the highway and turned so that he had the general in his line of sight. Laxman stood a couple of paces behind him.

After a trumpet blast, the army began its slow procession. Seconds later, Ramul's steed was within the range of Maryu's *goras*. When Maryu shut his eyes to search, the general's spark fairly leapt at him, hungry dark flames that licked at the weft of the world. With a cry of fury, Maryu send his shattering along the skein that joined him tenuously to his father's murderer. Immediately the nirodores drew their mounts about; with ducks of the head, mantras, and hand signs they deflected his attack. The recoil was a mailed fist striking his forehead: Maryu collapsed like so much dead weight, barely able to remain focused on the champing horses and the face of his brother, bent close to him, muttering questions that the older boy could not hear.

Straining his eyes at the gaps between horses, Maryu was able to make out the form of Numat: the Narsimyu had discarded his broken collar, and his face was twisted with a rage that would have made Maryu tremble were he not so innervated by his own reflected shattering. As his mind teetered on the verge of darkness, the boy felt a long-pent-up wave of terrifying power ripple across reality.

Screams sounded faintly in his deaf ears, and then he understood the true cost of revenge.

The simian's rage was too great, and years of enslavement had eroded his control. The general's nirodores were indeed shattered, bone and blood blossoming outward in a spherical blast. But the thrumming puissance was unfocused, broadcast wildly, and dozens of bystanders crumpled like discarded marionettes, their limbs unnaturally akimbo.

And before Maryu's eyes, tumbling down in the dusty road, Laxman fell lifeless.

Icy knives wrenched at his innards. Bereft, he surrendered himself to the oblivion of unconsciousness, his eyes dropping shut, blocking out the horror.

Then he was wrenched to his feet, slapped back to awareness. Soldiers had hold of him, were shaking him and shouting. His bones ground painfully together.

Ramul was standing over Numat, their magicks locked in a struggle that made the fabric of the cosmos howl about them.

A grin split the general's face of a sudden, and the narsimyu tottered, blood streaming from his eyes, nose, mouth, pores.

With a groan, he crumpled, dead and broken.

Maryu's hearing was coming back, a ringing roar of sound. The cries of the multitude, mainly, gathered weeping around their fallen friends and family.

"Kill him!" came the screams as the citizens of Baratu gestured wildly at Maryu, overcome with grief and rage. "Kill him!"

Maryu was amazed to see Ramul shake his head and raise his hand, demanding silence.

"The boy was consumed by grief," the general called out above the hushing din. "The one he loved the most was taken from him by the will of God. Ah, vainly does Man strive to find human targets for his anger at the First Father's plans. I hear your righteous rage, compatriots. But soft, now. I was the intended victim, after all. The law lays justice for this attempted murder in my hands. If I choose to forgive, who can gainsay me?"

No one spoke. Sullen eyes sparked in the morning sun.

"Of course, your losses must be compensated. Let the boy stand trial for the unintended deaths, the collateral damage. The holdings of the Aivandor are vast; dismantled, they will help to ease your grief."

For a moment, the general held them all by the power of his will alone. Then a mother rushed screaming from the crowd, swinging a club that smashed into Maryu's head.

The darkness took him at last.

#   #   #

"Wake, boy."

Maryu rose up through layers of black, struggling toward the dazzling white of consciousness. He heard soft, muted sounds all around him: padded steps, rustling fabrics. The smell of herbs and unguents hung thickly.

A healer's hall. He gently moved his limbs. If at some point they'd been broken, the healer's skill had mended them.

"Open your eyes, Maryu Maarcu Aivandor."

The general's voice. Alive.

Slowly, unwillingly, Maryu obeyed. The villain grinned down at him. He still wore his mail and purple cloak, which suggested that only a few hours had passed.

"Good boy. I must admit, you've impressed me. Not many of my enemies have gotten as close as you to ending my life. I suspected you might try, but using your *narsimyu*… well, that was the mark of a true tactician. Of course, it cost you dearly. Three dozen innocent bystanders. Your own brother."

His voice hoarse, Maryu moaned, "Your fault. Bastard."

There was a predatory glitter in Ramul's eyes. He gave a brittle laugh. "You'll have plenty of time to meditate on blame, boy. It's been arranged. Once the trial is over, you'll be sent to a monastery in the North. To join the Palitas Order in their devotion to the Way."

Maryu rose on his elbows, his distress boiling away as hatred surged from within.

"With your brother dead and you in exile, what remains of the Aivandor estate, after the jury awards the families of the dead, will fall to me. It may be that your widowed mother, once my victory is secure and her bereavement over, will consent to be my bride."

It was too much to bear. Maryu balled his hands into fists, tried to attack with body and soul, but his goras would not respond. It was as if all power had been stripped from him. Ramul pushed him back onto the bed with a sigh.

"It's unfortunate. At the temple, I sensed such potential in you. I could have honed you like a sword, used your keen edge in battle. But you'll never wield magic again, Maryu Maarcu Aivandor. Never."

The boy's hands went to his neck then, groping in spasms, and found runes carved upon a silver collar, dumb yet ineluctable words that silenced the spark of his heart. ♜

THE BLACK DOOR

By Deborah Daughetee

CORA SAT IN THE CORNER of the classroom, willing herself to be invisible, as a tornado of color and sounds whirled in response to the final school bell of the week. She closed her eyes and pretended she was a ghost, disappearing into some other place where she floated in a world of nothingness. On the periphery of her consciousness, she heard the teacher turn off the light and close the door as she exited the room. Still, Cora floated, a ghost caught in the in-between, in liminal space. She learned of liminal space when she read Jane Lindskold's book, *Child of a Rainless Year*.

She wasn't actually invisible, though sometimes it felt that way. She waited until the halls grew quiet before she eased out of her seat and skittered to her locker. It was Friday afternoon. There was cheerleading practice out on the football field, so she should be safe. And yet she sucked her breath in quick and shallow as if breathing too deeply would alert the predator to its prey.

She stuffed her books inside the locker and took out her backpack, slamming the door with a metallic clang that echoed eerily down the empty hall.

She paused at the door and forced herself to take that deep breath. She eased out, wincing at the loud click the door made when closing. The door opened out onto a kind of porch with two walls on each side, the door behind her, and the wide-open world in front of her. There were five steps leading down to a sidewalk that led to the paved, two-lane street, which led to the graveyard and past the house at the end of the lane. Her house. Cora heard a sound coming from around the corner and sprinted down the steps a few steps onto the sidewalk before a girl, Candy, caught the strap of her backpack, jerking her around.

"Well, will you look at this? It's the suicide's daughter."

"Let go, Candy."

"I don't know, I'd like to take a look at what's inside that backpack; wouldn't you, girls?"

There were four girls in Candy's gang, four girls who now surrounded Cora. Cora clutched her backpack to her chest.

"Oh, come on, we just want to uncover the mystery."

"What mystery?"

"Why, the mystery of how your father hated you so much he shot himself in the head."

Cora's legs lost all their strength and she fell to her knees, instantly transported back to the moment she walked into her father's study and found him with his brains splattered across the wall. She couldn't breathe. She doubled over as Candy jerked the backpack out of her hands and emptied it onto the sidewalk. But Cora was only peripherally aware of the other girls. Her father's mouth was open, his eyes wide as if surprised by what he'd just done. The room reeked of blood and gunpowder and death and Cora thought she would vomit, just like she did on that day.

The girls tired of their bullying and left Cora collapsed there, sucking in tiny bits of breath until her gorge settled in her stomach and her chest loosened. A long, shuddering sob escaped but she mentally slapped herself. She wasn't going to cry, not anymore.

Scattered around her were charcoal sticks which, miraculously, survived Candy's inspection, paper, and tape. There was also a plain paper bag with her dinner that Candy had stomped. She carefully put them back into her backpack and got up. Her knees stung from having scraped them on the cement; she welcomed the pain as it helped clear away the picture of her father. She ran all the way to the cemetery.

The little gate whined as she opened it… a proper welcome to a haunted cemetery. Cora thought that saying "a haunted cemetery" was redundant, but that's what people called the cemetery that Cora's father inherited from his aunt. Mother had moved them here after. She said they had nowhere else to go.

Walking into the cemetery was like entering another world. Willow trees lined the paths. Leaves and weeds littered the ground so thickly that Cora couldn't hear her own footsteps. Bright green moss covered the gravestones, some with strands of ivy and some with tiny pink flowers. High in the trees, birds sang their high joyous songs. It heartened Cora to hear that joy still existed somewhere in the world.

Cora's father taught her how to do rubbings of the gravestones. That was before he went away to war. He didn't do much of anything after he came back except drink beer until Mother had to help him walk up to bed. But before he went to war, Father told Cora she had a knack for coaxing the letters out of the most damaged headstones, the ones where the letters were so worn off you couldn't see them anymore. He said she had the gift of restoration.

The last time Cora made a rubbing was on Father's Day. Cora wanted to make him feel better, wanted to restore him like she did the gravestones. She made her father a rubbing from a stone that read, "World Greatest Father." When her father opened it. He looked at it for a long time, tears coursing down his face. Cora went to her room and curled into a tight little ball, leaking tears of her own. Later, Mother came into her room and told Cora it wasn't anything she did; Father was just very sad. Cora never made another rubbing, until now.

Father didn't use to be so sad until he became a soldier in the war. When he came back, he was different. He sometimes woke up screaming. Mother told Cora to stay away from him when he was sleeping because sometimes, he would wake up swinging his fist at some invisible enemy. Mother said Father might accidentally hurt her.

Cora thought that she would never make a rubbing again. But then they'd moved next to this old cemetery. The first time she walked through it, the whispers of good memories with her father pushed the bad away. She stole a few pieces of charcoal from school and spent her allowance on butcher paper and masking tape.

A willow tree had grown around a headstone and looked as if it wrapped it in a loving embrace. The stone was so old and worn that Cora wasn't sure even her talents would be able to bring the letters out, but she decided to give it a try. She unwrapped a wet soapy sponge and gently washed the moss off the gravestone. It wasn't crumbly, so she knew she wouldn't damage it if she was careful. Masking tape secured the paper to the headstone, which was challenging with the tree growing around it. Then she went to work with her charcoal stick.

It was a stubborn stone, but Cora talked to it, coaxing out the letters one by one and then dates.

"Please," she said. "Let me see your name and the dates you were alive. I want to know your story."

She talked to the stone as if it was an extension of the person buried there, for that is what she believed it was.

The letters slowly began to appear. "Let me remember you, though I never knew you."

Little by little, the name became visible, *Louella Davis*, then beneath *Birth 1664, Death 1693*. And then, *Beloved Mother*.

Cora was surprised at how plain the rubbing looked. She carefully removed the tape and pulled the rubbing from the stone. It just wasn't as beautiful without the tree that enclosed it, so she carefully drew the way the roots twisted around the outside of the stone, framing the inscription.

It was late afternoon by the time Cora finished. She sat and leaned back against a willow tree and pulled out her smashed dinner. The potato chips were crumbs but she ate them anyway. Her sandwich, garlic bologna with Swiss on white bread, was smashed flat, but still good. She took a bite and was chewing when a huge, black dog, a rottweiler, walked up and sat down right in front of her. Cora stopped chewing forcing a swallow and looked at the dog. It looked back. Finally, after moments of this staring contest, Cora offered it half of her sandwich. The dog downed it in one gulp, then lay down and put its head in Cora's lap.

Cora ate the rest of her dinner, then gently moved the dog's head, and said, "I need to go home, now, but I'll be back tomorrow." The rottweiler looked at her, then rose and walked right beside her, his side gently brushing against her leg.

She loved twilight. It was the in-between, that perfect moment between light and dark. She loved the way the shadows of the cemetery disappeared, and the world became grey. No color, no red blood or grey brain matter or blue, dead eyes staring.

The dog whined as Cora got caught up in the memory, pulling her back to the present. Then it growled, and Cora looked up to see a black door in front of her. Ice flooded her veins and stabbed at her heart. It was a black door in a doorframe with no building to hold it up. And yet it stood there as if beckoning for her to turn the knob.

The dog looked up at her, his head cocked sideways, eyes on hers. Open the door and walk through or continue down the path and go home?

Carefully, Cora stepped around the door. The opposite side looked just like the first. You could enter from either side. But enter to where?

"Home," answered Cora.

Night took the land and the door faded from view. Cora realized that she'd been holding her breath and released it, the exhale as shaky as her hands. Then she turned and hurried to the edge of the cemetery where the dog stopped and sat down.

Suddenly, Cora didn't want to be alone; she knew there was no one to welcome her, no one to ask her how her day was, no one to question her tardiness.

"You can come home with me if you want. My mom won't even notice. You can sleep in my bed."

But the dog just sat there, ignoring the open space of the gate.

"Okay, then. I'll bring you your own sandwich tomorrow," She reluctantly pushed the gate open, the squeal sounding loud in the gathering darkness. And she decided to run home instead of walking.

It was full dark by the time she arrived at her house, breathless. Her mother was still in bed, wrapped in grief and shame and guilt. Used to be her mother required her to come home right after school, do her homework, then eat dinner as a family. Now, her mother really didn't care where Cora was, if she did her homework or whether she had dinner. Now it was up to Cora to make sure her mother ate something.

Cora made another garlic bologna sandwich and took it upstairs. Her mother was asleep in a tangled knot of dirty sheets. Cora left the sandwich along with a glass of iced tea, on the bedside table. She took away the plate that still had a partially eaten sandwich on it and left without waking her. Then she went to her room and pulled out a box from beneath her bed. She sat with it on her lap for a long time before she got the nerve to open it.

The box was filled with drawings that her father made after he got home from the war. One of them was of her reading a book. She didn't even know when he did it; she only found it after... She put it aside and pulled out the rest. He'd used butcher paper using the same kind of charcoal she used for her rubbings. Drawing after drawing was of a door floating in nothing. A black door against a sea of white.

Cora stared at the drawings until she felt the tears coming. Then she stuffed them all, except the drawing of her, back into the box and shoved it under her bed. The sketch of her she taped to the wall across from the foot of her bed.

#   #   #

The next day the rottweiler was waiting for her in the same spot as if it has sat there all night. She gave it a pat on the head, then headed into the cemetery with her backpack full of supplies.

She wandered among the broken and nameless tombstones. It wasn't like it was a massive cemetery, but there was something about how quiet it was, about the way the trees and moss grew, and the gravestones spread out in uneven rows that made it seem like a different world than the one where Father's died, and Mother's stayed in bed all day. The birds sang to her, and the tree branches whispered in the wind. The scent of earth and moss and rock embraced her and made her feel at home.

She stopped in front of a grave with a statue of a young woman with short wavy hair and hands clutched to her chest. A rose bush grew where

Cora assumed the grave was. She wondered if the roots had pierced the coffin and if the bright, red roses were the color of the woman's blood. The scent was sweet and powdery, and Cora thought she might get lost in that scent, the way Father used to get lost in his drink. She couldn't get to the actual gravestone because of the thorny bush, so even though she wanted to know this woman's name and story, she moved on.

She finally stopped at a stone that had an effigy of a cat resting curled up asleep. The marker's face was worn, but the cat was still beautiful in the detail of its fur, its ears, and its tail which wrapped around its body. Cora imagined she could almost hear it purr. She lay out her supplies. If this person loved her cat enough to have it memorialized with her, then she deserved to be remembered. Cora was sure it was a woman interred here because a man wouldn't be caught dead with a cat on his grave.

The letters emerged. Martha Johnson. Born 1842. Died 1875. Born a slave. Died free.

"She was a slave," she said to the dog, who growled in agreement.

There was nothing at all about the cat that slumbered on her grave. But, thought Cora, it must have been important to her, part of her story, so she carefully removed the tape and the rubbing and drew the cat to complete the picture.

By then the sun was high and Cora decided to picnic in the shade of the willow that embrace the stone she worked on yesterday. As she sat down, she glanced over at Luella's stone and fell back on her rear in shock. On the clean surface of the stone, carved deeply for all to read, was Louella's name, date of birth, and date of death. For moments, all she could do was stare, until finally she ran her fingers over the letters and felt their deeply grooved edges.

"You're seeing this too, right," she said to the dog. While it didn't answer, it did regard her with a huge grin on its face, its tongue hanging out the side of its mouth

Cora sighed. "Okay, whatever. This is a haunted cemetery, right? I just wish it could have done that before I made my rubbing."

As she was pulling lunch out of her bag, two bologna sandwiches, chips, and an apple cut into wedges, a large, black cat came and sat down beside the rottweiler. She looked at the two of them sitting side by side.

"You see that cat too, right?" she asked the rottweiler. The dog turned its head and looked at the cat, who rubbed up against him, then walked over to rub up against Cora and finally settle in her lap.

She gave the rottweiler his sandwich and pulled the bologna out of half of hers and tore it into little pieces for the cat. Every now and then she glanced at the gravestone, just to make sure she hadn't imagined the reversal of the damage.

Later, Cora stood in front of the headstone of Martha Johnson. Like Luella's stone, the words were deeply chiseled into the stone. The two animals flanked her. Finally, she turned toward them and kneeled. She took the dog's head in her hands and brought her face to hers.

"You are Luella," she said, breathing the musky scent of dog. Then she turned to the cat, scratching it behind the ears.

"And you are Martha." The cat mewed.

Cora spent the rest of the day with Luella and Martha walking through the cemetery, trying to decide which stone to do next. Finally, she asked the animals, "What do you think? Who's next?"

The dog instantly turned and led her to a grave where the cat leaped up onto a stone so badly degraded that Cora couldn't see anything on the front except a shadow of a groove and roses carved all around the three sides.

"I don't know if I can do this one." The two sat down and stared at her, giving her a vote of confidence. Cora sighed and pulled out her tools.

It didn't take her long to coax the name from the stone. *Elizabeth Singleton, 1710-1735*. It was more challenging to tease out the inscription beneath, and when she finally did, it wasn't until she sat back to look at her work that she realized what it said.

"She was too sensitive for this world, so she walked through the black door."

Cora fell back on her haunches. The roses carved into the headstone began to bloom and the letters appeared behind her rubbing.

"Have you seen my dad?" asked Cora. The roses bobbed their heads at her.

Martha and Luella accompanied Cora, carrying a handful of perfect red roses, to the gate. It was full dark, so the black door didn't appear. Somehow,

Cora knew it only existed in the in-between, in luminal space. The animals sat down at the gate. Cora turned and gave each one a pat and promised to bring food again tomorrow. Sunday. She had one more day.

When Cora walked through the gate, the roses withered and dried, and the petals fell to the ground becoming dust.

#   #   #

Cora was shocked to see the downstairs lights on in her house and her grandmother's car in the drive. Her father's mother. They'd been estranged before he went to war. Her mother told her she had a lot of money and expected to get anything she wanted. She didn't want my mom. "Why marry this skinny, little hillbilly? You need a big, strong woman; one who can give you many sons."

She was sorely disappointed in both the marriage and the birth of a girl and was so vocal about it that her father cut her off.

The smell of sausage and dumplings hit Cora as soon as she opened the door. Her mother sat at the kitchen table, her face washed, dressed in jeans and a T-shirt, staring vacantly at the wall across from her. Her eyes were sunken with dark circles and red rims. Her face sagged and her mouth looked like it would never smile again.

Cora remembered the woman with shining, auburn hair that curled no matter how much she tried to straighten it. She remembered green eyes that sparkled every time Cora came into the room. Her mother encouraged Cora to find what inspired her and learn everything she could about it. She remembered the woman who used to believe in following your dreams.

Her grandmother stood at the stove ladling some soup into a bowl. Cora silently took her place at the table and her grandmother put the bowl in front of her. It steamed and sent up delicious tendrils that made Cora's mouth water.

It was a trap, Cora knew. If she ate, she would have to pay a toll. Her father said it was, "paid with the soul."

So even though her stomach growled, she fought to not pick up the spoon. Her mother knew it was a trap as well for her bowl no longer steamed and her spoon remained untouched.

Her grandmother sat down opposite her. "You realize that if your father had listened to me, he'd be alive today. Or at least have a male heir to carry on the family name."

"Smith?" asked Cora. "I think there are plenty of people carrying on that name, grandma."

"Hmph. Even so, every man wants a boy to raise."

"Not my father," said Cora. "He told me he was glad she was a girl because if she were a boy, his mother would be around all the time."

Her grandmother glared at her. "He killed himself because he made a mistake marrying your mother."

"No." Cora's mother's voice was thin and weak. "He killed himself because the war killed him first."

Hope flooded into Cora. It was the first time her mother had spoken in months and Cora thought maybe this meant she was getting better. But her mother hadn't stopped staring at the wall in front of her, and her body sagged as if the words had cost all the energy she had.

Cora glared at her grandmother. "Why are you here?"

Her grandmother sat back with a sigh. "Because despite being a girl, you are my firstborn's firstborn. Your mother is clearly unable to care for you, so I have started proceedings to have her declared unfit. You'll be coming home with me where there will be no more running around to all hours of the night, no haunting cemeteries—I never understood your father's obsession with those macabre rubbings."

"I have the gift of restoration."

Her grandmother got up and took away her mother's dish. "Restoration! Your only gift, my dear, is at destroying your father's life, quite literally. But you're still half Smith. It will just take some work and discipline to bring it out. Now, if you're not going to eat, go upstairs and pack your things. We leave in the morning."

Cora looked at her mother and was shocked to see her mother looking back. Her eyes were deep wells of sorrow, grief, guilt, and terror.

"I need to look after my mother."

"Your mother is a grown woman. She'll just have to suck it up and look after herself. You're simply enabling her by letting her wallow."

Cora knew her mother would simply waste away if Cora was gone.

Something snapped inside her mother's eyes. She got up and shambled over to the soup, got the bowl grandmother had just washed, and put in one ladle. Then she sat down and picked up her spoon and began to eat.

"It makes no difference what you do now, Evelyn. Cora is mine. On Monday, it will be official. So go back to bed and die and save yourself the effort."

Cora leaped from her chair and slapped her grandmother across the face. There was shock in the old woman's eyes, then anger and pure malice. She grabbed Cora by the arm, wrenching it so hard Cora cried out in pain. She half dragged Cora up the steps and pushed her into her room.

"Pack!"

Cora's mother appeared behind her grandmother breathing heavily from the effort of climbing the stairs. She put her hand on her mother-in-law's shoulder. Grandmother turned and pushed; Cora's mother fell down the steps backward.

Cora stayed in her room while the police came and took her mother's body away. Her grandmother mustered up a tear or two and said she was trying to help the poor woman, but she was so weak and fell on the stairs. She said Cora was too distraught to talk to them.

Cora packed her things, then went to bed and stared at the drawing her father made of her. She got up and pulled the other drawings out from under the bed.

#　　#　　#

Before dawn, Cora shrugged into her full backpack, slipped out her bedroom window down the slope of the awning, and dropped to the ground. The dog and the cat were there to meet her. All three walked to the grave with the beautiful, red stone roses, and gorged themselves on garlic bologna, Swiss cheese, and bread, all that had been left from her last grocery run.

Then the cat climbed into her lap, put its front paws on her shoulders, and bumped her forehead against Cora's. The dog licked her cheek. She put her arm around the rottweiler as it leaned against her. They stayed like that, waiting for the color that preceded the rising of the sun. Cora waited until that perfect time between light and dark, then hugged the animals and rose. They accompanied her to where the black door was waiting.

#   #   #

Cora's grandmother didn't notice Cora was missing until she came in to collect the girl and her things. There were two small suitcases on her bed, packed as if she planned on leaving that morning. Her closet and drawers were empty. The only thing left in the room was the picture on the wall of Cora reading surrounded by her father's charcoals of the black door. ♜

1/1

By Julian Michael Carver

BATHED IN GOLDEN SOLAR RAYS that pierced the overhead canopy, the baseball card looked angelic. Encased in a penny sleeve, Tristan twirled the card around, revealing the player photograph on the front and fact-ridden back.

Freshly pulled a day earlier from a blaster box, Tristan Weitz wasted no time in calling his best friend, Matt Thompson, down to their secret hangout to unveil his latest prize. The secret hangout – which was nothing more than the ruins of an old house foundation deep in the woods – was situated at the foot of an overflowing creek. Though little more than a few bricks that formed an imperfect square, the pair claimed the location as their hideout in their childhood. Now that both boys were now eighteen, Matt found himself wondering why they still haunted the area.

He also wondered why he was still friends with Tristan after all these years. For the most part, Tristan only bragged about his accomplishments and aspirations, which lately had hit critical mass. The constant bragging was driving Matt insane – so insane that Matt debated on ghosting the friendship altogether.

"What do you think?" Tristan asked, spinning the card back and forth. "Pulled this rookie from an old blaster box from the attic. Thankfully Dad never throws anything out. Not sure why he never opened these. This guy is worth over *three hundred grand* right now, ungraded! And if I do get him graded, I guarantee it'll come back a 10. And a 10 graded card of this guy would be *over* one million dollars easy!"

The "guy" Tristan was referring to was a player named Cooper Robbins who played for the Scranton Stingrays from 1999 to 2006 before retiring. As the Stingrays' star pitcher, he led the team to three straight World Championships, shattering several records along the way. He led the league in strikeouts for five consecutive years, making his baseball card one of the most valuable cards on the market.

Judging by the appearance through the card's penny sleeve, Matt saw that the card was in pristine condition, despite sitting in a musty attic for over twenty years. The edges of the card weren't frayed, and the card's front and back were free from blemishes. The product would undoubtedly be graded a perfect 10, Matt thought – whatever that meant.

"How about that," Matt feigned a smile, taking the card from Tristan and inspecting it.

"Be careful!" Tristan scowled. "You know how much these cards drop in value once they're tampered with."

"Right," Matt replied, flipping the card around to check both sides.

In reality, Matt didn't know about the drop in value. In fact, Matt didn't know anything about sports, other than the fundamentals. The most he cared about sporting events was the delicious food and attractive cheerleaders.

After a quick inspection, Matt carefully handed the card back to Tristan. As his friend took the card back, Matt noticed some gold embossed lettering on the front near Cooper Robbins' tennis shoe just above the pitching mound.

"What's that mean?" Matt asked, gesturing to the glittery numeric symbols.

"What?" Tristan replied, looking back at the card. "Oh, that's how you know this baby is worth money. It says 1/1, which means that this is the first card out of one card ever printed. Simply put, it's a one of a kind; the only one in existence. Lots of baseball cards have similar numeric lettering. There can be many number combinations on cards like 37/250 and 140/500 and 23/50. But a 1/1 card is the most rare."

1/1, Matt thought, the numbers transitioning into cartoon dollar signs in his head.

"And how much do you guess that this card is worth again?"

"Oh, easily a million dollars once it's been graded," Tristan admitted. "But maybe even more according to some internet sites I've been on. This could easily set me up for life, Matt! I'm talking pay for a new car, house, even my four-year college in Miami – everything. I could even start investing into *more* baseball cards and selling those off."

"Sounds cool," Matt replied. "And, more importantly, have you told anyone that you have this card? I mean, people could try to steal it from you if you aren't careful, you know."

"Nah, I haven't told anyone," Tristan smiled, turning back to the card with a bright smile as if to marvel in its brilliance. "I think the baseball card store down on Fifth is open until five. Maybe after we hangout here, I could –"

THHWWWAK!

The attack was savage and fast – so fast that Matt guessed Tristan never knew what hit him.

Grabbing whatever nearby loose foundation brick he could salvage from the ruins, Matt brought the weapon down on his friend's head from behind. On the first hit, Tristan uttered a helpless yelp before his attacker repetitively slammed the brick repetitively against his skull, slathering the soil in a coat of blood and gray matter.

After a minute of non-stop pounding with the brick, Matt backed away, shooting cautionary glances in all directions.

Nothing. Just trees and empty wilderness...

When he confirmed that no one was around to see the attack, he breathed easy. Apart from the distant rumble of traffic on the Interstate through the trees, there were no signs of human life in the foliage. The pair had been alone – no witnesses.

And who would see it? No one ever comes down here anyway. I can't believe I let Tristan take me down here all these years and bore me to death with his perfect life....

Imagining himself as Cooper Robbins some twenty years ago, Matt chucked the bloody weapon into the overflowing creek, hoping the block would land somewhere obscure where forensics would have trouble recovering it.

Fingerprints would long be gone in the water. No one even knows I was here anyway. No one knows this was our hangout! That's why it was always a secret hangout! And best of all; no one knows about the card, thus no one knows about the motive! It's perfect. Ha, so long, Tris'.

Wasting no time in scooping up the Cooper Robbins card, Matt gave one last look at the lifeless cadaver, shoved the card into his pants pocket, and departed from the area, smiling gleefully as he went.

#   #   #

Calm down! Tristan's dead. That was like – what? Twenty blows directly to the head? You're freakin' out, Matt! Honestly, no one ever goes back there. I think me and Tristan were the only ones that even knew about that place. Jeez, if you're that worried about it, go back, and bury him later somewhere else. But then what if someone catches you returning to the scene? Might look suspicious. Enough! Let the body rot there. No one even knows that place exists. Tristan didn't tell his parents he was meeting with me – I know that for a fact because I bumped into him on the walk back from school. And he didn't tell them he found that card either. Relax, Matt. Once you pawn off this card, you'll be set!

Wrestling with his inner demons, Matt shuffled down the sidewalk of downtown Bridgewater until he saw the glorious sign of the trading card store dead ahead.

The building didn't look like much. Erected in the mid 1980's, the building's facade was comprised of chipped, faded wood. Old outdated promotional posters for upcoming card and comic releases hung on the dusty windows that ran along the storefront. He breathed a sigh of relief as he saw the open sign hanging in the doorway. From the looks of it, no customers were inside, and the owner was sitting behind his desk, cataloging his new purchases.

Nice! Okay, here we go –

With the chime of a brass bell to announce his arrival, Matt eased into the store, earning a hearty wave from the vendor.

"Welcome!" called the owner of the store. "How may I help you?"

Matt walked up to the front desk, passing by the droves of highly priced sporting cards that remained encased in protective sleeves on the wall, displayed proudly on varnished wooden shelves. Many of the cards were highly priced, but none as valuable as Matt was hoping to earn for his Cooper Robbins card.

"Hey, *uh* – Doug," Matt replied, reading the nametag on the man's faded flannel shirt. "Just hoping to see what I could earn for this little beauty."

"Well, let's take a look," Doug said, taking the card and inspecting it. "*Wow!* This is a Cooper Robbins rookie card from 1999. And it's a 1/1, must've been pretty exciting opening this from a – what the heck is this?"

"What?"

"*Ugh*, is this... *blood?*"

Matt's heart sank as he saw the card collector's eyes go from happy to disgusted. At first, Matt had absolutely no idea why Doug's mood had shifted – until he saw the red stains plaguing the edges of the card.

Oh no! Tristan's blood! It's all over the whole card!

His skin turning pale, Matt realized the horrifying truth. Since Tristan placed the Cooper Robbins card in a simple penny sleeve, there was a large opening at the top where the card could fit through. When he bashed Tristan over the head, the blood from the attack must've seeped through the opening, contaminating his treasure.

Doug retrieved a small magnifying glass, aghast by the grim discovery.

"The blood's all over Cooper's uniform too! I couldn't tell at first, since it's a red jersey. And there's something else – mud maybe? Yeah, mud all over the pitching mount and slopped all along the side. Wow, man. You took a card that's potentially worth over a million dollars when graded and devalued it to – hmm, maybe a few cents? But honestly, it's worthless now. And also – hey, wait a minute."

"What?" Matt asked, trying to hold back his lunch.

"My nephew Tristan just called me last night about a 1/1 Cooper Robbins rookie card that he had and wanted to sell. I thought that he was stopping by later today to –

No! Tristan did tell someone about the card! He lied! Of course – how could I have been so stupid! He always talked about his Uncle Doug! Doug was the one that got him into baseball card collecting.

"There's *no* way that this is a coincidence," Doug scowled, reaching for his cell phone. "The card. The blood. How did you get this? If something happened to my nephew... I don't know what this is, but you stay put while I call the *polic –*"

The rest of Doug's sentence melded into a blur as Matt streaked for the exit. As he hurdled himself past the aisles of trading cards and comic stands, he tried to grapple with the potential end of normalcy to his life.

Doug would call the police. Based on the store's camera feed, the authorities would have his image. In a small town like Bridgewater, they would capture him almost immediately. Matt knew he wouldn't last two seconds in an interrogation room, and a lie detector test? He couldn't even stand up for himself in debate club – how was he supposed to defend his alibi to the cops?

No! No! This was all a mistake! Why did I do this! Yeah, I was envious of Tristan, sure? But killing him! Sure, I fantasized about trading places with him, but never did I think I'd ever go this far! Now look what's happened. You idiot! Now it's all over! It's all –

Matt's rapid-fire thoughts were so rampant that, as he fled from Doug's desk, he failed to notice the yellow wet floor sign placed just around the corner of the comic kiosk stand. With a lack of traction from his slip-on shoes, he went sliding forward. Pent up momentum sent him airborne half a second later, bringing his face forward and his legs flailing behind him like a clumsy superhero.

To his horror, his face approached the edge of a sturdy shelving unit until it consumed his vision.

THHWWWAK!

Pain jolting through his head in agonizing waves, Matt's forehead struck the hard edge of the shelf, before the rest of his face cracked on the tile floor just below, breaking bone and shattering teeth.

As Matt lay dying on the floor, his consciousness waning, the last thing he could hear was the muffled sounds of Doug talking to the police.

And the last thing he could see – the crumpled-up Cooper Robbins card, still clenched in his hand. now covered in his own blood. ♜

THE CURSE OF AMRITSAR

By Ammar Habib

IN THE TIMES OF OLD, dense fog during a full moon was considered a bad omen. It signaled the coming of the *jinns* and ghosts from the netherworld. It was nights like these when past generations would keep their children indoors and stay away from the lonely alleys.

And it was during a night like this when the city of Amritsar once burned.

However, those fears and beliefs had weathered with the ages, and they had grown into myths. Though a pale moon hung low in the heavens over Amritsar while mist hid most of the city, Arjun felt little trepidation as he walked the old roads. With Hisham at his side, the two teenagers' footsteps echoed up and down the deserted street as they made their way through the foggy night.

Although the fog was thick, it could not conceal the Golden Temple of Armistrar. The temple rose above the mist as the moonlight reflected against its bright surface. It was the city's immovable object – the one structure that gave Amritsar its identity. On nights like these, it became a lighthouse. Resting over the water, the Golden Temple towered above every structure in sight as it reached for the moon.

During the day, countless pilgrims would crowd the temple's grounds and just as many would line up along the lake's banks. However, at this late hour of the night, the temple was as empty as the street the two teenagers traveled. Shadows remained Arjun and Hisham's only companions, as if nothing existed beyond the fog.

"Couldn't you have picked a better night for this?" Hisham asked, breaking the silence that had plagued them since they started their journey.

"You're not scared, are you?" Arjun scoffed.

"I'd just prefer if I could see where I was stepping. This fog is hell."

"It's the monsoon season. There won't be a clear night for weeks."

"And you couldn't bear to wait a few weeks?"

"Why wait, Hisham? Everyone does an initiation to join the robotics club. Remember when Nikhail had to run naked across campus?"

"Running across campus and spending a night in a haunted palace are two completely different things," Hisham replied. "You do know that Anil put you up to this just to try and keep you from joining the club, right?"

Arjun didn't reply. Looking at his friend, Arjun noticed how the moonlight brought out Hisham's green eyes – an eye color that was a rare find in Amritsar.

"He really hates you," Hisham continued.

"Only because he's afraid of losing his spot as club president." Arjun put his arm around Hisham and shot him a smile. "Just think about it, buddy. We spend one lousy night in that stupid old palace, and then we've got the keys to the robotics club."

"You're an idiot," Hisham said with a smirk.

"But I'm *your* idiot."

Chuckling, Hisham pushed Arjun's arm off.

When their words ended, the only sounds that remained were the echoes of their shoes striking the cobbled road. Arjun's focus remained straight ahead while Hisham's kept turning to their left and right. The *shalwar* and *kurta* they each wore did little to protect them from the elements. However, the loose clothing did make it easier to bear the season's humidity.

Seeing a structure start to emerge from the mist, Arjun slowed his gait before coming to a complete halt, and Hisham followed suit. Hisham's gaze focused ahead, and he took a deep breath when he saw what awaited them.

"There it is," Hisham said in a low voice, the smile from his expression now gone. "Rasheed Palace...in all its glory."

The mist seemed to move, allowing the palace to break through the wall of fog. Though nothing compared to the size of the Golden Temple, the three-story palace possessed the Mughal architecture of generations past. A low-lying wall fenced off its property, and the palace sat in the middle of the garden. Beneath its old age, the palace still demonstrated a hint of its past majesty. It was constructed from red sandstone, and a vaulted gateway comprised its entrance. The ground floor possessed several large windows, and the two upper levels held smaller ones. Though once open-air, wooden window shutters had been later added.

Much of the palace's outer wall was deteriorating, and the palace itself appeared just as weathered. Cracks ran rampant, and the wooden shutters resembled dying trees. The garden itself was rotting, overgrown weeds infesting everything and wrapping around tree trunks. Many trees had started leaning into the palace, their crooked branches hanging over the property's grounds.

Without saying a word, the two teenagers scaled the wall with little effort. Its rough edges were jagged, but it did not deter either of them. Arjun went first, and Hisham remained only a step behind. Landing in the garden, Arjun felt the grass reach his knees, and the soil beneath the grass felt soft.

"You heard what happened to the last family that lived here?" Hisham asked.

"They died, like all the others...or so people say."

Arjun and Hisham waded through the grass like two adventurers hacking their way through a forest. The greenery was damp, almost soggy. Some bushes and patches of weeds rustled, but no critters or animals appeared.

"They didn't die," Hisham said as he swatted a bug off his neck. "The father hacked his wife to bits with a machete, murdered his own children... and then he drowned himself."

"Do you really believe that?" Arjun retorted. "This place has been abandoned for as long as I've been alive."

"But not always. A Muslim family once lived here before independence – the Rasheed family. They'd lived in this palace since the days of the

Mughal Kings."

The moon hung a little lower than before, and the crooked trees seemed to be watching them, studying the movements of the teenagers as they ventured further into the palace's shadow. For a moment, Arjun thought he saw a yellow-eyed crow hiding in a branch's shadow. However, the two of them persisted.

"They say the curse began during the 1947 partition," Hisham said. "The British finally left India, and the nation fell into riots. Hindus were killing Muslims, and Muslims were killing Hindus."

With each step, the teenagers marched closer to the palace. It continued growing taller and enveloping them in its shadow. It felt like the walls had eyes – eyes that kept their observant gaze on Arjun and Hisham.

"The Muslim family that lived here was slaughtered during the riots, and their deaths put a curse on this palace and a curse on anybody who ever steps foot in it."

The two teenagers stopped under the archway of the palace's entrance. The two wooden doors were closed and loomed over Arjun and Hisham. They appeared heavy. Intricate designs and patterns were carved into their surface, but the ages had caused them to fade. Arjun ran his hands over the patterns.

After staring at the doors for what felt like a long time, Arjun turned toward Hisham. "Do you know what ghost stories like that are for?"

Hisham did not answer.

"To keep little kids from trespassing here and getting hurt."

Again, Hisham did not respond.

"Besides, I don't see any reason to believe it." Arjun motioned toward the palace. "If this place was really cursed, I'm sure it would have been demolished by now. You know how superstitious our government can be."

Hisham stayed silent.

"So, I'd say that your ghost story is simply that," Arjun said as he smirked. When he did, the moonlight reflected against his expression, and the light turned his face pale, mirroring the appearance of a ghoul. "...a ghost story."

Focusing on the doors, Arjun leaned forward and gave them a mighty heave.

They swung open as they released a loud creak. It seemed to awaken the creatures of the night as the grass and branches behind them rustled. A gust of cold air blew from the palace and brushed against Arjun and Hisham's faces, but Arjun remained undeterred.

Not wasting another moment, Arjun stepped into the palace.

"Believe what you may," Hisham whispered. "But remember one thing."

Arjun disappeared into the palace's foyer.

"Not all ghost stories are myths."

#   #   #

Hisham followed Arjun into the palace and was enveloped by coldness. An old-wood smell was the first thing Arjun noticed. The frigid temperature was the opposite of the humid monsoon season, and it rattled Arjun's bones. The tiles beneath them were built from something hard – perhaps some kind of marble. However, it was rough and uneven.

With the window shutters closed, the foyer would have been shrouded in darkness if it was not for the moonlight seeping in through a few cracks in the ceiling. The pale light illuminated some of the foyer's sections, and an omniscient aura captivated the scene. Nonetheless, most of Arjun and Hisham's surroundings remained trapped in the blackness of the night.

Arjun squinted his eyes as he scanned the area. The foyer's ceiling reached the palace's rooftop. A magnificent staircase was to his right, and the second and third story's interior balcony encircled the foyer. Much of the palace's grandeur seemed to be lost in the darkness. Up ahead, on the other side of the foyer, was a hallway that led to a different section of the palace. Portions of the wooden balconies and staircase seemed to be eroding, just like so many other parts of this palace.

At first, neither boy said anything. Hisham waited for Arjun to speak, and Arjun took in their surroundings. He wondered how long it had been since a soul stepped foot inside this–

Creak…

Hearing the sound, both teenagers whipped their heads in its direction.

The front doors – they were shutting! Hisham took a step toward them, panic overtaking his expression, but he was too late. They slammed with a loud thud.

"The doors!" he exclaimed. "They–"

"Look there," Arjun said, his voice calm.

Hisham followed where Arjun pointed and saw the counterweights connected to either door by a pulley. Both weights sat on the ground.

"The counterweights closed the doors. No curse there," Arjun commented with a smile. "Just simple physics."

"Yeah…physics."

Arjun slapped Hisham's shoulder. "Lighten up, pal. We have the whole palace to ourselves. Maybe there'll be–"

Floorboards creaked, ending Arjun's words. Hisham's heart jumped to his throat. The boys stopped moving, but the floorboards groaned again. Slower this time. The sound hung in the darkness before disappearing. It wasn't from above them; no, it was from up ahead.

Arjun and Hisham exchanged glances, one horrified and the other startled.

"…what was that?" Hisham asked, his body tense.

"It was nothing–"

The floorboards creaked once more, closer this time. Hisham took a step behind Arjun as Arjun faced the direction of the sound. The night's blackness kept them blind to their surroundings, but quick footsteps approached.

Just as Arjun's hand formed into a tight fist, something stepped out of the darkness.

…a dog.

The old mutt didn't hesitate as it approached them. Its legs trembled, and its frame mirrored a malnourished child's. Seeing the dog, both boys breathed a sigh of relief as Hisham stepped from behind Arjun.

"It's just that stray dog we always see," Arjun said. "What's his name again?"

"Kuta."

"Ah, yes. Kuta. Very original."

"How did he get in here?" Hisham wondered out loud.

"Probably jumped the wall. He's a sneaky one."

Kuta let out a whimper as it neared the two of them.

"Did he scare you?" Arjun asked as he shot a smirk at Hisham.

"Just startled me is all."

"Sure," Arjun laughed. "Whatever you say."

Kuta stopped between the boys, its attention going from one to the other. It let out a whimper as the moonlight reflected against its big eyes, showing the look of a beggar.

"You hungry?" Hisham asked as he reached into his bag.

The dog whimpered, louder this time.

"How'd you like this?" Hisham pulled out a paper bag and unwrapped it to reveal a sandwich.

Life returned to the dog's eyes when he saw the sandwich. Kuta let out a bark as he briefly stood up on his hind legs, reaching for the sandwich.

"Are you really giving that to him?" Arjun asked.

Ignoring the question, Hisham cocked his arm back and then launched the sandwich into the air. Kuta pursued his meal. The sandwich soared into the darkness ahead, the dog disappearing behind it. Kuta's loud barks echoed through the palace, and his steps were hard and fast.

Hisham smiled to himself, his eyes staring in the direction he threw the sandwich, while Arjun spoke. "You do realize that you just lost your sandwich, right?"

"It's all right. I wasn't going to eat it anyway." Hisham turned to Arjun. "So, what now? We'll need to do something to pass the time."

"It's a big place. We can head to…" Arjun's words trailed off as his expression changed.

"Head where?" Hisham asked.

Arjun didn't answer as his smile faded.

"Hey!" Hisham said as he waved his hand in front of Arjun's face. "Anybody home?"

"Do you hear that?" Arjun asked.

"Hear what?" After a pause, Hisham's eyes widened as a realization washed over him. "The dog's footsteps are…"

"Gone," Arjun finished.

Silence.

"Maybe he's too busy eating," Arjun guessed as they both faced the direction the dog had run. "He might be a quiet eater."

"Or maybe…" Hisham began without finishing his thought.

More silence.

Arjun stepped in the direction the dog had run. Hisham grabbed his shoulder to stop him, but Arjun waved it off. He plunged into the darkness. Hisham hesitated, but only for a moment, before following him.

Stepping into a long and narrow corridor, the two of them followed it. The hallway took a turn, and the limited light hampered their visibility. The deeper they traveled, the narrower the corridor became and the lower the ceiling hung. Arjun could not decide if it was his imagination or reality that made it so. Either way, his heart began to race.

As they dove deeper into the unknown, the air turned colder. The echo of their footsteps remained the sole sound in the palace. An icy sensation traveled up both of their spines. Their lungs grew numb, and it was not just the frigid temperatures that caused it.

Hisham nearly ran into Arjun when Arjun stopped walking. Peering around his friend, Hisham's eyes widened, and he held his breath. Lying on the ground was a scene Hisham's eyes refused to believe.

The dog…it was dead.

#   #   #

Blood painted the ground as it continued pouring from the dog's lacerations. Some blood stained the wall, running down its surface.

A foul odor – the stench of death – seized the teenagers as their faces turned white. Their heartbeats and breathing grew fast and loud, a contrast to the dead silence that gripped the scene. Arjun's vision tunneled on the carcass, and he was unable to turn away.

Moonlight spotlighted the carcass, bringing it into full view. The dog's guts were spilled around its body, as if a beast's claws had ripped the dog's abdomen apart and turned it inside out. Its skull had been bashed in with the sort of force that could topple a brick wall.

Arjun's focus broke when Hisham grabbed his shoulder. He turned toward Hisham before following Hisham's gaze to the wall. What he saw nearly stopped his heart. Written with the dog's blood were the words:

The soul of the son must pay for the sins of the father.

The blood that painted those letters in short, choppy strokes continued to drip down the wall, but the words remained legible. The pale light turned the bloody letters sinister. Arjun read them once. Then again. And a third time. Each time, he took a small step back from the wall and felt his breathing become more rapid. Trails of cold sweat streaked down his face.

"A – Ar – Arjun…"

"We have – have to go – go to the – the entrance!"

Neither boy hesitated in abandoning the dog's carcass. Their footsteps were frantic and sloppy, their legs barely staying beneath them. Arjun's vision remained tunneled as he barreled ahead, and his movements were wild. Turning the corner, Arjun caught sight of the palace's entrance as the moonlight illuminated it.

Arjun barely stopped himself before slamming into the heavy doors. His hands ran over its surface as he searched for a doorknob or latch. Unable to find any, he pushed the door.

Nothing happened.

Setting both palms against the entrance, Arjun yelled at Hisham. "Help me!"

Both boys dug their heels into the ground and pushed against the door.

The door did not budge.

"It won't move!" Hisham cried.

"Push harder!"

"I'm trying!"

Reaching deep down, Arjun drew a long breath as he focused and discovered strength he'd never felt before. He pressed his shoulder into the door and crouched down. Hisham did the same.

Both boys pushed the door together.

"Aargh!" Arjun yelled as he leveraged all his weight. Veins popped out of his neck. Arms trembled. Jaw became clenched.

It was to no avail. The doors were deep-rooted mountains, and not even Bhagwan himself could move them. Again and again, Arjun tried. Until his legs began to grow weak. Until his breathing turned ragged. But the doors remained a mountain.

"Arjun!"

Arjun turned to see Hisham no longer at the door. He was attempting to pry open one of the window shutters.

"They won't budge either!" Hisham exclaimed.

"Are they locked?"

"No, there's no lock. I can't–"

Clang!

A sound echoed down the corridor, and it froze both boys.

Clang!

Again. Louder this time. It was the sound of metal plates slamming against each other. Arjun remained immobile, praying to Bhagwan that it was only the night's illusions playing tricks on him. However, then he heard the rattling of a metal chain…heard something sharp dragging across a sandstone wall…and then footsteps. Wooden sandals beat against the tiled ground. Each heavy step grew nearer, each echo a little stronger.

Arjun turned to face the direction of the sound and stared into the abyss. A cloud now blocked the moonlight, making him blind to what was coming, but it approached, nonetheless. His very spine shivered as the air turned colder. A paralysis overcame him, and it was impossible to blink.

Hisham was trapped in the same state. The footsteps neared, a foul aura accompanying whatever was coming. Arjun was not sure what courage overcame him, but, when it did, a whisper escaped his lips.

"Run…"

The footsteps continued.

"Run."

A shadow appeared in the darkness.

"Run!"

With this final cry, Arjun broke through his paralysis and dashed toward the staircase. Hisham followed less than a step behind him. The monster continued its unhurried approach, its odor filling the entire palace. However, Arjun and Hisham did not turn to see it. They scrambled to the second floor, both barely able to keep their balance.

Sprinting down the hallway, they passed closed door after closed

107

door. Arjun was afraid to stop at any of them, fearful that they would be locked. Cold sweat flew off his forehead. Some of it ran down his face, stinging his eyes.

A streak of moonlight revealed an open doorway ahead. Pointing at it, Arjun called out to his friend without slowing down.

"In there!"

Hisham followed Arjun into the two-door entrance. Grabbing either door, the boys shut it with such a force that the entire wall tremored. Arjun locked the bolt into place, barricading them inside.

Like all other rooms, this one's window shutters were closed, and the two of them were encircled by darkness. Arjun heard the heavy footsteps continuing their slow advance. Along with them came that stench – that hellish odor Arjun could not recognize. He began to retreat from the entrance, nearly tripping over a wooden stool as he did.

The steps grew closer…

Arjun could hardly breathe.

And closer…

Arjun's bones rattled.

And closer.

The steps ended outside the door. A moment of silence. Arjun heard what he thought was a growl…or maybe it was breathing. When the doorknob rattled, Arjun's heart dropped into his stomach. However, the door did not open. Not even when the beast began to push against the doors. Not even when the beast began to claw and scratch at them like a tiger hunting its prey. The doors shook. They creaked. They pounded against the bolt that kept them secure.

But they did not open.

Arjun's mind screamed for him to barricade the door with whatever furniture was inside the room, but he was immobilized. As he stood there, all he could do was silently pray that Bhagwan kept the beast out – that the doors held their ground. Horror trapped his thoughts like the room trapped his body.

Arjun did not know how long the beast tried to enter – how long those doors were shaken and scratched. But when the chaos ended, it did not end

Arjun's paralysis. His legs remained weak, and his mind remained numb.

It was when the beast began to retreat from the door that Arjun finally fell to his knees. Exhaustion plagued his veins as he listened to the beast's footsteps grow softer and softer...until they could no longer be heard.

#   #   #

At some point in the night, Hisham found a candle in one of the room's cabinets and lit it with the lighter from his *kurta's* pocket. He sat across from Arjun and put the candle between them. Its dim light created shadows on the wall as it flickered in the night's cold, foul air.

Arjun's face remained pale, and he could not help but glance at the now-barricaded door every now and then to remind himself that they were indeed safe. Hisham stayed silent as well, his legs crossed, and his gaze aimed at his lap. It sounded as if he was reciting some sort of prayer to himself.

When Arjun finally mustered the strength to speak, his voice was raspy. "What was that thing?" Arjun asked. "Was it the curse?"

Hisham nodded.

"The story you were telling me about the family who once lived here," Arjun continued. "Can you tell me all of it?"

With a sigh, Hisham raised his gaze to meet Arjun's. The candlelight reflected off half his face, but the other half was cast in shadows. The image mirrored something from a ghost story, and the dim illumination brought out Hisham's green eyes, granting them an eerie quality.

"Like I said," Hisham replied, "a Muslim family lived here for centuries: The Rasheed family. But when the British left in 1947 and India and Pakistan split, the religious riots began on both sides of the border. Hindu refugees tried to reach India, and Muslim refugees tried to reach Pakistan. The Rasheed family planned to escape the city, but a rival Hindu family – the Haldar family – had held a grudge against them for generations. They were jealous of the Rasheed family's legacy and claimed that this palace should have originally been theirs."

"What happened?"

"On a night much like this one, the city burned with riots. The police stood by as families were slaughtered and homes were set ablaze. Siddharth Haldar – the head of the Haldar family – galvanized a group of rioters and broke into the palace. They swarmed down like vultures, torches, and machetes in hand."

Arjun did not interrupt his friend, his mind fixated on Hisham's words.

"The Rasheed family was dragged out by the rioters." Hisham's voice was low – a whisper. "Some were beaten to death, and others were slaughtered or strung up from the trees – the very trees we passed in the garden. The women and girls were – well, I'm sure you can imagine what the rioters did to them."

Arjun shuddered at the thought and tried to keep his mind's eyes from envisioning the scene Hisham described.

"Somehow, the youngest member of the Rasheed family survived," Hisham continued. "He was no older than a boy. He hid in the bushes and watched his entire family tortured and slaughtered. The boy could do nothing to save them, and he hid in the mud and dirt for three days until the riots subsided. It is said that on that last day, as hunger and thirst nearly killed him, he put a curse on the Haldar family. And his hatred brought the curse to life"

"What was the curse?"

"All those present at the murders would die. And from each generation, a member of the Haldar family would die as penance for what they did."

The soul of the son must pay for the sins of the father.

Arjun remembered the words written in blood as he replied, "Did it happen?"

"After the killings, Siddharth Haldar got what he wanted – the palace. He and his family lived in these very halls…for a while at least. But months later, the murders occurred. Siddharth Haldar killed his wife with a machete, the same machete that he killed the Rasheed family with. He hacked her to pieces. Then, he slaughtered his own children." Hisham paused. "They say that his family's blood sprayed the walls and soaked the floor. The odor of their corpses was so strong that nobody could enter the palace for days to recover the bodies."

Arjun gulped as those words rang in his head. There was a silence before he asked, "And what happened to him?"

"He drowned himself in the Golden Temple's lake. It's said that ever since that day, a member of the Haldar family has mysteriously died every few years – committed suicide after going insane."

"The soul of the son must pay for the sins of the father," Arjun echoed.

Hisham nodded.

Silence. Arjun did not break his gaze from Hisham. He let his mind digest Hisham's words, imagining the carnage of the murders. Could this be true? How could it not after what he'd seen? Staring at Hisham for what felt like a long time, Arjun responded, "How do you know all this?"

"My father told me, and his father told him."

"I remember…" Arjun shut his eyes as breadcrumbs from a forgotten memory rose to the forefront of his mind. "I remember my mother's mother once saying something about the riots. Maybe it was this curse."

Hisham did not reply or break his gaze from Arjun.

Arjun opened his eyes and took a deep breath.

"What are we going to do?" Hisham asked.

Silence.

"We'll…we'll survive," Arjun replied as a flash of confidence splashed across his expression. "Neither of us is involved in the curse. My last name is Malhotra, and yours is Khan. The curse has no reason to kill us." Arjun paused and turned toward the closed shutter. "It has to be close to midnight by now. If we…if we survive until morning, maybe the beast will disappear. If nothing else, people will come looking for us."

Hisham silently watched Arjun stand up.

"I don't think the beast can go outside and enter through the window. If it could, it would have already done it. So, we just need to continue barricading the door." Arjun reached down and helped Hisham to his feet. Turning from Hisham, Arjun continued, "All we need to do is hold out until the morning. If we can do that, if we can survive until then, we can make it out of this nightmare."

The glint of hope Arjun displayed was not shared by Hisham. Though Hisham remained quiet, his eyes grew darker.

#   #   #

Hours later, the door remained shut and locked, and the boys remained huddled around the candle. There was no sign of how long the night had lasted, and Arjun prayed that dawn came swiftly. A sliver of peace washed over the scene, though the memory of their encounter with the monster remained fresh on Arjun's mind.

However, the stillness did not last. Trees began to rustle outside. It was soft at first, but the branches soon started to creak as the wind intensified. The window shutters rattled. Though the shutters remained closed, trails of the gust entered the room.

Though Hisham remained motionless, the commotion motivated Arjun to turn toward the shutters. He felt some of the blast's cold air. It was stronger than he predicted, almost unearthly. A thought came to his mind to protect the candle, but he did not react quickly enough. The fire leaned with the wind...

And the candle went out.

Heart panicking, Arjun reached and felt for where Hisham had placed the lighter. His fingers grazed it before he took the lighter in his hands. He fiddled with the lighter in the darkness as it refused to ignite. He tried once more, and then a third time. Arjun's hands grew sweaty as he half-cursed and half-prayed.

The fire ignited.

Arjun wasted no time in lighting the candle. Looking in Hisham's direction, Arjun breathed a sigh of relief and broke the silence. "That was a close—"

Hisham was gone.

Eyes wide, Arjun grabbed the candle and scanned the darkness. He glanced in every direction, his eyes frantic. The candle's flickering light seemed to weaken with every passing moment, and Hisham was nowhere to be seen. It was as if he had vanished.

"Hisham..." Arjun whispered.

It was when Arjun saw the room's entrance that he truly felt horror – more horror than he had felt the entire night. He blinked one, and then once more, hoping that he was hallucinating.

The door to the corridor was open.

All the furniture they had used to barricade the door had been moved from its place, and the bolt also lay on the ground. There was nothing between the room and hallway, nothing to keep the beast away.

"Hisham?" Arjun repeated, as if saying Hisham's name would make him reappear.

Every rational part of Arjun's mind begged him to stay in the room – to close the door and again barricade himself inside. However, his legs were no longer his. Against every rational thought, he rose to his feet and stepped into the corridor.

The hallway was still dark, except for the thin trails of pale moonlight seeping in through cracks in the ceiling. Standing next to the corridor's interior balcony, Arjun had a perfect view of the foyer below. It was lost in an abyss, but he could discern the vague outline of the heavy entrance doors – doors that were still shut.

Looking to the right and left, Arjun could not see more than three steps either way. His candle did little to help. The darkness seemed supernatural, as if–

"Arjun..."

That voice. It belonged to Hisham.

"Arjun...come here!"

It was a bit louder this time, too real to be a hallucination. Arjun did not make a move. The fog in his mind matched the mist surrounding him, making him unsure of what to do.

"Arjun! Where are you?"

His legs took on a mind of their own. He began to move in the direction of the voice, as if something was drawing him toward it. The echoes of Hisham's voice hung in the air as he continued calling Arjun to him. Arjun could not ignore it, could not do anything but plunge into the darkness. He was an insect captivated by a bright light.

When Arjun came to a halt, he was faced with a wall of blackness. His visibility was next to none, but he felt something – a dark presence. First, there was nothing. Then a shadow appeared in the abyss. Finally, there were eyes...green eyes breaking the night.

The beast appeared, and the candle fell from Arjun's hand.

Its looming figure was covered in a haze of smog, and its blackness matched the shadows. However, the only thing Arjun could stare at was its eyes. Those green eyes stood out from everything else. Its gaze met Arjun's, and he felt something touch the core of his very soul.

Arjun's entire body shook, and, as the beast enveloped him, his mind became lost in the night's abyss.

#   #   #

Amritsar was ablaze.

Homes and shops burned. Cries rang through the city. Corpses littered alleys.

The world was ending. Flames kept the night's mist at bay. Rioters – torches and machetes in hand – flooded the streets and neighborhoods. Their faces mirrored those of demons, their eyes wild and expressions demented. They broke into houses and dragged the inhabitants out. Pleads for mercy were cast aside. Rioters beat their victims to death or carved them with their machetes, and the blood of the dead watered the grass.

Burning brightest was the masjid. It was consumed in an inferno, and the thick smoke emitting from the flames blackened the sky. The glow and heat of the fire touched every corner of Amritsar. There was no moon today, no stars to brighten the heavens. There was only the burning city – a city consumed by screams and blood.

Arjun stood amongst the rioters; his mind trapped in a body. He could not control his movements and could only watch the monsters he stood amongst do their sinister work. His mind screamed as he witnessed the butchering, begging for the visions to end.

But it was when the rioters came to the palace that Arjun realized what he was about to witness.

The flames that consumed nearby buildings reflected against the palace's walls. There was carnage in every direction, and it was as if hell itself surrounded the palace. It could not withstand the storm. The mob broke through the front gates, soon overrunning the palace.

Arjun's spirit trembled as he watched the Rasheed family dragged out of the palace. Many were yanked by their hair; others were forcefully carried into the garden. Fear – no, horror – consumed their eyes. Children cried, and women begged for mercy. However, there was none to be had. The rioters were hungry wolves, and the only thing that would satisfy their hunger was death. They surrounded the family, torches, and machetes still in hand.

The family was thrown at the feet of the riot's leader – Siddharth Haldar. Siddharth's features mirrored Arjun's. He possessed the same eyes as Arjun, but painted across his expression was pure hatred. Siddharth stared down at the family as they pleaded for mercy. The father offered himself for his family's safety. If nothing else, he begged Siddharth to let the children go free.

Siddharth did not say a word in response to the father's pleas. Instead, a wicked smile spread across his face, and he raised his machete.

Blood spilled onto the grass.

When the father's corpse hit the ground, the rioters set upon the rest of the family. Their screams mixed with the inferno's heat and with the cries that rang across Amritsar.

Arjun witnessed the carnage from the eyes he was trapped behind. Unable to turn away, he watched the rioters descend further into barbarians as they tormented and slowly killed the family. How could mankind display such vileness? Where had their humanity gone?

The screams of their victims only increased the rioters' sadism. People were strung from the trees, their corpses left dangling. The rioters did not simply kill the family; they tormented them until death would be nothing but a relief. And Arjun could do nothing but witness it all.

Arjun was not sure how long it was before he noticed something – something hidden and unseen by the bloodthirsty rioters. It was a boy. He was covered in dirt, hiding in the palace's shadows. Fresh blood – blood that was not his own – clung to the boy's skin.

But underneath the boy's sad state was his eyes. They were not afraid; they were angry. They matched the hatred Siddharth showed. As he watched the rioters kill his family, the boy's jaw became clenched, and his eyes filled with a fiery rage greater than the flames surrounding him.

Sensing Arjun, the boy's gaze locked with his. There was something mystical about the boy's eyes – something unearthly. Arjun realized what it was. The boy's green eyes…they matched the eyes of Hisham…the eyes of the monster.

His expression unchanging, the boy raised a finger and pointed it at Arjun. As blackness washed over his vision, Arjun heard a menacing voice rise above the chaos and screams, a voice that echoed the words written on the wall:

The soul of the son must pay for the sins of the father.

When the scene changed, the riot was over. Instead, Arjun sat in a circle alongside several children. In his hands was some flour as all the children worked to prepare *naan*. It did not take him long to recognize that he was in the palace. The open doorway revealed the palace's distinguishable foyer not too far away.

Siddharth Haldar stepped into the room's doorway, blocking Arjun's view of the foyer. He was visibly older than the night of the riots. Siddharth's eyes were wild, his breathing heavy. In his hand was the same machete as before. Inhaling and exhaling deep gasps, his eyes set upon Arjun.

There were no words spoken, but Arjun saw the malice in Siddharth's gaze. With a mighty roar, Siddharth raised his blade and sprung at Arjun.

Arjun could not react. He watched the blade come down, unable to turn away. The machete split Arjun's skull, slicing into his brain. His body slumped to the ground. Blood dripped from the machete and poured from Arjun's open wound, but Siddharth did not stop. He again brought the rusting blade down.

Helpless, Arjun could not move, but the pain was more than real. He was a piece of meat, and Siddharth was the butcher. Again and again, the blade came down, no mercy in Siddharth's blood-stricken eyes. Arjun's limbs were hacked off, his bones split, and his muscles shredded. Blood poured out of his wounds like a geyser, and life abandoned him. A pain like nothing Arjun had ever felt overcame him.

But death was not the end.

As death's grip took Arjun, he awakened, and the memory began anew. Arjun sat there preparing the *naan,* surrounded by the same children. His wounds were gone, and so was the blood. The children spoke the same lines and wore the same expressions.

But then Siddharth entered the room, the same animalistic expression

116

washed across his face. He raised his machete and shouted his curses. And the murder began again.

Arjun was killed, and then awoken. Killed...and awoken. Killed... and awoken. The cycle did not break. It only became bloodier with each death. Arjun was not sure how many times it happened – how many times Siddharth murdered him like Siddharth murdered his family. Was it hours? Days? Weeks?

The pain intensified each time Arjun died. He could not scream for mercy or resist. All he could do was die. Again...and again...and again...

Until death was all that he knew.

#   #   #

The morning sun sat above the horizon when Arjun exited the palace. The fog had cleared, replaced by the clarity that a new day brought. Arjun's *shalwar* and *kurta* were ripped and tattered. Dry blood covered his skin, much of it mixed into his hair and staining his clothes. His hair was raggedy, his eyes blood red. A hollowness possessed his eyes.

He walked under the sun's watch, traveling down the path he had walked the night before. The street was no longer deserted. People went about their business, some going to open their shops while others headed toward the bus station. Many stopped and gawked at Arjun when they saw his condition, but his foul aura kept any from approaching.

Arjun walked, and then he walked some more. His feet turned swollen, and his legs became stiff. When he was almost a kilometer from the palace, he saw something that forced him to pause: a dog.

Kuta.

The dog he saw dead last night was alive. It looked no different than when Arjun had last seen it alive. Kuta went from person to person, begging for food. When it saw Arjun, it only hesitated for a moment before moving on to the next person. Even it would not approach him.

Arjun's journey continued. His blank eyes were still trapped in the nightmare. He saw Siddharth Haldar with the machete. He still felt the blade's steel cutting through his skin like a hot knife cuts through butter.

117

Arjun was butchered, hacked to pieces. He was slaughtered like an animal – slaughtered *by* an animal.

Entering under the shadow of the Golden Temple, Arjun felt a hand on his shoulder. His footsteps ended. Pausing for a moment, he turned around, and his blood eyes met a gaze…

Hisham's gaze.

Arjun's friend appeared the same as before. He bore no injuries, and his clothing was not ripped. The Golden Temple's shadow turned Hisham's face dark. He wore no smile or horror in his stoic expression. However, in Hisham's green eyes Arjun now saw the boy's eyes…and the monster's eyes.

Arjun did not react to seeing his friend alive. A silence hung over the two of them, a long stillness. When Arjun finally spoke, his low voice remained bare of any emotion. "Your name?" Arjun asked.

Hisham was silent.

"What is your full name, Hisham?"

Once again, Hisham remained quiet, but only at first. When he replied, his stern tone matched his expression. "My true name is Hisham…Rasheed."

Rasheed. The name of the murdered family.

"And your mother's maiden name," Hisham continued, "Was Haldar." Silence.

"The father of my father was the boy you saw," Hisham revealed. "He was the lone survivor who cursed your family. After that fateful night, he changed his last name to Khan in order to survive, but he never forgot. *We* never forgot what your people did to us."

The truth Arjun feared was correct. His mind did not fight the acceptance of Hisham's claim. There was no other explanation for what he'd seen or the torment he had endured. "I am the…" Arjun started. "I am the soul…the cursed soul."

Hisham nodded, and his hand fell from Arjun's shoulder.

Turning from Hisham, Arjun continued toward the Golden Temple's lake. People parted for him when he came near and kept their distance, as if he was some kind of leper. Taking one slow step at a time, he soon found himself at the lake's banks. All strength became lost, and Arjun fell to his knees.

His eyes brimmed with tears. Tears of sorrow, and tears seeking forgiveness for a sin that was not his. Staring at his reflection, Arjun blinked once. And then once more. Something – no, someone – now stood behind him. It was the face from the visions – the face of the lone survivor of the Rasheed family. Just like Arjun, the boy remained covered in cuts and blood, and his *kurta* was torn to shreds.

The soul of the son must pay for the sins of the father.

The boy did not blink as his green-eyed gaze met Arjun's. His expression remained cold, blood still running down his face and soaking into his clothing. At first, neither one of them moved. Finally, the boy raised one of his bloody fingers and pointed it at Arjun's heart. Blood dripped off the fingertip, and Arjun felt a stake driving into his soul.

Losing all his strength, Arjun fell into the water and sank to its depths. ♜

HOUSE OF MANY ROOMS

By Jess Hagemann

THOUGH WE ATTENDED THE SAME school, I didn't know Carson personally. Couldn't have picked him out of a crowd based on name alone until he became a household name.

By that time, he'd been missing for weeks. Long enough for an investigation to be opened, for all the local news outlets to carry the story. *College student headed home for winter break disappears, car found in field.*

Not just his car, but his wallet and cell phone, thrown carelessly in a console cup holder. His clothes were spotted in a crumpled heap maybe twenty yards from the car. All of them: jeans, shirt, underwear, socks, shoes. Like he'd stripped down in a hurry. Like he was hot.

There was no sign of damage to his clothes or his car. The old Toyota started when the sheriff turned the key, still in the ignition. *Drugs*, law enforcement speculated, holding up a baggie of pills stashed under the seat. *He must have been high. Hallucinating. Pulled over, took off his clothes, walked into the field. Kept walking.*

But if that was the case, how far could Carson have walked, really? They'd swept a sixty-square-mile swath of corn and sorghum rows, meadows of Coastal hay just tall enough to hide a body. There was one pond in the area, and more of a damp dirt tank at that. A diver had felt his way through every inch of the murky water anyway, just in case. Just in case in some altered state the twenty-year-old had wandered in, sank—or as was more likely, been sucked down by the mud—and drowned.

Even if all they could return to Carson's parents was his bloated corpse, the couple deserved that much. You don't raise a kid into adulthood, then look the other way when he disappears.

I watched them on the five o'clock news. Carson's dad did all the talking. His mom stood in the back and cried. Still operating, then, under the assumption that it was drugs, the middle-aged man pleaded for Carson to forgive himself. "Whatever happened, whatever you did, it doesn't matter," the father said. "We love you, and we just want you to come home."

Behind the mother, a lighted candy cane blinked on and off festively, reminding us all that it was almost Christmas. Decembers in Texas are warm; wherever he was, Carson wasn't at risk of hypothermia. But the impending holidays made it harder—the thought that his mom might wake up on Christmas morning, her baby lost or dead. Or just gone.

I remembered the Stoics we'd studied in Philosophy that semester. Seneca, in his thirteenth letter to his friend Lucilius, wrote: "There are more things ... likely to frighten us than there are to crush us; we suffer more often in imagination than in reality." Which is true. I agree wholeheartedly. But also, in the absence of explanation, what is one to do but get creative, to try to come up with an angle authorities have not yet considered?

Which is where the conspiracy theories started. "Alternate facts" circulated on internet forums by armchair sleuths. Someone said that Carson hadn't been alone. He'd driven at gunpoint, a crazy person telling him where to go and when to get out, what to do with his clothes.

Someone else said aliens. Clearly, he'd been beamed up by the big boys in the sky. What use had pod people for jeans, wallet, a cell phone? All they needed was the specimen. **FOR THEIR EXPERIMENTS!!** This last typed in all caps and bolded, an attempt to emphasize the grave nature of Carson's sorry fate.

I didn't know what to think. Where was the evidence, the clues? Weren't there scent dogs and strands of hair to tell us what had happened? Couldn't they check his cell phone history? CCTV footage?

They could and they did. The last call Carson made was to his parents, ostensibly to tell them he was on his way home. But he never made it home. While his car could be seen passing under the toll road camera, his digital footprint stopped where his car was found.

Sometime in the intervening hours, it was as though Carson had ceased to exist. Even now, he lives only in memory, in cell phone videos and the sad eyes of the Dachshund he left behind.

It's all we have of any of them, the Walkers.

It's all they have of me.

The same thing happened to me about a month ago. When it did, I was ready. Most of my friends had Walked by that time. My grandpa. The kid across the street I used to babysit. After a while, the cops stopped investigating anything. The government quit making excuses. It was always the same story, never a satisfactory ending. We lived, some in fear and some in curiosity, of the moment we, too, would disappear.

It felt like a whisper. Like the world exhaled, cool, against the back of my neck. I slipped through time and then I felt nothing. Not cold, although I was naked. Not hungry, though I haven't eaten since I Walked. I get lost wandering around this house of many rooms, but the loss is not a feeling. It's a state of being. A fact as undeniable as the jean shorts still crumpled in the window seat of my bedroom. I was sitting there staring out at the empty street below, and I had long enough to wonder if someone had opened up a window. Where was that breeze coming from? Then the view outside dissolved, was replaced by a no-color wall.

At first, I thought the no-color wall stretched forever. I walked along it for hours without encountering a bend, a single room to break up the sameness. All the while, I trailed my fingers lightly upon its no-texture surface, suddenly sure that if I ventured too far away I would lose it. And then there'd be nothing but the no-color floor. A flat dimension. And what if I was then reduced to circles and rectangles, a child's conception of the human form? So long as I touched the no-color wall and the no-color floor *and kept on moving forward*, I could, I reasoned, continue to exist in three dimensions. Even if the house of many rooms refuses to be governed by pedestrian concepts like height, width, and length.

Eventually, the no-color wall ended at a right angle. It ran off to the left and kept running, and I kept walking. Kept trailing. Long after it felt like the sun should have set at home, I came upon the first room. Hugged the wall as I went through the opening. Circumscribed its interior perimeter. Arrived back at what I can only assume was the same opening, then continued walking and trailing my fingers along what must have been the same wall. Never once did I grow tired or faint. Never once, in those first few days, did I meet another Walker.

Nothing lasts forever, though. Not even the no-color wall. Stasis, dormancy—these are fallacies. Everything is always growing or dying. Speeding up or slowing down. Evolving or returning to the earth. So, too, the house of many rooms is always changing. One day, I noticed the no-color wall had begun to curve. Following it, I couldn't tell whether the spiral was collapsing in on itself or expanding outward.

As I was pondering what might lie at the heart of a spiral, if such a thing could exist, another Walker appeared before me. She didn't have any eyes or a mouth, but somehow, I knew she was female. She'd been trailing her fingers along the wall also, and when she got to me, when her fingers brushed mine, she flinched. Keeping one hand on the no-color wall, she reached out with her other hand, groping for what she couldn't see. Her hand passed through me—though, again, I could not feel it—and when it did, I saw what she had seen when she still had eyes. I understood the things you don't need eyes to see.

I saw that the spiral was indeed expanding outward, and also that it lay within a larger spiral. The larger spiral was but one red blood cell in the body of a still larger spiral, ad infinitum. Within my spiral was a smaller spiral, and a smaller one within it, and at the center of the smallest spiral was something like a black hole. The black hole was growing bigger at the same rate as the largest spiral was expanding. One was eating. The other was being eaten. All that remained for me to figure out was who, between the other female Walker and I, was eating, and who being eaten.

But she was the one lacking eyes, without a mouth. She was disappearing from this world the way we'd disappeared from the last one. Stepping forward, I walked all the way through her, collecting her inside me. We walked on together. There were many more rooms to discover. ♜

A TALE AS OLD AS TIME

By Carmen Gray

HER NAME WAS PERLA. SHE was named thus because Mama Cuqui, her grandmother, insisted on it. "She looks like a luminous pearl," she had told Perla's mother when she saw her as a newborn. The name stuck and Perla was raised mostly by Mama Cuqui, as Perla's mother was busy cleaning houses and waiting tables to make a living.

Mama Cuqui had all kinds of interesting things in her small, unassuming room, inside the apartment where they all lived together. There were little plastic saints on the shelves surrounding the twin bed and there was a special chest in the corner that Perla had opened a few times. Inside the chest was a vial of holy water that Mama Cuqui kept replenished and some dried herbs stored in little empty leche quemada jars. But there was one thing Perla was not allowed to access, and that was Mama Cuqui's special lace tablecloth. She had told Perla, when she was a little girl, that it contained all of the malos puestos (curses) from the limpias (spiritual cleansings) that she'd performed in their tiny living room for neighbors, friends and strangers that called upon Mama Cuqui from time to time. That tablecloth was off limits and Perla, being an obedient little girl, refrained from opening the frayed yellow box that contained the forbidden item inside the chest. Years passed and Perla grew into a curious young teenager, and as teenagers do, she often found herself questioning the adults, including her dear Mama Cuqui.

One overcast Friday morning, Perla headed to school on her regular walking route. She ambled down the busy street they lived on, crossing over to the quieter, residential one that had the pretty houses lined up neatly. She dreamt about what it must be like to live in one of these houses: a picket fence, a garden, plenty of room inside. In a yard like this, Mama Cuqui would be able to grow all of her herbs in a giant garden instead of in the pots crammed outside the door of their apartment. She kicked a pebble she came across as she was walking along, minding her own business until she saw Laura Miller emerge from the prettiest home on the block.

Laura was the quintessential popular girl in middle school. She had long, beautiful hair, wore expensive clothes and always landed the best parts in theater class because she truly was a good actor and had lots of self-confidence. Her parents had money to pay for private acting and singing lessons. Perla had become acquainted with Laura recently during rehearsals for Beauty and the Beast. Laura was playing the part of Belle. Perla was part of the running crew. Her job included moving the props, opening and closing the curtains and ensuring that the actors got their cues. Although Laura was playing Belle, she'd been decent to Perla and had even invited her to her post dress rehearsal party this weekend. Laura noticed Perla and waved at her from the driveway. "Hi Perla! Hope to see you tomorrow night at my party!" She smiled broadly. Perla waved back and nodded. How was it possible for a 7th grader to have such perfect skin? Perla touched the pimple forming on her nose.

"Don't pick at it!" Mama Cuqui had reprimanded her that morning at breakfast. "I'll make something for you to put on tonight, mija." Perla imagined Laura could buy the best skincare products that she'd seen ladies using on Tik Tok. Mama Cuqui would probably make something stinky for her to try again and it wouldn't work, just like the last time she'd had a bad break out. Mama Cuqui set limits on Perla's screen time on their shared phone because she believed there were lots of ways to acquire empachos (blockages) and sustos (frights) from Tik Tok videos. Perla just figured Mama Cuqui was old and didn't get it. Plus, Mama Cuqui watched Tik Tok

125

videos herself. Ugh. When would she finally get her own phone? She'd been saving up some money from helping her mother clean houses on Sundays. Just a couple more Sundays and she'd have the amount that she needed for the iPhone she'd been wanting.

Perla noticed Laura's mom, a slender, tall woman was waiting in the white Tesla for Laura to join her. What a life! Perla thought. She continued down the 3 more blocks it would take to get to school. Anya, a recent immigrant from Ukraine, rounded the corner on the next block and met up with Perla, as they normally did each day.

"Hi!" she said cheerfully when she saw Perla.

"Hi!"

"Are you going to the.. what is it called again?" she asked, searching for the English word. She pulled out her phone to Google translate it. Even Anya had a phone. So unfair, Perla thought.

"The post rehearsal party?" Perla finished for her, before Anya had a chance to speak.

Anya nodded, smiling.

"Yes, but I can't stay long. My grandmother won't let me stay past 9 pm. That's my curfew."

"Curfew?" asked Anya, pronouncing the word wrong. Again, she began to search it up on Google.

"It means the time when I have to be back home. You know my grandmother is strict. I don't want her to come knocking on Laura's door— that would be horrible. So, yeah, I can go. But I'll have to leave by 8:45 to be home by 9. Maybe you could spend the night? I can ask." Anya nodded.

Anya and Perla had become friends in school. They had a lot in common. Both of them lived with family members that didn't speak a lot of English and neither had wealthy households. Perla didn't have to feel self-conscious when Anya came over because Anya also lived in a small apartment with her family. Mama Cuqui approved of Anya, too, because she was interested in the plants that Mama Cuqui had. And the girls could watch lots of Tik Toks on Anya's phone together and try out new make-up techniques. Anya had a skilled hand and an eye for art. She was especially good at applying eyeliner. Anya also enjoyed Sailor Moon and Totoro, which were two of Perla's favorite movies. Plus, they were put on the running crew together in theater class because neither of them was brave enough to try out for parts in Beauty and the Beast. Although Anya was so good with make-up, that Laura and the other young actors often requested her for touch ups. Anya was definitely becoming more and more popular with Laura and the others in theater class. Perla hoped that she'd be able to keep Anya as her close friend, but it was entirely possible that Laura would try to pull her into her friend group, which was so unfair. Laura could have any friend she wanted in school. She was basically perfect. It took Perla a long time to get to know others and to form friendships, as she was shy.

During theater class that afternoon, Laura excitedly flitted about, singing the opening song, "Little town, it's a quiet village..." as Anya and Perla were gathering the props to place them on the little wooden stage.

"She has such a pretty voice," Anya said, admiring Laura.

"Yes, she does," sighed Perla.

"You have a pretty voice, too. I've heard you sing to yourself," Anya whispered.

That made Perla feel good about herself. There was no way she'd ever have the courage to be on stage like Laura, but she had to admit, she did like to sing, and she sounded good, from what she could tell. Bruce, the boy who was playing Gaston, was right behind them skulking around.

"Ju af pretty voice, tuuu." He mocked Anya's accent.

He made Perla's skin crawl. He was so full of himself. He was actually the perfect person to play Gaston because he had the same narcissistic personality as that character. Laura was right behind Bruce and punched him playfully in the arm, "I bet you have a mad crush on Anya. Imitation is the sincerest form of flattery, you know." She winked at Anya, who's fair cheeks were turning red from embarrassment.

Bruce responded, "Ummm.... nope. I would never be interested in someone who isn't from here." He stormed off.

Laura patted Anya on the shoulder. "Pay him no mind. He may be one of the cutest guys in class, but he's a spoiled brat, with a helicopter mom and a dad that buys him everything. I mean, I know I don't have room to talk, but my mom doesn't hover over me like his mom does. She practically wipes his ass for him after he goes to the bathroom." Anya smiled at Laura for defending her. "Hey, I need you to do my eye make-up for the party, can you? You can come over early if you want!" Anya's eyes lit up. Definitely a sign to Perla that Laura was trying to coax a friendship.

"Can Perla come early with me?" Anya asked. Perla wished she could crawl into a hole. "Umm, sure," Laura responded hesitantly, flashing her winning smile.

"And will he be at the party tomorrow night?" asked Anya, looking over at Bruce, on the stage now.

"Well, yeah, I mean he's a major part of the show. I can't not invite him. Mr. Bellingham said that I have to invite everyone to the party and he's practically besties with my mom. So, I didn't really get a choice in who to invite," Laura answered.

Perla kept quiet. Of course, Laura's mother and Mr. Bellingham, the theater teacher, were good friends. Anya smiled weakly at Laura, trying to be nice, after all, Laura had come to her defense and had even invited her over to the party early.

"Laura, come on over here to run through the opening scene once more," called Mr. Bellingham.

Laura ran off and Anya looked down at her feet, still embarrassed and feeling conflicted.

"You know, Bruce is a total asshole. My mom cleans his house, and I've helped her clean it before. His mom does everything for him-she leaves post-it compliments for him for everything and thinks he's the most amazing person on this earth. She has this portrait painted of him hanging in the living room. It takes up nearly the entire wall. He leaves an absolute mess every time. He has no idea I know so much about him-he doesn't know I've helped my mom clean his house. Don't worry about him. And Laura, well, that's Laura. She may not like Bruce much, but they aren't that different," Perla said.

"But Laura seems nice?" Anya questioned.

"Well, she is nice to you because you have something to offer her: good make-up skills! But she and Bruce both have everything they could ever want; their parents drive fancy cars, and they live very different lives than you or I do. It's a different world for them. A much easier world. Their parents haven't had to struggle to belong here. They've had it easy." Perla said, a little resentful.

Anya nodded her head. Perla decided it was best not to talk anymore about either of them and get back to the tasks at hand. It wasn't clear if Anya really understood everything she was saying, anyhow, but she thought Anya caught on to the gist of it.

When the school day finally came to an end, Anya and Perla walked together to their meeting point. They would see each other at rehearsal and then the festivities and planned for a sleepover at Perla's after the party.

Perla continued along to her apartment where Mama Cuqui had prepared a special facial mask for her. "Come on, mijita. The yerbabuena will feel nice on your skin." She was right, the peppermint in the mask had a pleasant aroma and felt cool on her skin. It tingled slightly and she enjoyed a little extra attention from her grandmother. She hoped this would work to clear up her skin for the rehearsal and party later the next day. As she waited for the mask to dry, Mama Cuqui began to prepare some chamomile tea. "Is someone coming over for una limpia?" Perla inquired, as this was the tea her grandmother would make for anyone before a spiritual cleansing. "Yes, mija. Minnie is coming by; she's having a terrible time after her son passed." Perla nodded. She watched as her grandmother carefully strained the tea into a chipped porcelain cup with roses on it. The smell of the tea was comforting to Perla. Then, her grandmother disappeared into the bedroom to prepare it. Perla peeked in while Mama Cuqui opened the chest and took out the lace tablecloth. Perla watched as she rubbed herbs on it and murmured some incantations over it. "Go on, mija. I need you to clear the table for Minnie. She'll be here very soon." Perla wiped the little wooden table off from where she'd been sitting and removed the little napkin holder and the small round vase that contained a few marigolds. She went into the bathroom to wash off the mask and was about to head to her room when Mama Cuqui asked her to help her set the table. "Don't touch this after Minnie comes. You don't want any of her susto," she reminded her. Perla nodded her head and headed to her room so Mama Cuqui could assist her guest.

Perla played with her eye make-up techniques in her room while she overheard some chattering in the kitchen between her grandmother and Minnie, the downstairs neighbor. Perla knew that Minnie's son, Elias, had died a year ago. Apparently, he had been in a terrible car accident on his way home from work. Poor Minnie had been inconsolable for months. Elias was an adult and had worked as a travel agent in a nearby city. Minnie managed a little candy shop in town and Elias would come by to visit her once a month, bringing her candies from his travels to faraway places. Perla always enjoyed trying out some of the fun treats that Minnie would let her sample from these exchanges. She felt so sorry for Minnie and hoped that her grandmother could soothe her sadness. After the sobbing and chattering calmed down, Perla heard the front door close, and she came out to the smell of beeswax candles burning and watched her grandmother gently fold up the lace tablecloth.

"Mija, I have to get dinner started. Please do me a favor and put this back in its place. Lavate los manos after touching it," she instructed Perla.

"I know, Mama Cuqui. I know." She knew the routine. It contained the "malos puestos" (curses) from the limpia. As she was folding it carefully, a piece of candy fell onto the ground. Perla picked it up and observed the pink cellophane wrapper. It was a strawberry Hi-Chew. She loved Hi-Chews and stuffed it into her pocket. Minnie must have brought it with her from the candy shop, Perla mused.

"Ven, Perlita. I need your help with dinner," Mama Cuqui called to her. Perla shoved the tablecloth into the old yellow box and headed into the kitchen to help her grandmother, blowing off washing her hands.

Mama Cuqui and Perla made a traditional Mexican dinner together, as they did most Friday evenings. They always made extra for the weekend. After finishing dinner, Perla went to her room to finish some homework, watch some Tik Toks on the phone, sing the Beauty and the Beast songs to herself and went to sleep.

That night, Perla had a strange dream. In her dream, she saw Minnie in her candy shop crying as the transparent body of a man wandered through the shop. The man tried to comfort her, but Minnie could not be consoled. A snake slithered by on the shop's floor. Perla woke up startled, her heart racing.

She went to the bathroom to splash cool water on her face and went back to sleep. She had the distinct sensation that she was being watched. She pulled the covers up over her head and fell back into a fitful sleep until morning.

The next day arrived, and Perla went to dress rehearsal for Beauty and the Beast, where she went through the motions of moving props and rearranging the furniture in between scenes on the stage. Right before Bruce was to go on for the second scene, Perla saw a flash of light pass by and almost tripped into him.

"What the frick?" Bruce whisper-yelled at Perla, "Do your job right. You people." He snarled.

Perla moved quickly away from him and felt Anya's hand slip into her own.

"He's a jerk," Anya whispered into her ear. The way she said the word jerk made Perla smile. Anya was picking up middle school English quickly.

The rest of rehearsal went relatively smoothly. After the final scene, Laura tossed her hair and smiled on the stage.

"Don't forget! Party at my house at 5!" Laura announced. Everyone clapped wildly. Again, Perla saw a flash of light, this time it passed by Laura. She strained to see it again when Anya noticed her squinting her eyes.

"Are you okay?" she asked Perla.

"I think so…. I just keep seeing funny things." Perla responded. Anya looked curious. As they headed out of the auditorium together, Laura came running over.

"Anya! Come straight over, okay?" Anya nodded her head.

Anya and Perla walked the three blocks it took to get to Laura's house. Laura was getting dropped off by her mother in the driveway when they arrived.

She ushered the two girls inside a very beautiful home. The floors gleamed; the walls were painted a bright white. There were floor to ceiling windows and tall French doors looking out into a perfectly manicured backyard with a pool. Even though it was exceptional, Perla felt a strange sensation of sadness in the house. Laura led them upstairs into her room, which was larger than Perla's entire apartment. She had her own attached bathroom, with monogrammed napkins that could be disposed of after washing hands and there was a giant oval mirror on the wall above the sink. While Anya got to work on Laura's make up, Perla made an excuse to use the bathroom-she wanted to check it out further. She'd never seen a bathroom like this, even at the fanciest houses she'd helped her mother clean. She inspected herself in the giant mirror. Her skin looked pretty clear today. Mama Cuqui's recipe must have worked this time. Suddenly, she saw that same flash of light she'd seen during rehearsal out of the corner of her eye. She turned around to follow it into the closet, where it was moving. Inside the closet, she heard the sound of a little girl wailing. She pushed through at least 20 dresses to search for the source of the crying.

"Perla, did you fall in the toilet or something? What are you doing?" The sound of Laura's voice from the other side of the door brought Perla back.

"Sorry, I'm just washing my face."

She stepped out of the bathroom and into the bedroom where Anya was carefully finishing up a beautiful make up job on Laura's pretty face. Perla looked past the girls to a picture of younger Laura with what looked like another version of her in a meadow together.

"Oh, I didn't know you had a sister," Perla exclaimed.

Laura's face fell. "Well, that was my cousin-we looked a lot alike. She's in heaven now." Perla mumbled an apology, feeling awkward now.

"Okay, I look party ready now, don't I?" Laura was quick to change the subject back to the present moment. Anya and Perla nodded in agreement. "Well, let's just get ready, then. Everyone's going to be here in an hour!" Laura said and offered her bathroom to the girls while she went downstairs.

Anya helped Perla with her make up in the giant oval mirror.

"Are you okay, Perla? You seem, what is the word, distract?" Anya asked.

"Yeah, maybe I didn't get enough sleep. I had strange dreams." Perla said.

"About what?" Anya kept on.

"Well, just weird things. Maybe because my grandmother did one of her things last night with a neighbor." Perla thought it may be too strange to explain her grandmother's limpias to Anya. The language barrier was already difficult enough at times.

"Hmmm, I think I know. I think I see your grandmother speak to plants," said Anya.

"Speak?" Perla furrowed her brow, confused.

"Well, in my country, there are special people who speak to plants. I know your grandmother is very care of the plants. I see her." Anya said.

"Oh, yes, she is caring of her plants," Perla corrected.

"Yes. In my country, there is a word – let me see," Anya took out her phone and used Google translate.

"This." She handed the phone to Perla.

The Carpathian Shamans of Ukraine are known as molfar, the females being Molfarki (female molfary). They are known for their unique understanding of nature and its workings and have the ability to speak to the spirits of the plants with which they work. There are special Molfary, known as Wind Whisperer, Dreamer, or Black Shamans. They are also the ones who walk between the worlds of shadow and light with power. Often, they have acquired this power through their individual ancient karma or shadow lifetimes, or it has been passed down to them from their ancestors. This particular Molfar/Molfarki can also access the magical energy of earth and its consciousness, passing through the shamanic veils, entering the natural forces from their inner spaces in both time (waking mundane life) and no-time (dream time). A Molfar/Molfarki such as this has lived many lifetimes on earth to possess this deep connection.

The words struck Perla. She felt even closer to Anya. Never had she met a friend who understood what her grandmother did without giving her funny looks. Anya nodded her head knowingly and smiled.

"My great Aunt Nina was this," she said. "I think you are this, too." That surprised Perla, but maybe it explained what was happening to her. She never had thought of herself as anything other than ordinary.

The doorbell rang, interrupting their conversation. The first cast members had arrived. Perla and Anya finished up and headed down to the festivities. The party was fun, and Laura's mother had provided extra pizza for everyone. It got hot inside the house with so many people filling up the living room, so Laura opened the French doors leading out into the backyard and brought a karaoke machine out. All of the main actors were having a great time outdoing one another with singing. One of the girls playing the teapot commented on Laura's perfect eye make-up after singing a Celine Dion song.

"It was Anya! She's soooo talented! I bet she can sing, too," gushed Laura. She handed the microphone to Anya, who looked like a deer in headlights. Her eyes darted over to Perla, pleading with her to help her out. Perla felt a rush of something she'd never felt before: courage. "Canta, mija," she heard her grandmother's voice from somewhere. She took the microphone from Anya's hand and began to sing along to Beauty and the Beast.

"Tale as old as time
True as it can be
Barely even friends
Then somebody bends
Unexpectedly"

The words came out of her mouth perfectly, surprising even herself. All of the chattering stopped. All eyes were on Perla. Perla sang the rest of the song with perfect pitch. All of the cast members applauded her. She felt so happy. She felt like she finally belonged. And then she felt somebody push her. It was Bruce.

"Great job." He clapped slowly and sarcastically. "It's time to get wet!" He shouted to everyone. People began cheering. Perla resisted; she didn't want all of her make-up to get ruined. She certainly didn't want her clothes to get wet-she had changed from the black shirt from rehearsal into a white tee. He pushed her closer to the pool, leaning his body into hers. "Come on, wetback," he breathed into her ear, "I bet your mom swam here illegally." Perla panicked, searching for Anya in the crowd. "What's the problem, you can't swim?" Bruce's voice was hot in her ear. Perla continued to resist the force of his body against hers. A bright light wavered in the distance. It hovered over Anya. Anya looked at her and mouthed a word. Perla recognized the new word that Anya had taught her, "Molfarki."

She squeezed her eyes shut. Suddenly, she was a part of the stars in the sky, looking down upon the scene below. She watched herself summon up an extraordinary strength, like that of a man, wielding Bruce's body into the pool, where he slammed his arm into the diving board. Everything went black for an instant. In the distance, Perla could hear someone howling in pain loudly. She opened her eyes to see Bruce's right arm contorted. He was screaming in pain, trying in vain to swim with his left arm to the shallow end of the pool. Laura's mom came rushing outside, "What on earth is going on out here?" she yelled, taking in the scene.

"Perla flipped Bruce into the pool and broke his arm!" shouted Laura, still in disbelief.

"It's time to go home. I'm calling Bruce's mother. Party's over!" yelled Laura's mom, eyeing Perla suspiciously, "you, young lady, are in big trouble. Bruce's mother is going to be fit to be tied." Perla didn't exactly know what she meant by that, but it couldn't be a good thing. Anya rushed to her side. "It was an accident. Bruce was push..." she began. Laura's mother cut her off, "Just go. The both of you. I hope he's okay for the show next week." She waved the both of them away. The girls went upstairs to Laura's room to gather their things. Laura came running up after them. "Perla, how could you? I mean I know Bruce can be a D, but geez...." She looked to Anya to say something similar. "I think he deserved it." Anya responded. Laura gasped and covered her mouth. The girls left and giggled the whole way to Perla's apartment.

"See, I told you. Molfarki," Anya said. Perla smiled and shoved her hands in her pockets. She felt something there-the strawberry Hi-Chew. She gave it to Anya. "Yum! I love these. Where'd you get it?" Anya asked. "From Minnie, the neighbor. It fell out of the tablecloth when I was putting it...." Perla stopped. She suddenly remembered. "What?" asked Anya, chewing the sweet candy.

"I was supposed to wash my hands after touching the tablecloth-maybe I have the malos puestos!" Perla was now questioning her newfound powers and could hear Mama Cuqui scolding her for not washing her hands.

"What is malos puestos?" Asked Anya.

"Curses from Minnie's limpia-the spiritual cleansing."

"No," said Anya. "you learn your powers now. My great aunt Nina was our age when she found hers. You can go between places."

"Which places?," asked Perla.

"The living and the non-living," said Anya.

"Maybe so," responded Perla.

They were almost at Perla's place. A transparent figure of a man followed closely behind them. ♜

THE LIGHT AT THE END OF THE TUNNEL

By Sam Knight

TREMORS IN THE EARTH FORCED Tracy to stop walking and hold a handout to steady herself against the side of the tunnel. One of the Old Ones on the surface above must be restless, she thought. Only a small amount of dirt fell from the cracks in the ceiling, most of the loose stuff having fallen a long time ago. When the passageway around her no longer swayed, she brushed the dirt off her raggedy clothes and out of her hair.

"You okay?" Kim's voice echoed up the tunnel from behind. They had just parted company at an intersection fifteen feet back. Kim lived another hundred yards down the other tunnel.

"Yeah," Tracy answered. "You?"

"Fine. See you tomorrow."

"See you." Tracy turned back up the tunnel towards her own home.

Not that she was in any hurry to get there. Her mother had gone insane and killed herself when the Old Ones had first come, ten years ago, and her father had been on whatever mind-altering substance he could get his hands on since. Tracy was surprised the Town hadn't put him Topside as an offering long ago. Of course, he was quiet and kept to himself, and there seemed to be no end to people who broke the Rules of Civility and got sent up.

Not to mention the people who just vanished.

That was the latest topic of discussion at school. Where did they go? How did they disappear without anyone knowing? There were only two known exits from the underground city, and they were both guarded at all times to prevent raiding parties from stealing the food. No one had any answers. Teachers were asking everyone to report anything unusual and trying to convince kids to never travel alone.

That had made Tracy laugh out loud. If she hadn't managed to turn it into a cough in time, she would have gotten extra labor this week. Kids already traveled in packs, either to pick on other kids who were stupid enough to wander around alone, or in a group to avoid getting picked on. Almost no one traveled alone, no matter how protective the Rules of Civility were supposed to be.

As she walked the last few yards to her home, the rags wrapped around her feet crunched down the newly fallen detritus. A brief memory of Topside, triggered by the smell of the freshly exposed dirt, crowded into her thoughts. It was of a park with green trees, grass, and a dog chasing a Frisbee. That was all. She didn't have anything else to go with it. The thought tantalized her. Had she been there with her mother? She didn't know.

Tracy didn't remember much of the world before the Night of Madness. She didn't even remember the night itself, as she had only been four years old, but that was nearly all they talked about in school. And they celebrated it each year with one evening when the Rules of Civility could be broken.

She didn't like Remembrance Night. It hadn't taken her long to realize that even if everyone said it was all right to break the Rules of Civility on Remembrance Night, it really wasn't. People remembered what you did, and they held it against you. Her older brother, Randy, had been beaten to death by a mob, two days after Remembrance Night, for stealing food from the Farm. He hadn't even stolen that much, just what fungi he could eat off the cave wall himself while he was in there.

No matter what anyone said, she was sure Remembrance Night was just an excuse for adults to get drunk, high, fight, and have sex. She always did her best to stay hidden until it was all over.

Nearing the door to the cement shelter she called home and shared with her father and eight other people, she decided not to go in. She didn't want to be around other people right now. Between going to school and farming the food cave, it seemed like she was always around other people, always being told what to do.

The quiet stillness of the tunnel seemed so soothingly peaceful now. It called to her.

Walking on past the row of doors into the shelters, she didn't even drop off her make-shift plastic backpack. She feared someone would notice it and come looking for her, unlikely as that was.

The Rules of Civility might make it so the people she lived with had to tolerate and pretend to respect her, but there was nothing that said they had to actually care about her. There was very little caring in this gloomy subterranean world. Even the teenagers who thought they were in love were really just acting out elaborate mating rituals and then moving on to their next conquests. No one really cared for anyone down here. No one cared for her.

Not even her father.

For the briefest of moments, Tracy remembered what it was like to have her mother hold her, love her…and then it was gone. She tried to pull the feeling back, to hold on to it, but it was elusive as a forgotten dream.

Echoing her mood, the tunnel around Tracy had dimmed considerably. She looked around and saw very little of the green phosphorescent fungi that lit most of her world. A nervous chill made her shiver as realized this tunnel was unfamiliar. How long had she been walking lost in her thoughts? She thought she knew all of the tunnels down here. She had explored them many times searching for anything she could eat.

Looking back behind, she saw nothing familiar. Her pulse quickened, whether from fear, excitement, or both, she wasn't sure. Should she turn back? She considered it. It would be the safest thing to do, but then, she couldn't remember the last time she had seen something—anything—new or unfamiliar. She felt the ache of a need she hadn't known before.

A sound caught her attention. A quiet mewling some small part of her remembered from somewhere and called 'kitty.' It came again from up ahead.

The tunnel was dark, but looking carefully for the source of the sound,

Tracy spotted a branch not too far ahead on the left. She was sure the sound was coming from there.

Creeping forward, the worn rags on her feet making no noise to give her away, Tracy went to the edge of the junction and peered around the corner.

Her eyes went wide. A small, pink, fuzzy, glowing worm-like creature was frolicking in the tunnel. Tracy hadn't seen the color pink since she was four. Her world was one of grays and greens now, and the new color mesmerized her. And this creature…

Tracy couldn't remember the last time she had seen anything other than an insect. She had never even heard of this kind of creature. It was batting at a small rock with one of its many stubby tentacles. Two long eye stalks waved in the air above its grub-like body, carefully tracking the rolling pebble. The soft pink fur, gently glowing in the dim tunnel, rippled across its body as it wormed forward like a caterpillar and swatted at the rock with another small tentacle. Tracy thought it had six tentacles, but they seemed to grow out of, and disappear back into, the chubby little body, making them hard to keep track of.

A dark spot appeared on the side of the thing. As Tracy squinted at it, trying to figure out what it was, the spot opened, and an eye looked at her.

Before she could react, the creature spun its eyestalks to view her and began mewling with the saddest voice she'd ever heard.

Inching forward awkwardly, listing side to side like a rolling egg, the pink betentacled fluff-ball cautiously approached Tracy. It wormed over the top of one of its own rubbery limbs and tripped, turning clumsily onto its back, eyestalks and tentacles waving desperately in the air.

Tracy giggled.

The little pink tentacles couldn't coordinate well enough to push the creature back up. As soon as one side would start to lift, limbs from the other side would also lift, or worse, whip around and knock free the ones already lifting. More eyes opened on its sides, all sadly looking at her, begging her to help it right itself.

Caution stopped Tracy from reaching out and touching it, but it began crying real, heartfelt little sobs that shook its whole body with fuzzy ripples. Finally, Tracy couldn't resist. She couldn't remember having touched anything furry before. What would it feel like? And that bright color! What would that color feel like? She stepped forward and kneeled down.

The pink glow brightened in anticipation of her touch as she reached out and gently stroked the fur. It was the softest thing she had ever touched. And it was warm.

Several flailing tentacles gently caught at her hand, wrapping about her fingers and wrist, softly tugging, trying to pull the creature over onto its belly.

Using both hands, Tracy righted the little thing.

With a squeal of pure joy, the creature scurried up her arms and nuzzled her neck, purring. Gentle tentacles groped around her neck, brushed her ears, tickled her nose and softly probed her lips and eyes.

Tracy giggled and hugged the creature close. This is what she remembered love felt like.

"What's your name?" she asked as a big green eye opened up to look into her face. "Do you have a name?"

"*Growlf?*" A small mouth on the larger end of the creature opened and made an odd high-pitched sound.

"Growlf? What kind of name is that?"

"*Growlf.*" A slimy tongue darted out and licked the end of Tracy's nose.

It tickled, and she had to wipe her face with her shoulder. Growlf seemed to think this was funny and squirmed upwards in Tracy's arms to lick her again.

Tracy laughed and wiped at her nose while Growlf's tongue licked at her face with increasing fervor, its body wiggling with joy.

A tremor rocked the tunnel. Tracy lost her footing and fell hard. Growlf landed on her lap with a startled yip, then rolled off as the shaking continued. Dust fell from new cracks in the ceiling and walls, then rocks began to fall. Tracy tried to protect Growlf with her body as larger rocks bounced round them.

With whine of pain, Growlf shot out from under her, disappearing down the tunnel impossibly fast, its pink glow fading in the distance.

"Growlf!" Tracy staggered to her feet as the tremor subsided. "Growlf!" She tripped over some of the larger rocks in the dim light as she tried to give chase. "Come back!"

A feeling of loss came over her. She couldn't remember ever feeling so empty as she did in the deepest parts of her heart right now. "Growlf?" Tracy staggered on calling out. "Where are you?"

The tunnel darkened to the point Tracy could no longer see without Growlf's pink glow. Having been underground her whole life, the dark didn't bother her, but she didn't know where she was. She had no idea where this tunnel led to, and, as she turned and looked for any sign of light behind her, she realized she was no longer sure of the way she had come.

Panic tightened her stomach. She was lost. She was now one of those people who disappeared, and no one knew what had happened to them.

Feeling out for the edge of the tunnel, Tracy found the wall and kept her fingers on it to stay oriented. She had to get back to someplace familiar. The strange feeling of curiosity about the unknown she had felt earlier was gone. She didn't know where this tunnel went, what it might lead to, but she did know that none of the people who disappeared ever returned.

Dragging her fingers along the wall, she moved slowly back the way she had come, lifting each step high and setting it down gently to avoid stubbing her toes or twisting her ankles on rocks. She had gone no more than a dozen steps when she heard something behind her.

"Growlf?"

Tracy looked over her shoulder and spotted a dim pink light flowing over the rocks on the tunnel floor. Her chest tightened and her breath caught as emotion overwhelmed her. "You came back!"

"*Growlf!*" the creature squeaked in response and hurried toward Tracy, dodging larger rocks and scurrying over smaller ones.

Falling to her knees, Tracy held out her arms and the fuzzy pink worm crawled up them, again wrapping tentacles around her neck and nuzzling her. Tracy held Growlf tightly, pushing her face into the fur that brought back memories that she could only name as 'flowers.'

The slimy tongue went into Tracy's ear and then brushed her cheek and lips. Tracy laughed and moved her face away but didn't put the creature down. She fell back into a sitting position and snuggled Growlf until she fell asleep.

#   #   #

Waking to Growlf's soft pink glow lighting the tunnel, Tracy smiled and resisted the urge to hug the creature close again, fearing she would wake it. Growlf slept in her lap, a soft snoring sound coming and going with the pulsing of its chubby little body.

Tracy shifted her weight a little, and a single eyestalk popped up and opened. When Growlf saw she was awake, it began wiggling and climbing up to lick her face again.

Giggling, Tracy stood up, cradling Growlf in her arms. "Come on. Let's go home. I can't wait to show you to Kim! She's gonna love you."

"*Growlf!*" Tentacles and a slimy tongue all tried to reach for Tracy's face.

As Tracy started walking back up the tunnel, Growlf began to squirm and whine.

"What's wrong?" Tracy stroked the soft fur as she walked, but the creature wriggled even more, using tentacles to try to push out of her arms.

With a final shove, Growlf managed to get free and fell to the floor, landing with a moist thump and a painful squeal.

"Are you okay?" Tracy quickly bent to scoop Growlf back up, but it moved out of her reach.

"*Growlf?*" It moved a little farther back down the tunnel. "*Growlf?*"

"What are you doing? Come here." Tracy patted her thigh. "Come here."

"*Growlf.*" With a playful jump, it moved even farther away, wiggling excitedly. Tracy stepped to pick it up and it moved again. "*Growlf.*"

"That's the wrong way. Home is this way."

"*Growlf!*" It scurried the other way.

"No! This way!" Stepping forward again, Tracy reached for Growlf, but it ran down the tunnel and disappeared. The darkness of the tunnel swallowed Tracy up again. "Hey! Where'd you go?"

"*Growlf!*" The pink glow reappeared as it peeked around a corner Tracy hadn't seen before.

"Come back. Come here..." Tracy stepped towards it. "Come on."

It pulled back, disappearing, then looked out again. Tracy sighed as she reached the junction.

"Come on—" She stopped and stared.

There was a dim light coming from the tunnel. Another color Tracy hadn't seen in years—blue.

"Growlf!"

Tracy watched as Growlf wormed quickly down the tunnel, one eyestalk on her, one pointed ahead. Other eyes on its body appeared and disappeared excitedly as its tentacles helped propel it over rocks.

"Growlf!"

Fear twisted in Tracy's stomach. She didn't know what was down the tunnel, but somehow, she was sure if she followed she would never come back. She would never see her father again. Never see Kim or the other kids at school…

A sense of calm came over her. She wasn't afraid of never seeing any of them again. They really didn't care about her, and she didn't really care about them. She was afraid of…the unknown that lie ahead of her.

Except that she wasn't. She craved it. She felt the same excitement, the same need she had felt before. She needed something new.

Taking a deep breath, she stepped forward toward the blue glow.

"*Growlf!*" The creature came back to her, circling and rubbing against her legs, wanting her to pick it up.

Tracy smiled and scooped it up, holding it in her arms and keeping her face away from its quick tongue. It wiggled happily and then settled down as she walked.

The glow became brighter, lighting the tunnel so she could easily see, and as she went, it intensified, becoming the brightest light she could remember. She stopped and played with her shadow on the cave wall for a moment, remembering it from when she was little. Growlf waved three tentacles to help her get the shadow's attention.

Tears formed in her eyes as she waved, and her shadow waved back. It was like finding an old friend she had lost. How had she forgotten about shadows? They were so beautiful!

A sound from up the tunnel pulled her away from the shadows.

"*Growlf!*" The pink fluff ball wormed out of Tracy's arms again and hurried up the tunnel excitedly.

The sound drifted down again.

It was…music.

Happy music, the kind Tracy remembered, not the sad, monotonous hand-clapping kind the people in the Town did.

She hurried up the tunnel, wincing as the light got brighter. She rounded a bend and the light shone down blazingly brilliant. Her eyes watered and her head hurt from the intensity of it. She stumbled on, covering her eyes, shielding them and wondering if the quiet, painless dark wasn't a better place after all. As the music got louder, her eyes hurt more and more until she could no longer bear to keep them open.

Even closed, with her hand over her eyelids, it was too much.

She stumbled on rocks and fell.

"*Growlf! Growlf!*" Fuzziness nuzzled at her arms, but she couldn't pull her hands from her eyes.

"Tracy? Is that you? Oh! My Baby! It is you!" Gentle hands touched her shoulders, and Tracy felt arms encircle her and pull her close. Awkwardly, she hugged the form back as she felt Growlf rubbing around her ankles.

"I never thought I'd see you again!"

Tracy recognized the voice.

"Mommy?" Tears seeped from her scrunched eyes as she managed to say the name.

"Yes! Baby! It's me!" Arms pulled her in tight again. "It's me."

Blinking her eyes with pain from the intensity of the light, Tracy looked upon her mother's face for the first time in over ten years. "You're beautiful!" she breathed. "Just like I remember." And she was. Tracy's mother looked just like the last memory she had of her.

"So are you, sweetheart! Look at you, all grown up!" Her mother cupped Tracy's face in her hands and kissed her on the nose.

Soft voices sang, whispered, and laughed with music in the distance, but Tracy couldn't focus that far yet. She blinked the tears from her eyes and looked up at the blue sky. The sun burned her eyes with its brightness, but its warmth kissed her face. Tracy held her hand up to feel the heat.

"Oh, my poor, poor baby. How awful it must have been for you down there." Tracy's mother put her arms around her again and held her.

145

Tracy hugged her back, tears rolling down her face. This is what love was. Not the way her father just sat and ignored her.

Her father...

"Dad misses you horribly," Tracy began.

"Shhhh. We don't talk about men here."

Leaning back, Tracy looked into her mother's face. "What?"

"This is not their world. This is our world, and we don't talk about them here."

"I don't understand."

"You will. Come." Taking Tracy by the hand, her mother stood and pulled Tracy to her feet.

"Growlf!"

Tracy bent down and held her arms out. Growlf wormed up into them in a flail of tentacles and eyestalks. In the bright light of day, its pink glow was gone and Growlf looked more like one of the white fluffy clouds in the blue sky.

"Are we in the park?" Tracy asked as she looked around at the green grass and trees. The smell of fresh earth and life filled her nose and made her happy. She had vague memories that there should be houses or buildings, but she didn't see any anywhere.

"No dear. This is our world, not the world of men. Look around." Her mother swept her arm in a wide gesture. "There are no roads, no cars, no buildings. Nothing of the blight men put upon the Earth. This is a new world. Our world. Not theirs."

Birds flew in the sky. Tall grasses at the edge of the clearing bent with the wind. Trees cast cool shadows upon squirrels and rabbits that darted between bushes. A group of women, all wearing light and airy sundresses that were so much nicer than her own rags, waved to Tracy and laughed with pure joy.

She smiled and waved back, feeling the urge to join them, to dance and play. There were no happy people in the Town. She had never seen a gathering of people having fun like this before.

"This is so beautiful." Tracy hugged Growlf tight, and it chirruped into her neck. After a moment, she thought, "But where are the Old Ones?"

Her mother smiled and pointed to a distant mountain range.

Tracy couldn't remember ever seeing anything so far away before. How huge must a thing that far away be? Purple and blue with distance, she made out the massive shapes that formed the ridges. Gargantuan heads, trunks, folded wings, limbs, and shapeless masses lumped together to become one, unfathomably large beast.

"Are they asleep?"

"As much as a being like that can be."

Tracy looked back the way they had come. The women appeared to have turned their song into some sort of game, chasing each other and laughing. Tracy realized there were no men at all.

"Why aren't there any men?"

"This isn't their world."

"But look at all of the happy people!" Tracy pointed at the women. "Can't the people of the Town come up here? There is so much food, and warmth! And love!"

"There is all of that, and more, with one exception. You are wrong, dear. There are no people up here. There is just one person. Only one."

Tracy looked at her mother, her brow furrowing.

"Only you, dear. You are the only person here."

"But…" Tracy weakly waved a hand towards the women before looking back to her mother. "But…"

Her mother smiled warmly. "This is not the world of men. Or women. Or mankind, or humans or whatever word you wish to use. This is our world. There is no place here for man. People will soon be a distant memory we will not bother to remember."

Tracy looked over her shoulder as some of the women giggled. The music had stopped, and they had all come closer without her realizing it. They smiled mischievously as they approached on tiptoe, still dancing and twirling, but never taking their eyes off her.

Tracy took a step back. Her mother's hand caught her shoulder.

"It's all right, sweetheart. No one will miss you any more than you missed them." ♜

I AM LAID TO REST IN MAINE

By Mike Owsley

TEARS SPILLED OVER MY COFFIN in great cold waves familiar only to those who lived near my parent's beautiful French villa on the east coast. He was too young, they wailed, he was too innocent. I disagreed vehemently. If I was too young, why was I wise beyond my years? If I was too innocent, how could I so simply distinguish the bitter taste of coffee from the scentless nip of the arsenic mixed into my creamer? Yet, as I am laid to rest in Maine, I could not distinguish whether I had been right or arrogant. People clearly mourned me as if I had been both selfish and selfless, pure and corrupted by a cruel and twisted world.

Cruel world. Twisted world. I bask now in nothing but the heat of nothing. My body is warm and stiff, but not so that I ache. There is nothing cruel or twisted about dirt. I might even call it beautiful down here. By the time erosion makes memories of the coast nothing will remain of me but bone dust. I can hear the school yard's whistling wind above me. Its Atlantic chill is the sound of shuddering grief. With the last of my nerve endings, I know nothing but warmth. My coffin is safe. My coffin is peaceful.

Father worked for the army when I was a kid. Maybe it was the National Guard. He was always traveling or buying guns or shooting. I remember when he ran for congress and the president came to town and campaigned for him. He bounced me on his lap - the president, of course. Never Father. I wonder if that old bastard is here now. Anger sits in overflowing stomach acid as the chance of this crosses my mind. It will not be long until this sloshes out and dissolves my organs.

Some days or months after my wake, I climbed from the safety of a maple bed to emerge in Maine. Something profunctually passed through my half-stone nasal cavity. Beyond where I stood, a field of broad white headstones were irregularly interrupted by mausoleums. Nested in the chaotic branches of an old gray wolf tree was a Murder. They cawed menacingly, sniffed knowingly, at me. I could not defend myself if they set upon me. My sinews were like an unstrung guitar.

Father made me play both guitar and soccer. I remember the feeling of the ball against my foot for the first time. Strength is best in exertion, otherwise it is vain. Kick. Again. Kick. Again. Kick. Again. His dictatorial tone frightened me. I suppressed globs of snot and sobs behind my still-sealed tear ducts. Kick. Again. Again. Again.

I kicked into Loving Memory of Clinton Taylor Dewitt April 18th, 1769 - September 9th, 1844. If I could feel I might have named every broken toe. Instead, my mangled foot hung limp. From then on it plagued me as a large, flat, inconsiderate club. In my unbeating heart flashed unimaginable pain. It was fear. Frustration. What would Father say when he learned I broke my foot? Would he break the other in rage?

Mother Nature was quiet at the far-off sound of Father's inconsolable temper. Under a red cedar wood in the graveyard, I watched the igneous stained shores sink beneath the peaceful waves. Dying Earth sleeps like the nesting gulls on the cliff face. I didn't mind the nipping crows tearing at my exposed face and arms. To live in harmony with nature is the purpose of solitude, I think. To feed nature is the purpose of giving, I believe.

It came to pass that I would spend night after night watching the erosion work away in Maine. Children playing on the beaches built great silt castles and were dark wizards in dark towers. Father and I behaved similarly not more than ten years ago. He would run his hands through my free-flowing hair, now beset by lice in uneven patchwork. We would dance with unbroken feet and flail with unbroken arms and ask Mom what book she was reading. How fun life was. How different those times seem now. Now I am waiting for a rapture which will never come. Now, I hope he is waiting to see me again.

In the daytime I let myself waste away in my dirtbed. Being dead is intensive work and I'm so fucking tired. There is unspeakable pain from the maggots burrowing through my flesh. If my vocal cords were not frayed and snapped, I would scream myself hoarse. Every hour drags out in agony, every moment and second an infinity of suffering. The pain and the stench are two agents of evil. My own flesh is rotting into my nose. My muscles have atrophied for how useless they are. What remains of my flesh is purple and blue and bloating from asphyxiation. I don't sleep anymore because I'm always sleeping and I'm so fucking tired all the time.

In the infinite nights, when it is safe to leave my exile, I curse myself for being born with nerves. I have consulted with the ethereal moon and sprinkled stars. I ask them if God is real, and I think the silence is their answer. I beg and plead with the Earth to help me understand meaning and still the crows speak their garbled, antediluvian tongue. I've been inviting them to feed off me. They tear surgically. They trade me for language. It is nice to have someone to talk to, even in my stupor.

\#   \#   \#

Father comes and speaks to me from time to time. At first he was cold. Angry. I learned that it was bitter. He talks to me about politics. He talks to me about soccer (although he would prefer to discuss football) and my shared childhood with him. He talked about Mom. I haven't heard him do that in years. He leaves me space to respond. I caw at him, desperate for him to know I am finally listening. From time to time, I've heard him cry. He has apologized frequently. I have accepted profusely. Still, we are separate from each other. Each in our own worlds, speaking our own languages.

With time my eyes have melted into vaporious pools. I grope around like a blind drunkard, using the muffled sound of the world in guidance. There is no pleasure in nature anymore. I cannot see if it is still alive. I am shrouded in the darkness and shamefully stuck in my past. Maybe the world is dead and that is why it grows quieter every day. I don't even know if I am sitting under the tree with the birds anymore. There is no company in my solace. God truly is dead. I will exist forever in a state of remnant. Will my molecules still scream with the weight of my consciousness, or will one day I be cast into oblivion? Death is not an escape but merely a lobby to a waiting room of torture. I am alone. I am dead and alone. I am alone. Alone. Alone. Alone and dead. I want to scream from how alone and dead I am.

Except for when Father comes to visit. His voice still holds harsh command. When he speaks all the crows stop to listen in the trees. I stop to listen too. He holds court unlike how most men hold weight, with haughty grandeur and confidence. I think, despite my brain running down my nose, I understand his words. Remarried. New siblings. They are abstractions in my world. The things we share are less and less common. That is worse than the feeling of decaying. I am melting away and the complexity of my Father moving on is torment beyond torment in hell.

#   #   #

I did not realize how lonely loneliness is until I was dead, buried, and forgotten. Father has not visited me in eons. There is little left to visit. My body is a failed experiment in wax and humanity. My wicker runs thin as the fire draws close to my afflicted soul. I do not remember how to feel any more. I do not know how to speak other than the raspy caw I've grown accustomed to. I am hungry. So hungry. My teeth have long rotted out and turned to dust. My bones are broken and exposed but I can still shamble ceaselessly. Purposelessly. With my death came the rumor of the haunted graveyard. With my wailing came the warning not to draw near at night. I am dead and alone forever now. I would cry if there was any liquid left in me. It all dried up years ago.

I think about Father a lot. With his beautiful teeth and well-maintained hair. I wonder what he is doing with his new family. It is not jealousy I feel. I am sure he is looking at them with his two working eyes. He laughs at their jokes and speaks to them in a language not dissimilar from English. It is not jealousy that I miss him. He was so good in my youth, so thoughtful. I bet he uses his still solid brain. Maybe if I could pick it from time to time, I would know what to do next? Life seems so alone and stagnant, and our family feels so broken. Does he still live in my parent's beautiful French villa? If only Father would see me now.

But what stops me from seeing him?

I feel an outstanding rush of euphoria as I enter the town. They are cheering for me. I hear screams and gunshots and what sounds like a parade. There is honking and it smells delicious here, like fresh bread and warm flesh. Tears of joy wash over town in great cold waves familiar only to those in Maine as I shamble into stores and gas stations. The wind pierces through me in sharp bullets but that will not stop me. I have been rejected by oblivion and have faced an eternity of torture, there is no deterrent for me to return home. The pain of death has been replaced by the joy of living. As I fumble with familiar street signs and cars I know, I am nearly there. I know we have grown so far apart but I hope he recognizes me as his son. I know he will embrace me with open arms. That he will love and accept me for who I am. I want to hear him cheer like the rest of town at the return of the prodigal son. ♜

THE CREATURE IN JAY COOKE PARK

By Scott Pearson

June 1955

IT WAS JUST BEFORE MIDNIGHT, under a moonless sky, and Pete was driving his girlfriend home. A sudden, loud thump made Shirley scream as the Chevy started wobbling down the road through Jay Cooke Park.

"Just a flat," Pete said, pulling the car over onto the narrow grassy shoulder. "Nothing to worry about."

"Except for my dad when I get home after midnight."

As Peter got out and hurried to the back of the car, he heard whispers in the darkness. He quickly opened the trunk, fumbled with the flashlight, then turned it on, shining it across the road toward the sound. It was probably only the St. Louis River splashing along its rocky banks. After a moment of flashing the light around, he shook his head at himself and pulled out the jack and spare.

But then he realized where they were—right near the old pioneer cemetery. Hidden in the woods were gravestones sticking out of the ground like crooked, broken teeth. As he shined the flashlight that way, a wisp of fog floated like a ghost into the road. Pete shivered, then laughed at himself. He

153

hadn't believed in ghosts since he was kid.

Then... something yanked his arm.

"Hey!" Jack yelled, jumping to his feet after I'd tugged on his sleeve. He staggered on the the uneven ground of our campsite.

Wayne laughed, slapping his knee. "He got you!"

"No, he didn't," Jack said with a half grin, just visible in the dim light of the kerosene lantern I'd brought.

"Sorry, I couldn't resist," I said, smirking at them both. But then they seemed to remember they weren't speaking to each other. With a *humph,* Jack sat down cross-legged on the ground out of my reach. Wayne turned his back toward Jack, got out his comb, and worked on the ducktail his wavy hair wouldn't cooperate with.

With a sigh, I shifted around on the cooler I was sitting on and got back to the story.

Pete jumped. He hadn't heard Shirley get out of the car, and she'd come up right behind him and grabbed him by the sleeve. She said she was scared to be alone because she'd heard noises.

"Probably just the river," Pete told her, but she said the noises had come from under the car.

Grumbling, he got down on hands and knees to shine the flashlight under the Chevy. "See? Nothing there. Just wait in the car and turn up the radio."

She looked a little angry, but she got back in, and soon he heard "Rock Around the Clock."

Pete got to work changing the tire as fast as possible, swearing when the flashlight kept rolling away from where he put it. Just as he was tightening the last lug nut, the flashlight rolled under the car. He laid flat on his stomach to reach it, squinting because it had turned back toward him, shining in his eyes. Just as he got his fingers on it, he lost his grip—like it had been pulled away from him.

"Very funny!" he said, thinking Shirley was playing a trick on him.

But then from above he heard her say, "What're you yelling about?" She had rolled down the window over him and stuck her head out.

He looked back under the car, where the flashlight still sat, shining in his face. He must have bumped it away himself when he tried to reach it. This time he made sure he had a good grip on it, but when he tried to pull his arm back, the flashlight wouldn't budge, as if it had wedged between some rocks. With a grunt Pete gave it a hard tug, and it came loose, but it slipped from his fingers again, spinning around as he dropped it, pointing away from him.

Something was there, flinching away from the light, a tangle of clacking claws and twisting tentacles and too many unblinking eyes—

"Hold it right there," Jack said, leaning forward. "You said this was a true story."

Without turning to face Jack, Wayne added, "Yeah." Jack nodded.

Agreeing with each other was a step in the right direction, but I didn't mention it. I just folded my arms across my chest. "It *is* a true story."

"Bullshit," Wayne said.

"You know Pete Gran. The quarterback, he graduated last spring," I said. "And Shirley, captain of the cheerleading squad this year."

"So, you used real people's names." Jack leaned back and stared into the starry sky while swatting at a mosquito. "Doesn't make it real."

But I'd heard the story of the Jay Cooke Park monster from my big brother, Rich, and I believed him. "Rich's buddy Al heard it from Pete himself."

"Al Stone, that delinquent?" Jack said. Jack's uncle was a deputy in the Carlton County Sheriff's Department. "How do you know he didn't make up the whole thing?"

"'Cause he wouldn't lie to my brother, they're pals."

Jack stared at Wayne's back. "Hmph."

Wayne spun around on the log he was sitting on and glared at Jack. "I didn't lie, you lied!"

Jack just tilted his head to the side. "You're gonna get slivers the way you keep spinning on that log. Makes sense, because even though I didn't lie, you're a big pain in my ass."

Wayne stood up, so Jack stood up, and they stared at each other like gunfighters.

Before they could take a step closer, I stood up between them. "Guys, come on." I was sick of my two best friends not being friends with each other anymore. Ever since second grade, summers were all about the three of us riding bikes, going fishing, and lighting firecrackers—Eddy, Wayne, and Jack, the Three Musketeers. But things started going wrong the last quarter of ninth grade. That's when the new girl, Julie Wills, moved here. And then Wayne and Jack both got crushes on her. Almost every boy in the whole school did, but that didn't seem to make a difference to these two knuckleheads, who each somehow thought they had dibs on being her boyfriend. Before I knew it, they weren't talking to each other, which continued pointlessly even after she'd started going steady with a junior basketball player who never missed a free throw. So now I was looking at a summer of them feuding.

"Guys," I said again. I put a hand on each of their shoulders. They glared at me. I lowered my hands. It was the same glare they'd given me this afternoon when they'd first seen each other in my backyard and said at the same time, "What's *he* doing here?" To get them both camping in the park, I'd invited them separately without telling either about the other. Then, to keep them from leaving, I'd made a big deal about having a secret I'd only tell them once we were at camp. I needed something more amazing than Julie to get them talking again, and I figured the Jay Cooke Park monster was a big enough deal do it. If I could only get them to believe me.

"And you!" Wayne poked me in the shoulder.

I took a step back. "Me? What?"

"Tricking me into coming!"

"Yeah," Jack said, poking me in the other shoulder. "Tricking *me* into coming!"

Well, at least that was something else they could agree on. But I gave them both a push back anyway. "I wouldn't have to trick you if—" I stopped and listened, trying to ignore the frogs and crickets singing in the night. "You hear that?"

They both rolled their eyes at me. Jack slapped a hand on his flat top. "And now your made-up monster just happens by our camp."

Wayne laughed. "What a coincidence!"

"I didn't make it up. Stuff like this has been on the news. Something happened in Cloquet just a couple months ago, Mr. Therrien was talking about it in English—" I froze. I was sure I'd heard something in the underbrush again, a dragging, slithering sound, something behind the whispering of the pines and the splashing of the river. I stared into the mottled darkness, broken up by the light of a low-hanging moon shifting through the trees. We weren't that far from where Pete had seen the monster under his car.

"I don't know anything about that," Jack said. I wasn't surprised, he never listened in English class. He shoved his hands into the pockets of his jean jacket. "But even if *you* didn't make it up, then Pete or Al or—"

He stopped and shifted his eyes back and forth. I could tell he'd heard it that time too, a clacking sound, almost like lightly clapping a couple of two-by-fours together. I looked at Wayne, who was also peering into the trees.

"Who's out there?" Wayne said to me. "Is Rich in on this?"

All Rich was in on was telling Wayne and Jack's parents that he was watching all three of us. Instead, he'd dropped us off here and was having a party, because our parents were out of town overnight. He was covering for our camping trip, and I was covering for his party.

"Rich is on his third can of Hamm's by now," I said.

There was another loud clack, followed a weird gagging sound. Jack's eyes went wide, and I felt a shiver slither down my spine like a snake in my shirt.

"Then it's Leo, isn't it?" Wayne said loudly enough for someone hiding nearby to hear. Leo, though not one of our Three Musketeers, often went fishing with us.

"No one's—" I started but stopped as Wayne suddenly scooped up the lantern and ran toward the sounds, leaving Jack and me in the dark.

"Wait!" Jack called, and dashed after Wayne, following the lantern light as it bounced up and down and around trees.

I fumbled in my backpack and dug out a flashlight, then raced after them. They were already farther away than where the sounds had first seemed to come from. All I could hear now was their shouting and my own breathing.

Just as I thought I was gaining ground, I tripped on a tree root and took a dive like I was stealing home. The flashlight flew out of my hands and went dark on impact. The wind knocked out of me, I stumbled to my feet, gasping for breath while trying to spit dirt out of my mouth at the same time. I caught some glimpses of the lantern far ahead, and followed, going as fast as I dared under the dim moonlight.

"Wait up!" I shouted. I'd lost sight of the lantern, and there was no response. I stopped running and held my ragged breath. I tried to tell myself I was listening for them, but really, I was checking for the clacking, gagging sounds I'd heard before. I exhaled in relief, hearing nothing but crickets and frogs, a few mosquitos buzzing near my head, the river across the road, and an owl in the distance. The relief was short, as I then wondered about my friends. My eyes were adjusted to the moonlight now, so I started off at a jog in the last direction I'd seen them. I didn't know what else to do.

Then I tripped again, on something hard, and went sprawling. I rolled onto my side and curled up so I could grab my aching foot, wondering if I'd broken a toe. At first I thought the dark shape in front of me was a tree stump, but I flinched when I realized it was a gravestone. I must have tripped on a tipped-over stone, and luckily, I hadn't smacked my head on the upright one looming over me.

After taking a moment to tell myself I didn't believe in ghosts, I got to my feet and limped around in a circle, wondering what to do. I felt colder than the night, as if the ghosts I didn't believe in were wrapping themselves around me like icy blankets. I tried to shake that thought away, but the ghosts were just replaced by the monster. I'd told Wayne and Jack I believed Rich, but there's a difference between believing your brother's monster story and standing in a cemetery in the middle of the night wondering if that monster has already devoured your best friends.

I was just about to call their names when I heard something coming toward me. I huddled down behind the gravestone and peeked around the edge in the direction of the noise. As it got louder, it sounded a lot more like two scared kids running through the woods than any of the weird monster noises I'd heard before. I leaned further out from behind the gravestone and saw Wayne and Jack burst into the clearing of the cemetery just a few yards away, freezing in place when they realized they were surrounded by graves. They must have taken a more roundabout route through the woods than I did.

I stood up. "Hey, guys."

"Aaaahhhhh!" they screamed together as they jumped. Wayne dropped the lantern, which was already out.

Startled by their outburst, I jumped too, yipping like a scared puppy. After a moment of awkward silence, we all started laughing.

After we wound down and caught our breath, Jack said to me, "See any monsters?"

"Nope. No ghosts either." Bringing that up spooked all three of us, and we glanced at the tombstones scattered around. Moonlight shifting through the trees made it look like the stones were slightly swaying back and forth.

Quickly fumbling with the lantern, Wayne said, "I'm gonna get this lit again." He set it down on top of a stone with a clang, adjusted the wick, then lifted the glass chimney. He fished his Zippo out of his pocket.

"Careful with that," Jack said.

"Ha-ha," Wayne said.

A couple summers before we'd been at Wayne's house messing around with firecrackers, and when he had to refill his Zippo, he spilled lighter fluid all over his hand. When he flicked the lighter, his whole hand went up in flames, and somehow, he didn't notice until I said, "Wayne, your hand's on fire." He started jumping around, waving his hand all over the place to put it out. Jack and me laughed so hard I thought we were going to throw up.

Jack has never let Wayne forget it, and he watched like a hawk as Wayne flipped open the Zippo and flicked it. Jack waved his pointer finger at him. "Smokey Bear says, 'Only you can prevent finger fires.'"

"Hilarious," Wayne said. "You should go on Ed Sullivan." He lit the lantern and flipped the Zippo closed.

I was grinning like an idiot looking back and forth between them. They were acting normal, not snapping at each other like junkyard dogs. Jack picked up the lantern and moved it closer to my face. "What's with you? You're smiling like my baby cousin after she's filled her diaper."

Wayne snickered. Not wanting to jinx it, I couldn't tell them what I was really thinking, so I said, "You believe me about the Jay Cooke Park monster now, don't you? Both of you." I actually was happy about that too. My plan was working perfectly.

Wayne shrugged. "I don't know. Those were some weird noises. And I think we would have caught up to someone pranking us."

"Yeah," Jack said, "But we didn't *see* anything weird."

Wayne took the lantern back. "Maybe it was just a raccoon or something."

"A raccoon?" I said. "Making that gagging noise?"

"I don't know. Maybe it had a fish stuck in his throat."

"And had a couple wooden legs," Jack said. "They'd clap together when he was trying to get the fish out." He clapped his hands clumsily in front of his face, looking more like a seal than a choking racoon, but he did make convincing gagging sounds.

That set us off laughing again. Wayne had to set the lantern back on the gravestone. It took us a while to notice Jack had stopped laughing. When I did, I could tell, even under the lantern light, that he'd gone pale. His mouth hung open a little, and he raised a shaking finger to point behind me and Wayne.

I felt like I swallowed my laughter in one big painful chunk. I didn't want to see what was behind us, but I turned slowly, getting a glimpse of Wayne's unblinking eyes as he also turned. Across the clearing, a kind of blurry white shape rose up from behind a gravestone. I didn't realize I'd taken a step backward until I bumped into Jack, who was as still as a statue.

The shape, its back to us, was turning around as slowly as we had, coming more into focus, arms stretching outward, loose clothing and long, pale hair billowing around as if it were underwater. Within the gauzy material was a curvy silhouette to go with the long hair.

"No..." Wayne said.

The ghost's face finally turned toward us, pale and expressionless—it was Julie Wills.

"How?" Jack croaked, his mouth dry with shock.

The "ghost" took off at a run, not smoothly floating like a spirit, but with bare feet thumping on the grass.

Speechless, I turned toward my friends. Their expressions flashed between fear and confusion, then settled on anger, and they both glared at me.

"What—?" I started, then realized they thought I'd planned this, that somehow I'd talked Julie into playing the cruelest prank possible on both of them, never mind that I would never do that, or how impossible the whole thing was.

"Later," Wayne growled at me, and then he was off like a shot in Julie's wake.

"No, you don't," Jack yelled after him and sprinted into the woods after leaping over a half-fallen gravestone.

I stood there a few seconds, the lantern left behind with me, at a loss about what to do now. Just as my heartbeat was slowing to normal, it hit me: Mr. Therrien talking about rumors of what had happened in Cloquet. Witnesses swore that somehow monsters had looked like normal people, people they knew—

Grabbing the lantern, I charged after my friends. It wasn't a prank. Julie hadn't died and become a ghost. It was the Jay Cooke Park monster.

I could hear Wayne and Jack somewhere ahead, crashing through the brush and calling Julie's name. They were headed toward the road. When I came out of the woods, I saw Jack's back as he plunged back into the woods on the other side of the road. I hurried after him. It wasn't that far to the river here, and before I caught up, I heard a scream.

Soon I was stumbling on more and more rocky ground, and the trees thinned. Suddenly I was near a short precipice above the St. Louis rushing by below. The lantern had gone out again while I was running, but along the riverbank the low moon could shine clearly, glittering across the surface of the water.

Wayne and Jack were right on the edge of the small cliff, leaning forward, peering down.

"Oh my god oh my god, she went over the edge!" Wayne said.

Jack leaned back a bit and pulled Wayne back too. "Could she... survive? The rocks look sharp down there."

I carefully moved to the edge and looked down. There was nothing down there but rocks, water, and tree branches washed up by the river. "It wasn't her," I told them. "It was the monster."

They both spun toward me. I don't think they'd noticed me joining them.

"It *was* her," Jack said. "You saw her. We all saw her."

Wayne went back to staring over the edge.

I put the lamp down by Wayne. "Why would she be alone in the cemetery in the middle of the night wearing nothing but a… a nightgown? And why would she run from us right over a cliff?"

"Because you—" Jack stopped. I guess it had finally hit him that the idea of me talking her into doing any of this was crazy. He looked over his shoulder. "Wayne."

Wayne started to say something at least three times before letting out a long breath. "Have we all gone nuts?"

"No," I said. "That was the monster. They can make illusions or change shape or something. They mess with people."

Wayne looked back over the edge one last time, then took a few steps away. "Well, shit. Where'd it go?"

"Hell, the thing could have turned into a bird and flown away." Jack turned toward me. "Can they do that?"

"I don't know."

"So, what should we do?" Wayne said.

I knew what I wanted to do. "Go back to camp for our stuff. Then it's only a couple miles to walk back to my house." Our three bikes were in a heap in my front yard to demonstrate we were all there to anyone who drove by. Rich wouldn't be back for us until he woke up in the morning—and who knew when that would be.

"Come on," Jack said. "We'll make a fire. I brought marshmallows."

"You want to stay?" Wayne was relighting the lantern again. As soon as he was done, I picked it back up and we started walking.

"Well, the monster only scared the bejeebers out of us then ran away."

I shifted from one leg to the other. "Rumors are that some of the monsters have been violent."

Wayne glared at me. "You lured us out here to find a dangerous monster with no escape plan?"

"Uh… sorry?" I saw now that that had been a weak point of my scheme to reunite my friends, even though I'd succeeded. "And I don't want to be a spoilsport, but we can't have a fire. We're not supposed to be camping here, it's a state park."

"So, rain check on toasting marshmallows," Jack said. "But back to our monster… how exactly did Pete's story end? You didn't get to finish."

"You mean you didn't give me a chance to finish."

"Six of one, half dozen of the other."

I shook my head at him. "Well, after Pete shined the flashlight on the thing, it scuttled off. Pete jumped in the car as fast as he could and sped all the way to Shirley's house and got there five minutes after midnight, but they had the excuse of the flat tire, so they didn't get in too much trouble."

"See?" said Jack. "I think our Jay Cooke Park monster is a scaredy-cat. Nothing to worry about."

"But, but that's not…" Wayne stopped and took a deep breath. "It was in my head."

"What do you mean?" Jack said.

"How else could it be Julie? It must be reading our minds somehow, right?"

"Well, you're not the only one who's been thinking about Julie a lot." Jack's tone was a little sharp. I worried that we were going to lose ground here.

"It was a dream. *My* dream," Wayne said in an almost whisper. "It *invaded* my brain."

Jack stopped walking. "You dreamt Julie was a ghost?"

"No, no." Wayne stopped as well and looked between us, obviously embarrassed. "But I dreamed I saw her in a see-through nightgown. Just like she was. But not a ghost."

Jack looked at me and back to Wayne. "In your dreams she still had clothes on? In my dreams—"

"Take that back!" Wayne said.

Now Jack was the confused one. "Take what back?"

"Don't talk about her like that."

"I'm not talking about *her*, I'm talking about a dream."

"Still. I don't like it."

"Don't be stupid."

"Don't call me stupid."

I couldn't believe what was happening. "Guys, come on. Dreams don't mean anything. And I bet the monster was in all our minds. We were probably all thinking of ghosts in a cemetery, right? It blended it together." I started toward camp, and since I had the lamp, they followed me, one on either side.

"But why did it run away?" Wayne was still angry. "That wasn't in my dream. Maybe she was running away from Jack."

"Why would she run away from me?"

"Stop arguing!" I snapped. "You're *both* being stupid. We just saw a monster, and you're arguing about a girl who didn't even go out with either of you."

"But he lied!" Wayne said.

I grunted in frustration. "You said that back at camp."

Jack said, "But I didn't lie."

"All right, we're getting to the bottom of this right now. What did Jack lie about?"

Jack said, "I did not—"

I held up a shushing finger. "Not a word out of you, mister."

Wayne cleared his throat. "He promised he wouldn't ask her out if I did."

I turned to Jack. "Did you promise that?"

"No, I promised I wouldn't ask her out *before* he did."

"What?" said Wayne. "No, you said…" He trailed off.

I was confused. I looked at Wayne. "So, he asked her out before you did?"

"No, after I told him I had, but I thought he'd promised not to."

"But that's not what I promised. And I didn't even ask her out!"

"You told me you did!"

I turned to Jack. "You lied that you asked her out?"

Jack looked at his feet. "I was embarrassed that I chickened out. But I only said that after Wayne asked her, like I promised."

"Well, there you go," I glanced at Wayne. "He never—" I hesitated at Wayne's sheepish expression. "What?"

"I never asked her out either."

"What!" Jack and I said together.

"I never had the guts to do it, but I didn't want you to know."

"You knuckleheads," I said. "Not only did neither of you go on a single date with her, neither of you even got up the nerve to ask her out. You both lied to each other, and then spent the last month barely talking to each other because of a misunderstood promise. And the whole time, Julie was already going steady with someone, let's be honest, neither of you would've stood a chance against anyway. And I was stuck in the middle!"

All three of us were quiet as we stomped the remaining distance to our camp. When we got there, I lifted the lantern high to shine down on the destruction. All our backpacks were torn apart. Our gear and clothes and sleeping bags were scattered everywhere in pieces. The cooler of sandwiches I'd lugged along was ripped open like it was made of aluminum foil. Not even a bear could have done that.

"Maybe," said Wayne, breaking our shocked silence, "the Jay Cooke Park monster isn't such a scaredy-cat."

"Yeah," Jack said. "Maybe this was revenge for chasing it all through the woods."

But I had a different thought. "What if it was just hungry? It first approached us slowly, but we chased it away. Then it played its Julie trick and lured us further away, so it could come back here when we were gone."

"But it wrecked everything," said Wayne.

"It did only take the food," Jack said.

"It's super strong and we don't know what it's thinking," said Wayne.

"How about this: safety first." Jack rummaged around near the camp for some good sticks, then got out his knife to sharpen the ends into points.

"Just if we need to defend ourselves," I said.

Jack handed out sticks. "Yeah, just in case."

Wayne didn't say anything.

"Let's get going," I said. "We can come back in daylight to clean all this up."

We made our way to the road, then hooked a right for the walk back to my house in Carlton. We hurried past the cemetery. We hadn't gone much further before Wayne stopped and said, "Listen." He pointed toward the river side of the road with his stick.

I heard a few odd clacking sounds then silence. As if something was scuttling across the rocks on the riverbank, tracking us, but had stopped when it realized we were no longer moving. But the sounds were hard to distinguish against the background of rushing water. There was no way to be sure. We kept walking, but we'd not gone another fifty yards before Wayne stopped a second time.

"I heard it again, I'm sure of it," said Wayne. "It could follow us all the way back. It could destroy who knows what in town, looking like anybody."

"We don't know that," I said.

"We don't know anything! Where'd it come from? Outer space? You said it's not the only one, that they've been seen other places. It's an invasion. Like in *War of the Worlds*."

"So, what are we supposed to do?" said Jack. "The three of us with pointy sticks?"

"I just want to check. See if it's following us. Then we gotta tell the police. You can tell your uncle."

"Pfft. He'd never believe it."

But Wayne wasn't listening, he was already tramping off into the woods.

"Wait up," I said, hurrying after him with the lantern, with Jack in tow. When we broke through the trees onto the bank, Wayne was running carelessly across the rocks, jabbing his stick here and there.

"I saw it! I saw it!" He stopped for a moment when he noticed me approaching slowly over the rocks with the lantern. "It was following us, the ugly thing. It was just like you said Pete saw."

Then he turned away from us and half ran, half hopped across the rocks, yelling, "I'm gonna find it!"

"Damn, be careful," Jack called after him as we tried to pick a careful route to catch up with him. Before we got there, Wayne toppled over the edge with a shout.

We scrambled as fast as we could to the cliff, fearing what we'd find, but as we got onto our bellies to peek over, we heard Wayne call out, "I'm okay. Sort of." But there was pain in his gasping voice.

We were around a bend in the river that blocked most of the moonlight from shining on the bank. I held the lantern over the edge. Wayne wasn't that far below us, clinging to the face of the cliff. The cliff wasn't that high, but it was a straight drop down onto uneven, jagged rocks. It would be a nasty fall.

"Can you climb back up?" Jack said.

"I don't think so," said Wayne. "My foot is jammed in a crack. I think my ankle is broken. It really hurts."

"What should we do?" Jack whispered to me.

It took me a while to collect my thoughts. The night had been a roller coaster ride already, and now this. Finally, I said, "You stay with him with the lantern. I'll run to the first house I see and get help." I wouldn't have to go all the way into Carlton, because the little town of Thomson was on the way, only about a half mile up the road.

I handed Jack the lantern and got up to start back across the rocks to the road. I'd taken a few steps before I noticed it between me and woods. It was hard to make sense of the thing. There were tentacles and pincher claws and eye stalks and things I couldn't put a name to. None of it made sense, it was like a random bunch of parts stuck together. It was about the size of a large dog, but the strange shape of its body, especially since some parts of it were squishy like an octopus, made it appear to change size as it sort of walked, sort of slithered, sort of rolled over the rocks toward me.

"Jack." I took a step or two back, then stumbled because I wasn't watching where I was going. I fell backward but luckily onto a fairly flat spot, though it still sent a painful jolt up my spine as I landed on my butt.

"Wha—?" Jack said.

I glanced back over my shoulder. In the lantern light, I could clearly see the look of surprise and fear on his face. Then I turned forward again just in time as the monster skirted around me, so close I could have reached out and touched it—if I wanted to. Instead, I just watched, noticing some parts of it that looked like they belonged on a giant spider. I swiveled my head as it went by and continued toward Jack. The lantern started shaking in his grip.

"Jack?" Wayne called from below. "Can you hold the lantern out again? I don't like being in the dark here."

But Jack was frozen in place. He did pull his head back as the creature creeped past him, one of its tentacles sweeping right over his lap. I'd gotten up to follow along after it, just a couple of its body lengths behind it. I sped up as it disappeared over the edge of the precipice, right above where Wayne was. Fear for Wayne seemed to snap Jack out of it, and he once again held the lantern over the edge as I got down on my stomach beside him.

The thing shimmied down the cliff toward Wayne, claws and tentacles gripping outcroppings I could barely see in the flickering light. I reached over and turned the wick up a bit. Until that moment, Wayne had had his cheek pressed against the rock, eyes facing down river. But as the golden light brightened, he turned his face upward and first saw the thing descending toward him.

He flinched backward with a yelp, and I was afraid he'd tumble down to the rocks below or hang there upside down by his broken foot jammed in the rocks. But a tentacle stretched out and wrapped around one of his wrists just as he lost his grip. More tentacles appeared as if instantly grown and secured Wayne. The tentacles shortened, growing thicker in the process, and Wayne was gently lifted from the crack his foot was in. His eyes opened wider than I thought possible as he was suspended in the air in the thing's tentacles, at least three feet away from the cliff face.

Then the monster's crablike claws began pulling it back up the cliff. Only one eyestalk seemed focused on Wayne as the rest turned back toward the cliff, scouting any crevice or protrusion it could use as an anchor as it ascended.

None of us spoke during this unbelievable rescue, and shortly one of the monster's claws appeared over the top of the cliff, grabbing an outcropping near my right leg. As it continued its rise, Wayne's face appeared, jaw hanging open, eyes blinking rapidly. When half of the thing's body was above the cliff, it rotated, swinging Wayne over our heads before placing him carefully on a flat rock it had investigated with multiple eyestalks.

The creature divided its eyestalks between the three of us, examining each of us from multiple angles. Then it retraced its steps back to the woods with its unusual mixed gait and disappeared into the dark.

We hadn't yet spoken, but as Jack and I lifted Wayne onto one foot between us, Wayne said, "Did you see that? It had sticky bits of marshmallow on its legs."

"Good thing I brought them," said Jack.

"When we come back tomorrow, we'll bring extra food," I said.

And then we Three Musketeers continued our journey home. ♟

PENUMBRA

By S. N. Rodriguez

TOWERING STORM CLOUDS GREW ON the horizon as if lifting, heavy with the sea. The winds wailed and the mighty thunderheads darkened as they approached the coastline.

"Let's get out of here, Ruby. The storm's getting stronger," warned Alex, her black hair loose and whipping in the wind against her face.

"This is amazing!" Ruby's eyes were wild and electric. "Isn't it exciting? Just a few more pictures for my page, okay?"

"Forget it," Alex said, shaking her head. "We need to get back to the car before we blow away."

Ruby's camera shutter clicked. "Did you know they built this seawall after the Great Storm of 1900? It's seventeen feet high, and like, ten miles long or something like that."

"Spare me the history lesson, Rubes, you can tell me all about it later."

"At least six thousand people died, Alex. Can you imagine that storm?"

"I think I can," Alex said, her eyes fixed on the dark sky and roaring waves.

As they climbed up the seawall steps to the boulevard above, the tide licked their heels. Ruby spotted the remnants of the abandoned Pleasure

169

Pier that was wrecked decades ago. "I'm going to the old pier for some better shots. Pick me up over there," she said, her voice trailing behind her as she ran.

"Ay, Ruby. We need to go now," Alex demanded. "It's a ghost town for a reason," she shouted. "Ugh! You're so stubborn!" Alex shook her head and rushed to her car to follow her sister.

The hurricane arrived. The waves swelled with the wind and crashed against the rocks sending spray soaring through the air. The sea barreled beneath the pier and buried the beach. Tethered fishing boats rammed into one another, jostled and corralled into the docks like a flock of frenzied sheep.

"This is insane! I should've never agreed to this," Alex growled with the car's engine, "Mom and Dad are gonna be pissed."

Ruby snapped shots of the storm, its clouds blending like a mixed palette of deep blues and purples. "These are going to look great!" Her excitement rivaled the electricity in the air. Thunder rumbled toward her. "Whoa, that sea spray looks like a face!" She held onto the weatherworn posts. Her sneakers curved around the bottom plank as she bent over the rotted railing. The waves surged and swatted Ruby back onto the pier like hard fists. "Mierda," she muttered as she inspected her camera.

"Ruby!" Alex slammed the car door and ran to her sister. The water rushed over the pier sucking everything loose into the ocean. Ruby struggled to regain her balance on the buckling boards beneath her. Alex ran across the pier. "Let's go, we need to get out!" Before she could reach her sister, the weather-beaten planks snapped, and Alex fell through. A single scream escaped her lips before she hit her head on the pier and plummeted into the rising water below.

"No! Alex!" Ruby cried, but her screams dissolved around her. "Alex!" She looked at the violent scene and saw Alex's blood on the planks. It was as if a spell had been broken, and she suddenly realized the danger they were in. "What have I done?"

Down below, Alex's unconscious body swayed and rolled as the sea swallowed and spit her out repeatedly. Sea foam bubbled up around her and pale green and blue arms tugged at her limbs. Water-logged faces of people who sank to the depths grasping for life long ago opened their mouths like hungry koi beckoning and dragging her away from the shore. Alex's eyes fluttered. The cold rain hit her like hailstones. She felt the cold hands upon her and saw their macabre faces as they pulled her under. At once, she screamed, and salt water filled her mouth. She pried the dead fingers from her body and kicked desperately toward the surface. Her vision blurred, and she wiped blood and salt from her stinging eyes, but she continued kicking with the violent waves. The water breached the seawall and poured onto the abandoned streets. She clung to a streetlight as the waves briefly receded before battering the shore again. A voice called out to her through the howling wind.

"¡Señorita, aquí!"

She spotted a woman with long brown hair waving at her from a motel balcony.

"¡Nadar! ¡Nadar!"

Alex swam and noticed the stinking, rotted arms upon her once again and stared into their hollow, eyeless faces. "Let me go!" She thrashed against them until one by one they disappeared beneath the waves. Head thrumming, she swam toward the woman. The first level of the motel was submerged, and a large swell slammed Alex against its brick facade, crushing something in her side. She screamed and the pain sent a wave of nausea over her. The woman tossed a sheet out of the window and Alex wrapped it around her arm, the pain in her side winding its way up her muscles like a vine. The woman braced herself against the wall and pulled slowly. Alex strengthened her grasp on the makeshift rope and climbed the worn bricks until she was able to crawl over the railing and collapsed onto the balcony. A pool of blood and saltwater formed around her. At once the woman was at her side and helped her to a bed.

"Gracias," Alex wheezed. She felt as though she was still swaying, and her ribs ached with each breath. "What were those things…in the water? Did you see them?"

The woman nodded her head solemnly. The wind rattled the windowpanes.

Then Alex remembered, "Ruby's out there, mi hermana. I have to find her, I—"

"Ella está bien." The woman reassured Alex and covered her with a blanket. She had light brown skin and a small mole under her right eye. "No te preocupes."

Alex felt the side of her temple and remembered her head hitting the pier as she fell through and into the water. The area was swollen and any pressure against it made it throb even worse. When she looked at her hand, it was covered in blood. "Ruby," she sighed, and looked into the woman's soft smiling face.

The woman cupped Alex's hand in her own. "Tranquilla." She brushed matted strands of hair away from Alex's face as the young woman drifted into unconsciousness once again.

#   #   #

Alex awoke to the sound of the surf. She pressed a cold hand against her forehead, but the pain was gone and so was the woman who saved her. She looked at her hand and saw there was no blood and that her clothes were clean and dry. The sunlight poured in from the balcony window and carried with it the smell of sweet citrus smoke and murmuring. Alex felt her ribs for pain or swelling, but there was nothing, not even a bruise. "How long have I been out?" She walked to the balcony and looked at the street below.

Stacks of lumber and bricks dotted the streets. The city was devastated, but healing. Texas flags flew high and there was a parade coming down the street.

"What's going on?" Alex searched her pockets for her cell phone, but it wasn't there. "I must have lost it in the flood." Alex walked out of the room, down the steps of the beachside motel toward the lobby. To her surprise, the building looked pristine, not a single hint of flooding or wind damage. "How?" The decor was a little outdated, but still tropical and inviting. A woman wearing a vibrant flower crown atop beautiful brown braids sat behind the front desk with a phone against her ear and her hands typing steadily on a keyboard.

"Yes, it's been a busy season," the woman sighed, "but we still have room. I'll set it up for her right away." She hung the corded phone on the wall and turned her attention to Alex. "Ah, Alex, you're awake! So glad to see it. I'm Elena."

"Hi." Questions flooded Alex's mind amidst curiosity and confusion. "I—I have a lot of questions," she admitted, shaking her head in disbelief, "but first, may I borrow your phone?"

Elena shook her head, "No need." She walked around the reception desk and ushered Alex toward the front door. "You're just in time, your family is waiting for you outside."

"They're here?"

"Yes, if you go now, you can still catch them." Elena opened the door. "Ándale, chiquita. You can ask your questions later."

The street was filled with orange marigolds and people dancing and singing to mariachi music. Some people dressed in modern clothes while others wore colorful traditional Mexican clothing with their faces painted to look like skulls. Papier mâché skeletons were beautifully decorated and hoisted into the air on poles. A man dressed as an old cowboy leaned against the building and tilted his hat as he nodded to Alex.

"It's Día de los Muertos already?" Alex stood on the sidewalk perplexed. She remembered the terrible storm and the cold hands of the creatures that seized her.

She looked around but didn't see her family. Monarch butterflies fluttered from flower to flower as she walked through the celebratory crowd to a nearby cemetery. Gravestones were cleaned and decorated like altars with bright pinks, yellows, and purples. Some were lined with lit candles, and at the base of others burned sweet, pine-scented incense alongside photographs of the departed surrounded by marigolds. There were bowls of fruits and fresh water, sweet breads, and painted sugar skulls thoughtfully arranged among the graves and memorials.

Alex smiled and scanned over names and faces in photographs, some in color, some in black and white, and as she did this, she suddenly felt a sensation like a pull leading her toward someone as if summoned. She followed the feeling and then she saw her.

Ruby rested on her knees in front of a beautiful memorial site decorated with candles, marigolds, and offerings. She curled a strand of auburn hair

173

behind her ear and placed a photo beside a bouquet of sunflowers before lighting a candle. "I picked the best sunflowers for you. I know how much you love them." Her face wrinkled, and tears gathered between her lashes. "I'm so sorry, Alex."

Alex's eyes darted between her sister and the memorial. "No, no, I'm okay, Ruby!" Alex ran to her sister. "Ruby, I'm here!" She fell to her knees and placed her hands on her sister's shoulders. "It's me, I'm okay!"

Startled, Ruby turned and looked over her shoulder. Alex smiled and stared into her sister's brown eyes. "It's me, I'm okay, see?" Ruby said nothing and scanned the area around her. "Ruby?" Alex stared into her sister's eyes again and saw no reflection of herself in them. She gasped and her eyes widened as she stepped back. Ruby focused her attention on the picture. Alex stared in disbelief. It was an old picture of her and Ruby climbing their favorite live oak tree when they were children.

"No," Alex whispered. She shook her head and placed her hands over her face. "No."

"I couldn't find you, Alex. You were there, and then… I saw your blood on the pier. I was so scared. The water was coming in so fast I hopped in your car and sped away. I needed to find help. You're gone, and it's all my fault."

Alex looked helplessly at her sister and sank beside her. "Ruby."

Ruby buried her face in her hands. "How am I supposed to live without you, huh? You've always been there to look out for me and now you're not. You'd still be here if I hadn't been such a tonta." She pulled her knees to her chest and sobbed. "I'm so sorry."

Ruby wiped her eyes with a tissue and blew her nose. She picked up the photo and kissed it before placing it beside the sunflowers and flickering candles again. She stood up and slowly walked around the gravestones through plumes of woody incense and past families and ofrendas. Alex followed solemnly beside her. The two of them sat on a bench and watched as the sun set below the horizon. Alex placed a hand over Ruby's.

Ruby looked down at her hand and to the empty seat beside her. "Alex?" She placed her other hand over her own. It felt cooler than her other and she started crying again. "Oh, Alex, if it is you, I hope you can forgive me. I love you and I miss you so much. I wish the storm had taken me instead."

Tears streamed down Alex's face as she felt a subtle warmth against her hand. "I can't believe I'm dead and I'm sitting here with you right now. This really sucks. You can't even see or hear me, but I'm here." She tried to gently squeeze her sister's hand. "It was an accident, Ruby, you have to forgive yourself, okay?" She wrapped her arms around her sister like she had done so many times before. She wanted to comfort and reassure her, but she needed it as well.

"There you are, Ruby," her mother said, placing a hand on her daughter's shoulder. "It's getting late."

Alex turned around and saw her parents. Her mother's black hair was peppered with silver strands and her father had grown a thick beard. Both were thinner with a profound sadness swimming in their eyes despite their gentle smiles. She stood up and approached them with tears in her eyes. "Mom? Dad? Can you see me? I'm right here." She placed her hands on their cheeks and felt their warmth.

"And cold, too," her father added. "We'll have to leave soon, mija."

"I feel really close to Alex here, can we stay a bit longer? Maybe share some stories about her?"

Her parents nodded. "I'd like that," her mother agreed.

Ruby sat in between her parents on the bench, and they shared their favorite memories of Alex, whose spirit stood beside them listening, laughing, and crying along with them. As the candles grew dim, Ruby and her parents walked away from the bench and stood in front of the memorial for those who lost their lives in the great storm a year prior.

"We love you, Alex." They turned and walked out of the cemetery holding hands.

Alex stared at her family with a deep longing. "At least I was able to have this one last gift," she whispered, her voice trembling. Before she could follow, a soft breeze brushed her hair aside.

"Tranquilla," said a familiar voice behind Alex.

Alex started and turned around. "It's you, from the balcony."

The woman smiled and nodded her head. "My name is Sofía. I lost my life in a similar storm many years ago, just like you. I can see you are very loved. You will see them again." Sofía extended an inviting hand toward Alex.

PENUMBRA

Alex held Sofía's hand, and they watched her family walk out of sight. "Come with me, Alejandra, there is much to show you." As the candle lights faded behind them, plumes of smoke extended into the air like tall, curling crooks guiding them through the darkness. ♜

THE SILHOUETTE AGAIN

A Glazier's Gap Story

By Leanna Renee Hieber

Glazier's Gap, Colorado, 1999

THE SILHOUETTE THAT LIVED BEHIND the door that couldn't be opened softly knocked again. Roz froze. The silver knob turned. The hinges strained. There came a hiss and then an overwhelming rumbling sound as if there was a gale of a storm on the other side of the old mahogany wood, a door nearly as old as the town itself.

There was a peephole on that door, looking from the inside out onto what had once been a curious and ill-conceived landing affixed to the back of Roz's old family house, a three-story Victorian Queen Anne with peeling paint and the decided air of a lost cause. The landing was entirely in shadow, as it abutted the mouth of a cave.

If the door was able to be opened, Roz could wander from her attic room into the mouth of a cavern that adjoined the old silver mine shafts of Glazier's Gap. It was said some of those shafts and tunnels connected all the old houses in the town if one could figure out their pathways.

And now, someone was standing on that landing. Having come from an abandoned mine shaft, through a cave mouth, to try the knob of her bedroom.

Whatever stood on the other side of that door Roz had only seen once, on a particularly dark day of her admittedly young life. She didn't know if she was about to see it again and didn't know if she wanted to.

Roz was a being of conflict. At seventeen years of age, she supposed that was normal, it was punk, it was the way of things. She liked to read Victorian novels full of angst and pining, feeling comforted by old and unrequited miseries, her attitude a product of those pages. But at this moment, she didn't have the courage to look out the peephole again.

Not knowing what else to do in the middle of the night with an unknown entity just the other side of a wooden partition, fully aware she couldn't run downstairs to wake her anxious mother and potentially send her precarious mental state into a tailspin, Roz did what she did when she needed to relax. She played the piano. If it wasn't so late, she'd call her beloved bandmates, John and Victor. But a 1am call would attract too much suspicion from already jumpy parents.

It wasn't a *real* piano she was playing there in her small attic bedroom; it was an electronic keyboard with a volume control she used to play softly in the middle of the night. Perfect for times like this. She began tinkering with a variation on a dark Chopin etude she mixed with a few measures of *Bloodletting*. She wasn't some old soul entirely; she was still a product of her century. Roz stood for Rosalyn, but she preferred the shorter, edgier nickname.

The doorknob turned again. There was a press upon the door, as if something was putting its weight against it. Roz turned up the volume on her keyboard a bit more.

"It's just the angel," she muttered to herself. "Just the family guardian angel."

That had been the answer when she'd asked Grandpa about the silhouette after the first time she'd seen it; a couple of months prior. She'd dared to look into the peephole at the center of the door, at eye level, staring into the shadowy darkness beyond.

There, standing as a shadow within shadow, the outline only visible by a faint glow behind it and the slight light spilling in from under her bedroom doorway, Roz saw what looked like the shape of a tall, broad-shouldered figure in a long coat. Perhaps there was the glimmer of glowing eyes. The figure lifted a hand to her in greeting. She withdrew from the door, double-checked that the deadbolt still held, threw a towel over the bottom of the door to block any light or draft and went downstairs to watch television, hoping to rid her mind of the unsettling image she tried to convince herself she hadn't seen.

The next time Grandpa came over, as he was the keeper of all the family lore, Roz dared to ask: "Would you say I was crazy if I told you I saw a strange silhouette on the other side of my door, the one you said can't be opened, the one that connected forever ago to the old mine?"

Grandpa snickered softly, in a way that unnerved Roz. "Our family has an angel, kid," He explained. "Some call him the angel of death but I don't know that that's entirely fair. It's a matter of perspective." Grandpa took a long drag off the end of his cigarette, quashing it in a large glass ash tray on the gingerbread-laden front porch that needed more love and money than any of them had to spare. Roz widened her eyes. This was not the answer she had expected. She didn't know what she should have expected but it wasn't that.

"See, you're a Barreau, but you're related to the Glaziers via your aunt, the named *lords* of the town. They came to this pass between the mountains during the gold rush and silver boom, here where the Ute tribe wanted nothing to do with this land because they deemed it cursed. The Glazier's seemed undaunted, though, and legend had it that old Robert Glazier had been led here in 1850 by what he called his Guardian Angel."

"Was it actually a figure, a person?" Roz pressed.

"I don't know. That family was always *creative*, so I'm not sure what was truth or fiction, but that's the way of this town, no one ever knows." Grandpa laughed, then, shaking his head. "See, it's all mixed up now, though. A generation back, one of the Glaziers did marry a Denny, a sad, quiet man, and now this family is entwined with theirs too. I don't know whose side, the devils or the angels, anyone is on anymore. You'll have to choose your sides for yourself, and I don't know who is who or what is what. It's the trouble with curses in a small town. Eventually, everybody crosses its path."

"What do I do?"

"Don't do anything. If it's just watching, let it be. That's what guardian angels do, right? They watch?"

"Like a peeping tom? A voyeur?" Roz grimaced. "I'm just supposed to be okay with that?"

Grandpa stared at the stack of old cloth-bound books on the table, set beside one of Roz's open sketchbooks; a silhouette in a cave, illumined by a silver aura sketched in metallic pencil. He picked up a well-worn copy of *Dracula* that Roz had been known to take with her everywhere since she'd learned to read and waved it at her. "I think, kiddo, you always have been. *Okay*. Prepared for this."

Roz sighed, called out. It did scare and thrill her in equal measure.

"Thing is," Grandpa continued carefully, after a thoughtful drag on his cigarette, "if the angel comes for you once, he might just be trying to get to know you. But if the visits become more frequent, well, at some point, you might have to make a bargain, or stall for more time." Grandpa held his hands up. "I know, I can see that furrowed brow of yours. Aren't bargains for devils, not angels? You would be correct, my clever girl, but this is why this is not a regular angel and I leave that to you to figure out. You've always been better with strange things than I ever was. Maybe the angel, or devil, knows that too and that's why he's shown himself to you. He only made himself known to a few of the Glaziers before. But I can't make the decision for you about what you're comfortable with. At any point, if you're done with him, you say so. No one has any right to make you *scared*, kid. You got that?"

Roz nodded.

That was the end of their conversation. Her mother and father had started screaming in an argument and Grandpa went to go try to diffuse it, to no avail. He died of a heart attack the following week.

Roz never forgot that conversation and she soon was convinced the angel was listening outside the door that couldn't be opened whenever she played music. Her angel of music, maybe. Her classic-novel-laden mind had thought of Leroux and his Phantom, and she began to fancy herself a Christine. Only she wasn't below an opera house, she was adjacent to dangerous mine shafts and precarious minds. So, she would always keep playing, to appease whatever stood in the shadows, watching from behind a closed door.

So, on this night, coming back to herself in this present moment, nearly at the edge of the 21st century, when everyone was talking about what might happen in a Y2K shutdown like it would be the end of the world, Roz was thinking of angels as the ornate silver doorknob turned.

Be not afraid. Scripture declared that phrase when confronted with miraculous moments or beings, Roz realized, because they *were* scary. Angels. Demons. All a matter of perspective, after all; weren't devils just fallen angels anyway?

"Do you want in or are you just telling me you are here?" Roz asked finally, her voice just above the level of her piano, her fingers nervously dancing up and down a flourish of scales.

"Keep going, please," she heard the angel whisper. "You always loved music and sometimes old passions are all we have left."

Roz didn't know what he meant by that, but his voice was so soft and compelling, so sad and storied that she didn't feel she could let him down.

"I will play for you, then," she whispered back. "Whoever you think I am."

"You are as you always have been, and always will be. You are yourself. An eternal soul." His response was a strange riddle. "You should get some sleep."

Roz fell into bed as if pushed, as if dropped into sleep like a dead weight, and in that deep slumber, she had a strange dream in which she was herself and yet not.

She had been sleepwalking again, and when she came to, there was a curious note in her hand, written in a script not her own.

The note, her skin, and the sleeve of her white nightdress, designed in an old, Victorian style, were all luminously bright in a shaft of moonlight that managed to cut through a small break in the otherwise dense copse of Douglas fir trees looming large around her. Old, wide-trunked trees that had seen ages of strange things in these sharp hills of deep shadows and dark secrets.

"For Roberta" the note began. Bea didn't go by her formal name but whoever wrote this note knew it. Glazier family, then, or a friend… The note

181

continued, curiously, in an elegant, looping script. "The Devil may be in detail, my dear. But your Angel is in paradox."

She was standing at the main entrance to the silver mine, at the crest of Glazier Drive, a place she didn't remember walking to. The hulking wooden door of the entrance remained shut and locked. The mine had made the Glazier family's fortune. She whirled around, but no one was there. Only endless trees and curious silence, save for the occasional call of a night bird.

But suddenly the silence was broken by screams.

A bellowing voice hurled damnations and cries echoed up from the carriage house below, a structure to the side of the great Glazier mansion.

For all the grandeur of her family home and its surrounding environs, neither she nor her privileged status had been able to protect her best friend from cruel intentions.

Running down the hill, Bea watched in horror as a tall, imposing man in a long frock coat held his daughter by the hair and was dragging her down the narrow gravel lane of Glazier Drive. The moon was bright and illuminated his cruel features and the terror on young Camille Denny's face with equal clarity.

"Eustus Denny, you stop right there!" Bea cried, darting towards the man in hopes of extricating Camille from this violent indignity. The Denny patriarch cast Bea aside as if he were swatting a fly, his strength almost preternatural. She tumbled onto the gravel, skinning her hands and hitting her head. Through a flash of pain, Bea registered the parting words of this now-unhinged widower.

"You had your chance to have a say and you rejected me, Miss Glazier, and go put on some clothes, you're indecent," he snarled and kept dragging Camille, who had fought to right herself and shoved herself free from her father but he grabbed her by the wrist again and was down around the curve in the drive as Bea struggled back to her feet.

He hadn't always been like that; an utter boor and brute, he had been kind once. A possible prospect, even, after his wife's death. But this town had a way of either bringing out the best or the worst in someone, and the worst had been blossoming in Eustus. Rumors about the families had been burgeoning to new levels of wild speculation; that one was blessed by an angel, that the other had made a deal with a devil for their wealth and success. Depending on whose loyalty lay where, the blessed or the cursed was entirely a matter of opinion.

And now, Roberta Glazier out wandering in her nightgown, while Eustus Denny dragged his daughter down a hill to an unknown fate... Rumors had fresh grist for their mills.

Not knowing what to do, Bea ran back up towards the silver mine. Chilled, she noticed that the doors were open. A silhouette in a long black coat stood with a hand out, eyes luminous. An Angel, dark, in the night. A paradox.

"Can you help?" Bea asked, wiping her tear-stained cheeks with her scraped palms, letting the saltwater sting her abrasions. "Whatever you are?"

"Some things have to play out for themselves," the angel responded. "I'm not bound to those poor lovers. They've their own journey to take."

"Then what are you good for?" Bea cried. "What kind of angel lets suffering like that go unpunished?"

The silhouette didn't answer her.

"What are you good for?" Bea insisted. "Why are you here? What are you doing to me? My family?"

"Helping you become your best selves. The people you are truly meant to be. It takes cycles of pain, sometimes, to transcend to higher beings. You'll know when you're ready to join me."

Her grandfather had told her that the angel might come for her, and that sometimes she might have to bargain if she wanted more time.

Was that Bea's grandfather, or Roz's grandfather who had said that? Who was she?

Staring at the beautiful being, she felt air being pressed out of her lungs and she didn't want to die like this; snuffed out at the prime of her life. She wanted the chance to become a better self and live into some unknown future...

Roz shot up in bed and the door that her family had always said was rusted shut and triply locked, a door that couldn't be opened *was* open, the silhouette standing there, arm outstretched, long black coat rustling around his ankles as if in the wake of his own power.

He was beautiful. At least, Roz thought it was a man, but then again, Angels, or Devils, depending on the perspective, didn't adhere to mere mortal binaries and so this entity was simply *beautiful,* and Roz found herself aching in a way she did not know was possible, for something that thrilled her as much as revolted her. She, Bea, Roz, whoever she was and whoever she had become, wanted to be touched by this creature. Her neck strained towards that open hand, towards the arms ready to embrace her. To either kiss her or draw the last breath out of her.

But she didn't want it to be the end. She wasn't her best self yet. She wasn't ready to go. The angel of death had come too early for her.

"No..." Roz whispered. The beautiful creature's sharp face softened. It retreated at the disinvitation. The door closed behind it. Her breath returned and she collapsed, released back into a more peaceful sleep.

It was time to tell her bandmates, John and Victor, Roz decided. *Silverdeath* had been playing together since sophomore year, billing themselves as *Tori Amos meets the grunge scene.* Roz was lead singer at the piano while John West played the drums and Victor Denny played bass.

Roz's attic was the best place for them to rehearse; she had a small amp setup, a stand for her keyboard and a worn drum set. A trio of lost souls going into senior year unsure of themselves or what they wanted to do in life. But they loved music, their band, and, sometimes, each other.

"Guys, I have something to tell you," Roz said, trilling a few notes out on her keyboard.

"You love me," Victor said airily, clicking his black-painted nails together. "I know, no one can help it." He pursed his lips and batted his eyes which were ringed in black eyeliner, his black hair cut at a messy angle and styled with Robert Smith height.

"Guess again," Roz retorted, the airy trill of an upper scale shifting to an ominous chord.

"It's me, then," John countered nonchalantly, bright eyes glimmering mischievously.

"No, you *tools*, there's something out in the corridor beyond that door. An... entity. I don't know. It likes music. So just... wanted to tell someone."

"Like… a ghost?" Victor asked.

"Family called it a guardian angel."

John frowned, staring at her in disbelief.

"It's true though," Roz insisted. "There's something out there. In that corridor. It waits for me."

John's face transformed into something hungry, raking a lock of long ginger hair behind his head. "Then that makes two of us."

Victor scoffed and rolled his eyes.

"Guys, could you think with your heads for once, this one, up here," Roz tapped her skull with her fingers. "This isn't about us. It's something bigger, I think."

The truth was, they were all hot for each other and sometimes they let themselves experiment, but it hadn't gotten in the way of their wanting to make music, first and foremost. At least for now. But sometimes Roz wondered if their connection wasn't good for each other. She couldn't tell. Her head felt so fuzzy. Maybe they were all a drug they collectively needed to kick. Or maybe that's what the angel wanted her to think; so that she'd turn her focus back on *its* thrall alone…

"I can't see or think straight. That thing. It's… pulling at me. And I don't know what it wants from me."

"Pulling at you, like, how," Victor said warily.

"Like something old that wants me to remember. A past I lived. Pain I witnessed and did nothing to stop."

Victor kicked at his guitar chord. "Yeah, try living in a Denny mansion, the past always has you by the throat."

"What, are we all just repeating old, terrible things?" Roz spat, throwing herself on her bed in frustration. "I had a nightmare last night; that I was one of my ancestors, watching people be terrible to one another and I couldn't stop it. I'm scared I might be repeating things I don't even understand. And… I think whatever is behind that door…" Roz pointed to it. "Was there, then, too."

"It's just a feeling," Victor countered. He shifted on his feet, leaning towards Roz as if he wanted to go sit next to her but couldn't move. "It isn't real, it's in our heads. But I know what you mean; that sense of something

185

watching, controlling, but no matter what you do, you're never going to get it right and you're never going to satisfy the hungry shadows. At least, that's the curse of being a Denny and I hate it," Victor said, staring down at his worn black boots. "We're stuck here. Doomed to fail."

"No, we are not, though!" Roz threw a pillow at Victor which bounced off his *Downward Spiral* shirt and landed on his boots. "Don't sound so damned *goth* about it. We are *not* stuck here. We can always run." Roz felt her heart quicken, a sudden surge of excitement taking over. "I think we should leave, guys. Let's just tour. Let's take *Silverdeath* on the road. Screw senior year."

Her boys chuckled sadly. She stared at them and felt the excitement turn to hopelessness.

Grandpa had said, once, that there was a weight in this town and sometimes people just couldn't shake it and if a heart wasn't careful, they'd end up a ghost before they even died, full of regrets and unfulfilled promises. Were her best friends, her dearest ones, going to be like that, too?

"I can't leave, you know that, Roz," John said, twirling a drumstick between his fingers. "I'm all dad has at the bar. I can't leave him. I promised him I'd take over. You know I don't go back on a pledge I made to a loved one," he said, staring at her with an intensity that made her deeply uncomfortable. Images and memories of their first kiss; a violent explosion of pent-up energy and searing touches, ticked through her mind in blinding flashes, making her blush, recalling all the red marks left after they'd broken away.

"Yeah," Victor scoffed, interjecting pointedly. "Try leaving this town if you've got my last name. I think my ancestors cursed us all to stay here, wasting away."

Roz rose and took a step towards Victor. "Your family has had so many weird illnesses! Doesn't that say something to you; to get out? In my dream, the silhouette, the angel I am talking about, he was there, in the past. He talked about cycles, he talked about this…" she gestured around her wildly, "weird little place we're in, and that we have to break out of patterns. I mean, I never thought I'd say this about my dad, but maybe it makes sense he's not been around. Because mom's mind sure isn't handling life well. Maybe it's this town. These old, drafty houses. Ghosts we can't see, poking us until we're bruised."

Roz paced, trying to gather her scattered thoughts. "What if we broke out? Can't we do that, together? All of us? I feel like something bad is about to happen. I don't want to go alone."

"I don't know how to leave," Victor said, plaintively. John just shook his head.

"You just have to *run*," Roz insisted.

John started a slow beat. Victor picked up a soft bass riff. The boys were lost to music, unable to hear her.

Roz's shoulders fell, she sighed. She went to her keyboard and started singing, making things up as she went.

"You just have to run, break free, towards the sun, to the sea
The past is a trap, say no, hearts will snap, if you don't go
Run and keep running
Run and keep running
Because the angels and devils are always watching..."

The trio played for hours, their music able to speak better than they could about their angst, their hearts, their unrequited loves, and the apprehension about the future that was endemic among their peers. People growing up in small towns always wondered what the wider world actually held, it was like a light at the end of a tunnel whose distance kept shifting. No one really knew what was on the other side of that light, though. That too was scary.

That night, Roz woke to the creak of the door opening. The moon seemed impossibly bright through her window, a silver shaft dissecting her space into light and shadow. She had fallen asleep restless, in a vintage robe she'd gotten from a thrift store, something billowing and filmy, the stuff of old films and dramatic book covers.

She lifted her head from her pillow to see the silhouette standing there at the mouth of darkness, trailing long, silvery hair, skin luminous in the dim light of Roz's room, a beautiful, bold, and terrifying figure.

Again, Roz wanted to be touched by this creature and that desire

187

transcended time. The ache in her bones felt ancient. Her body strained towards the hand reaching for her, her back arching, and the subsequent gasp that tore from her lips was sensual. That she was lying on her bed this time felt paralyzing yet tantalizing and she wondered if this was the paradox the angel wrote about in its note to Bea Glazier over a century ago.

"You can come with me," the angel said, reaching a long-fingered hand from the darkness into the wan light. "You've always had that choice."

Her Grandfather's gamesome voice sounded in her thoughts. Panic won out over whatever spell this angel was casting. *Bargain.* It still wasn't time to go. She wasn't sure where she'd end up anyway... heaven or hell? Was there such a place and had this creature seen both poles? How could she bargain for time to think?

"I'd like more time," Roz choked out her words. "Not in the immortal sense, though. Time right *now*. In *this* life."

There was a low, sad, weary chuckle from the shadows. "What you always say. But remember, Roberta, Rosalyn, whoever you become, I'll always know to look for you."

Roz tilted her head. "And I bet I'll always think that sounds super creepy, dude."

The shadow laughed, mouth widening in delight, and that's when Roz noticed the impossibly long, sharp teeth. Maybe this being was something else *entirely*. Roz shuddered. The being closed its mouth, stared at Roz and damn if it didn't hold her breath within its gaze as if it alone controlled her lungs.

"There will come times when you'll have to make choices," the angel said. "I think this is one of them."

It was one of those moments in life when it just wasn't clear what to do. Roz had those frozen points before, concerning her band, her boys, their tangle of hearts. And this new creature only complicated things. Roz felt she'd been in this place before, far beyond seventeen years and lifetimes ago. She didn't know what choice to make or how to make it. A deeply human impasse. Everything spun and nothing made sense here at what Roz realized was a precipice between life and death.

The first time she'd seen the silhouette behind the door, not only had it been a dark day, but it had also been a moment when negative ideation had been getting the better of her. Inner voices would tell her that her art was pointless, her music, herself; that none of it mattered. She knew depression ran in her family, and she knew those voices lied. But suicidal thoughts could be seductive vipers, slithering in and working their way into the cracks in resolve and the recesses of thoughts, ready to strike.

But here, facing down a possible end, those thoughts were banished by her stronger and far more resilient desire to do more, see more, be more. And, perhaps, love more.

As if the being had read her thoughts, there came a quiet, fond response: "Then do so." The words felt like a gentle caress.

Whatever strange and rumbling sounds she'd heard now and then from deep in the rock beyond her attic door now crested to a new sound, a cross between an earthquake and an avalanche. She looked around in panic.

The earth was shaking, the house was creaking, and silt was building up on the upstairs windows. In school, they'd been warned about landslides; their town being nestled between two sharp rises.

Either the angel would take her soul, here. Or the earth would take her body, here. She didn't like either option.

A rumbling sounded from deep within the corridor. Shafts were collapsing. Hidden tunnels were disappearing. The past was being subsumed and the present was in danger.

If she didn't act now, the stalling she'd done with an angel of death might prove fruitless. So, she ran to her door. Looking back at the threshold of her room, the figure just stood there, placing a hand on either side of the doorframe, staring, holding up those posts as if those powerful arms were holding up the world. Maybe it was a guardian, after all.

Run and keep running. Her own refrain echoed in her ears.

Her mother was screaming downstairs, having run out from her room in her flannel nightgown, staring at the trembling floor and rattling windows. Roz gathered her, grabbing her hard by the arms and dragging her towards the door. Eventually her mother found her legs and the two ran out onto their sloping lane and up to Main Street, dashing towards higher ground as a landslide began to obliterate their house- and a whole half of the ski resort next door- in one hungry, fell swoop. Like the *Fall of the House of Usher*,

Roz thought morbidly. It had always been one of her favorite tales.

Of course, she thought as she ran, she might just be starting the cycle all over again; burying something deep down that she didn't want to be confronted with, buying herself time by running away towards distraction.

But that was the thing about surviving; that was the thing about banishing cruel ideations and depression's inertia. Sometimes you just had to keep moving, one life to the next. Never sure if it's a devil or an angel close on your heels; a soul has to make the choice to protect itself and propel forward.

The past was now buried, literally.

She made her choice to run and keep running. Whether she'd always feel watched, well, that would be for time to sort out now that she had more of it left to live. ♜

CONTRIBUTORS

DAVID BOWLES is a Mexican American author and translator from south Texas, where he teaches at the University of Texas Río Grande Valley. He has written over two dozen award-winning titles, most notably *They Call Me Güero* and *My Two Border Towns.*

His work has also been published in multiple anthologies, plus venues such as *The New York Times, Strange Horizons, Apex Magazine, School Library Journal, Rattle, Translation Review,* and the *Journal of Children's Literature.*

Additionally, David has worked on several TV/film projects, including *Victor and Valentino* (Cartoon Network), the *Moctezuma & Cortés* miniseries (Amazon/Amblin) and *Monsters and Mysteries in America* (Discovery).

In 2017, David was inducted into the Texas Institute of Letters. He now serves as its vice president. In 2019, he co-founded the hashtag and activist movement #DignidadLiteraria, which has negotiated greater Latinx representation in publishing. In 2021, he helped launch *Chispa*, the Latinx imprint of Scout Comics, for which he serves as co-publisher. Follow him on Twitter and Instagram: @DavidOBowles

JENNIFER BRODY, who also writes under the name Vera Strange, is the author of the popular *Disney Chills* series, *The 13th Continuum* YA sci-fi trilogy, and the Stoker Finalist *Spectre Deep 6,* prompting Forbes to call Brody "a star in the graphic novel world." She is the co-author of *Star Wars: Stories of Jedi & Sith,* where she penned the Darth Vader cover story. She's a graduate of Harvard University, a film/TV producer and writer, and a creative writing instructor. She began her career in Hollywood working for A-List directors and movie studios on many films, including *The Lord of the Rings* trilogy.

JULIAN MICHAEL CARVER is a pen name for documentary film editor Joey Kelly. Beginning his writing career in 2019, Carver has written books for both adults and children.

Carver describes his original works as science-fiction with a blend of horror and adventure. His most popular book is Triassic, a tale of space-marines in the distant future that get marooned in Earth's prehistoric past. Triassic is available through sci-fi and horror publisher Severed Press.

In 2021, Carver wrote the official novelization of the horror film Freshwater, earning him a place within the IAMTW (International Association of Media Tie-In Writers) an organization of professional tie-in authors writing licensed fiction. In 2022, the novelization was nominated for the Scribe Awards alongside the novelizations of Alien 3 and Halloween Kills, appearing in Locus Magazine.

Carver has also written for BattleTech, the wargaming franchise developed by FASA and currently licensed to Catalyst Game Labs by Topps. Carver is currently working on several other media tie-in projects across various licenses and is a frequent promoter of tie-in writers on social media. Carver loves to collaborate and aspires to land more media tie-in gigs in the future.

To keep up with Carver and his works, visit his blog at: julianmichaelcarver.home.blog or visit him on social media.

In 2013, Carver graduated from the now defunct Art Institute of Pittsburgh. Since college graduation, Carver has worked full time in the world of commercial advertising. His video content has been featured on Ancient Aliens, Roseanne, Forensic Files 2, and The Sinner.

DEBBIE LYNN SMITH DAUGHETEE has spent most of her career writing and producing such television shows as Murder, She Wrote; Dr. Quinn, Medicine Woman; and Touched by an Angel. She has published short stories in magazines and anthologies, including the Bram Stoker award-winning Dark Delicacies. In addition, she has also written audio dramas set in the world of the 60's classic television show, Dark Shadows, including her Scribe award nominated, The Lost Girl. Most recently, Debbie created Kymera Press, a comic book publishing company that supports women in comics. She writes the comic series, Gates of Midnight which was winner of the 2019 Irwin Award. She also publishes the Bram Stoker Award Winning Mary Shelley Presents Tales of the Supernatural.

Debbie travels the country with her husband Paul attending comic book conventions where they sell their books.

Probably the most interesting thing about Debbie is that she is a double lung transplant. Please become an organ donor. It saves lives.

Twitter: @kymerapress

Facebook: Kymerapress, D. Lynn Smith

IMDB: Debbie Smith

CARMEN GRAY is a Native Texan. She has appeared 3 times in different volumes of *RoadKill: Texas Horror* by Texas Writers. She also authored both a femme fatale short story and a YA fiction piece published by Castle Bridge Media.

As a freelancer, she has crafted a diverse portfolio that includes travel, education, arts and entertainment reporting for *Latino Magazine*.

Carmen enjoys bringing the supernatural to life in her fiction, employing elements of magical realism. Her Mexican-American heritage and the Spanish language is often reflected in the characters and conversations in her stories.

She is currently working on a novel in progress that would most likely be categorized as Latina Gothic.

You can also find her poetry on her blog: walkersonthejourney.com.

AMMAR HABIB is a bestselling author from Lake Jackson, Texas. He is the author of 12 books and 30 short stories. Ammar writes in a variety of genres, including historical fiction, historical nonfiction, children's fiction, and action/thrillers. His most popular novels include *The Heart of Aleppo* and *The Orphans of Kashmir*. He has also been featured in several anthologies, including *Predator: Eyes of the Demon*.

JESS HAGEMANN's recent work has appeared in *Southwest Review, Castle of Horror: Femme Fatales,* and *Into the Forest: Tales of the Baba Yaga*. She has an MFA from the Jack Kerouac School. Her debut novel *Headcheese* won an IPPY Award in Horror.

LEANNA RENEE HIEBER is an actress, playwright, tour guide, audiobook narrator and award-winning, bestselling author of over 14 Gothic, Gaslamp Fantasy novels for Tor and Kensington Books such as the *Strangely Beautiful, Eterna Files* and *Spectral City* series. Her debut contemporary Gothic Romance, *Ghosts of the Forbidden,* begins the Glazier's Gap series via Castle Bridge Media. She narrates her own speculative fiction for Scrib'd. *A Haunted History of Invisible Women: True Stories of America's Ghosts* marks Leanna's first foray into non-fiction, co-authored with Andrea Janes. Her stories have been featured in numerous notable anthologies and her books have been translated into many languages. Her *Strangely Beautiful* series was a 3-time Prism Award winner for excellence in Fantasy Romance and *Darker Still* was a Daphne du Maurier award finalist. A licensed NYC tour guide, Leanna has been featured on TV shows like *Mysteries at the Museum* and *Beyond the Unknown* discussing Victorian Spiritualism. She gives lectures and theatrical presentations around the country at prestigious institutions like New York University and Miami University to nationwide library systems, focusing on paranormal themes and 19th century women's history. leannareneehieber.com

SAM KNIGHT is the owner/publisher of Knight Writing Press and author of six children's books, five short story collections, four novels, and over 75 stories, including three co-authored with Kevin J. Anderson.

Once upon a time, Sam was known to quote books the way some people quote movies, but now he claims having a family has made him forgetful, as a survival adaptation. He can be found at SamKnight.com and contacted at sam@samknight.com.

New York Times bestselling author **ALETHEA KONTIS** is a princess, storm chaser, and adventurer. She has written over 20 books and 50 short stories, including *AlphaOops: The Day Z Went First*, *Enchanted*, and *Prince Phillip's Birthday Waltz* (Disney). Alethea is the recipient of the Jane Yolen Mid-List Author Grant, the Scribe Award, the Garden State Teen Book Award, and two-time winner of the Gelett Burgess Children's Book Award. She has been twice nominated for both the Andre Norton Nebula and the

Dragon Award. Alethea also narrates stories for multiple award-winning online magazines and contributes regular YA book reviews to NPR. Born in Vermont, she currently resides on the Space Coast of Florida with her teddy bear, Charlie. Find out more about Princess Alethea at aletheakontis.com.

MIKE OWSLEY is an author and activist. You can find him physically in Missouri, or virtually @BigMikeOwsley on Twitter. His short stories have previously appeared in the *Castle of Horror Anthology* and *The QRM Zine*.

SCOTT PEARSON is a full-time freelance writer and editor. He has published across a number of genres, such as literary fiction, mystery, urban fantasy, horror, and science fiction, including three *Star Trek* stories and two *Trek* novellas. His stories "The Ghosts of Glenmirror," "The Murder Couple," and "The Loneliness of Monsters" appeared in *Castle of Horror 4, 5,* and *7* respectively. He co-developed, with William Leisner, *Tales of the Weird World War,* an alternate history/horror/sci-fi series which debuted in 2021 with the short novels *The Big Dark & Meet John Doe*; "The Creature in Jay Cooke Park" takes place several years later in that same world, around the same time as "The Loneliness of Monsters." Scott and his wife, Sandra, divide their time between St. Paul and the wilds of northern Minnesota, where their cat, Ripley, lives with Scott's mom. He and his daughter, Ella, cohost the podcast *Generations Geek.* Visit Scott online at scott-pearson. com and generationsgeek.com. Follow him on Twitter @smichaelpearson and Mastodon @ScottPearson@mastodon.fraize.com.

S. N. RODRIGUEZ is a writer and photographer in Austin, Texas. She is a Writers' League of Texas Fellow, and her work has appeared, or is forthcoming, in The Journal of Latina Critical Feminism, Blue Mesa Review, River Teeth, Castle of Horror Anthology Volume 6: Femme Fatales, and elsewhere. As a Little Free Library Steward, she loves providing her community with access to a diverse selection of literature. When she isn't writing, she enjoys hiking and kayaking with her family, reading, and playing board games. You may also find her cleaning up local lakes and rivers, and helping wildlife in need. You may read her work at snrodriguezwrites.com.

BRYAN YOUNG (he/they) works across many different media. His work as a writer and producer has been called "filmmaking gold" by The New York Times. He's also published comic books with Slave Labor Graphics and Image Comics. He's been a regular contributor for the *Huffington Post, StarWars.com, Star Wars Insider magazine, SYFY, /Film*, and was the founder and editor in chief of the geek news and review site *Big Shiny Robot!* In 2014, he wrote the critically acclaimed history book, *A Children's Illustrated History of Presidential Assassination*. He co-authored *Robotech: The Macross Saga RPG* has written two books in the BattleTech Universe: Honor's Gauntlet and A Question of Survival. His latest book, *The Big Bang Theory Book of Lists* is a #1 Bestseller on Amazon. He teaches writing for Writer's Digest, Script Magazine, and at the University of Utah. Follow him on Twitter @swankmotron.

CASTLE BRIDGE MEDIA RECOMMENDS...

If you liked *The Castle of Horror Anthology Volume 9: Young Adult,* you might also enjoy reading the following titles from Castle Bridge Media available on Amazon or by order at your favorite book store:

Austinites
By In Churl Yo

Bloodsucker City
By Jim Towns

THE CASTLE OF HORROR
ANTHOLOGY SERIES
Volume 1
Volume 2: *Holiday Horrors*
Volume 3: *Scary Summer Stories*
Volume 4: *Women Running From Houses*
Volume 5: *Thinly Veiled: The 70s*
Volume 6: *Femme Fatales**
Volume 7: *Love Gone Wrong*
Volume 8: *Thinly Veiled: The 80s*
Volume 9: *Young Adult*
Edited By Jason Henderson
and In Churl Yo
*Edited By P.J. Hoover

Castle of Horror Podcast
Book of Great Horror:
Our Favorites, Top Tens
and Bizarre Pleasures
Edited By Jason Henderson

Dream State
By Martin Ott

FuturePast Sci-Fi Anthology
Edited by In Churl Yo

GLAZIER'S GAP
Ghosts of the Forbidden
By Leanna Renee Hieber

Isonation
By In Churl Yo

MID-LIFE CRISIS THRILLERS
18 Miles From Town
By Jason Henderson
Lost Angel
By Sam Knight

THE PATH
The Blue-Spangled Blue
By David Bowles
The Deepest Green
By David Bowles

SURF MYSTIC
Night of the Book Man
By Peyton Douglas
Dark of the Curl
By Peyton Douglas

Nightwalkers: Gothic Horror Movies
By Bruce Lanier Wright

Yesterday's Tomorrows:
The Golden Age of
Science Fiction Movies
By Bruce Lanier Wright

Please remember to leave us your reviews on Amazon and Goodreads!

THANK YOU FOR SUPPORTING INDEPENDENT PUBLISHERS AND AUTHORS!

castlebridgemedia.com

www.ingramcontent.com/pod-product-compliance
Lightning Source LLC
Chambersburg PA
CBHW050843180626
46814CB00007B/2599